ALSO BY MARIANNE WIGGINS

Novels

Evidence of Things Unseen
Almost Heaven
Eveless Eden
John Dollar
Separate Checks
Went South
Babe

Short Stories

Herself in Love
Bet They'll Miss Us When We're Gone

the
SHADOW
CATCHER

MARIANNE WIGGINS

Simon & Schuster Paperbacks

NEW YORK   LONDON   TORONTO   SYDNEY

SIMON & SCHUSTER PAPERBACKS
A Division of Simon & Schuster, Inc.
1230 Avenue of the Americas
New York, NY 10020

The Shadow Catcher is a work of fiction. Although parts of the novel borrow elements from the lives of Edward S. Curtis and the author, the novel is not intended to be understood as describing real or actual events, or to reflect in any way upon the actual conduct or character of real people.

First Simon & Schuster trade paperback edition June 2008

SIMON & SCHUSTER PAPERBACKS and colophon are registered trademarks of Simon & Schuster, Inc.

For information about special discounts for bulk purchases, please contact Simon & Schuster Special Sales at 1-800-456-6798 or business@simonandschuster.com.

Designed by Jaime Putorti

Manufactured in the United States of America

10 9 8 7 6

The Library of Congress has cataloged the hardcover edition as follows:
Wiggins, Marianne.
The shadow catcher : a novel / Marianne Wiggins. —1st Simon & Schuster hardcover ed.
p. cm.
1. Curtis, Edward S., 1868–1952—Fiction. 2. Photographers—Fiction. I. Title.
PS3573.I385S53 2007
813'.54—dc22   2007011842
ISBN-13: 978-0-7432-6520-1
ISBN-10:   0-7432-6520-3
ISBN-13: 978-0-7432-6521-8 (Pbk)
ISBN-10:   0-7432-6521-1 (Pbk)

for Lara

the
SHADOW
CATCHER

Let me tell you about the sketch by Leonardo I saw one afternoon in the Queen's Gallery in London a decade ago, and why I think it haunts me. The Queen's Gallery is on the west front side of Buckingham Palace, on a street that's always noisy, full of taxis rushing round the incongruous impediment of a massive *residence* in the middle of a route to Parliament and Westminster Abbey and, more importantly, a train station named Victoria. The Queen's Gallery is small, neither well maintained nor adequately lit, and when I went there to see the Royal Collection of Da Vinci drawings, the day was pissing rain and cold and damp, and the room smelled of wet wool seasoned in the lingering aroma of fry-up and vinegar, an atmosphere far removed from the immediacy, muscularity, and sunny beauty of Da Vinci's subjects. There were drawings of male adolescents, drawings of chubby infants, drawings of rampant horses, toothless women, old men with spiky white hairs on their noses and boils on their chins—and then, in a corner, there was a different kind of sketch, a map. It was drawn in ochre on a sheet of rough, uneven rag approximately the size of ordinary letter paper, the same color as southern California sandstone. I stood in front of it for something like *too long* because a guard stepped forward 'til I leaned away, still looking at it, mesmerized. Some things you re-member for a lifetime; other things, mysteriously, bleed away, or fade to shadow. Sometimes, you try to bring the memory of some-thing back, and can't. You try to see a face, recapture love, recapture rapture; but it's gone, that face, that vibrancy. Other images return without your bidding. Almost every night when I'm at home, alone, in bed, before I fall asleep, my mind presents that sketch of Leonardo's without warning. Onto that inner space where dreams take place, my mind projects its image. I see it, plain as day—a lit-tle piece of sandstone-colored paper on which an Italian coastal town is drawn from a perspective high above the ground, so high that no treetop, no cliff, no man-made promontory could have served as Leonardo's point of view. It's the view an airplane affords, a view Da Vinci must have drawn from an imaginary *self*-projec-tion; and judging from the scale of things, he must have been imag-ining himself ten thousand feet above the ground, or almost two miles up. Commercial airline pilots volunteer this kind of informa-tion—altitude and cruising speed—which is how I've learned to estimate how high above the ground I am, looking from an airplane window. I've learned what the Earth looks like from a great height—but how did Leonardo know? Are we hardwired, as a species, to imagine flying? We take it for granted now, most of us, this point of view, as a second site, because many of us have flown, many of us have been up there, and, even if we haven't, most of us have seen the pictures of our world as a distant object, beamed to Earth by satellite. We can adopt this point of view as a modern way of looking, but is it modern? What if there's something in our psy-ches designed to see things from above? Isn't it a possibility that, as humans, we were built to dream from heights? That Columbus dreamed of *flying* to America, dreamed his future landfall *from above?* That Lewis and Clark, bedding down on rocky ground, flew at night across the Cascade Mountains in their dreams, above sequoias, over the Columbia, toward the valiant coast to the magnificent Pacific? Maybe we are built to reconnoiter from above, survey the Earth from heaven, dream of flying. Maybe it's the angel in us. Gertrude Stein, the first time she flew, saw in Earth's crevasses and folds the antecedents of cubism and told Picasso that he'd stolen that artistic vision off the backs of birds. I want to think that Galileo flew, in thought. I want to think that all the peasants in the fields of history dreamed in flight, that all the slaves and all indentured souls whose dust still gathers on this Earth had wings at night, and aspirations swift enough for uplift. I want to believe we're built for soaring in our thoughts, and out here on the edge, in California, at night, in that fading wakefulness before sleep erases sight, my mind projects that sketch of Leonardo's, and then, before I realize it, I'm flying in, flying to America, making landfall on this continent, not from over the Pacific, not from Singapore or Australia, Fiji or Hawaii on routes I've flown in real airplanes, but I dream I'm coming in across the other ocean, over the Atlantic, like Columbus. Flying in, not as I've done from England and Europe in a jumbo jet with Greenland off the starboard side, down the Scotia coast with Halifax below, but flying in and making my first contact off the Carolina coast near the 37th meridian, where the English landed, equidistant from the Catholic French in Canada and the Spanish Jesuits in Florida. I dream I'm flying in across Cape Hatteras, where that little spit of land cricks around Pamlico Sound, where the Tuscarora were. Where the Tuscarora fished and lived and danced and laughed and loved before the measles and the smallpox took them. Here in California, on the edge, at night, after the coyotes end their braying, there's an hour after midnight when a silence drops into these canyons which persists 'til the first birdsong of morning, and, in that intervening lull, I give myself to flying in, west from Tuscarora marshland over Choctaw sands and Chickasaw meadows—*I project myself speeding toward myself*—flying, as the eagle flies, over Creek, Catawba, Natchez, Kiowa, Comanche and Plains Apache, Wichita and Zuni, Navajo and Hopi, above the First and Second Mesas, over Acoma and Chaco Canyon, across the Colorado toward the Paiute, Chumash and Morongo, here, where I am in Los Angeles. There are those who say the sound my country makes at night, the sound I hear when flying, the sound my nation exhales as it sleeps, is the sound of prayer, the sound of *Jesus Christ* arising from the basalt in the Rockies, splitting hearts of granite as he shakes off chains of time and is reborn, and there are those who claim the sound my nation makes at night is the metallic hiss of money in the forge or the sound of slavery's jism misspent in anger and assimilation, or that the sound my nation makes is the sizzle of cosmetic simulation, the sound the cutting edge of surgical removal makes, the sound of History slipping into coma, cosmic silence, almost total, through which, in my dream of flying, I perceive a hopeful distant note—*the sound my country makes*—a note so confirming and annunciatory that it seems to bend into itself, bend into its own impending future like an announcing angel *comin' round the mountain*, bend the way a shadow bends, conforming to the curvature of Earth, wailing gently through the night. That sound is the siren's sound of the iron road, a haunting whistle. I fly, in my imagination, over the abandoned Plains, the Rockies, and the ghost

Mojave—toward myself, toward *home*—and, turning in my bed, I hear it. Out here on the edge, in California, turning in my bed, the nation at my back, I hear a single note, heralding arrival. The sound of a train whistle. The sound my country makes. And I feel *safe*.

take fountain

All writers have these moments—all *people* do—when Realization forms from air.

I associate the phenomenon with finding a perfect word, a telling gesture, an insight into character, a crux on which a plot must turn. But that's because most of my Realizations strike during work and are related to the shape of my profession. My work is strung on moments when I realize something—a novel is, by nature, one long Realization, which is not to say other pursuits aren't dependent on discovery: sailing is. Cooking is. Playing music is. Sex always is. Loving is a series of discoveries: it starts, significantly, with a Realization: that moment when you *know* that you're in love. If writing were as exciting as falling in love, I'd get a lot more written, but most of my Realizations come as pinpoints of light while staring at the dismal tundra of an empty page. Given my average event horizon, most of my ideas don't have the bursts, the color spectra of world-altering discoveries like Newton's did, or Galileo's. Mine are minor stellar occurrences, but strung up as a necklace of small lights, my bright ideas dot the boundaries that define my life. When one occurs, then, it's a Birth Day, like the birth of a new star far off in the universe.

Won't necessitate the reinvention of the calendar.

But it makes another piece of heaven, all the same.

So when one of these Realizations struck one day when I was crossing Melrose after lunch with my friend David, I thanked my lucky star(s).

David likes to go to Angeli's on Melrose, where, at lunch, only the sound of steam from the espresso maker at the bar enlivens the lacunae in the sullen dialogues between distracted screenwriters, including between me and David. He was well and truly disillusioned with writing for Hollywood that afternoon, as was I, and I was seriously planning to start picketing the studios to CUT THE CRAP and start funding films with socially responsible story lines. Stop being pipelines for product placement, a propaganda machine for consumer consumption. Stop waving guns and tits at everybody. Between the two of us, though, David made the more convincing opponent to the way Hollywood is operating these days, because he'd actually written scripts that had been made into films, whereas all I'd done was write, get the boot, and grouse. His complaints had validity, whereas mine gave off the scent of sour grapes. I had tried to work, and failed. He, at least, had worked with Hitchcock. In another century.

When we finally wandered out into the hyper-daylight, pausing, curbside, waiting for the light to change, David said, "Hey. Where are you? You've left your face.

"Are you *writing?* Christ. Can't it wait 'til you get *home?*"

"Actually," I confessed, "I was trying to decide if it's better to take Highland to the 101, or quicker to take Crescent Heights."

"George Burns story."

I looked at him.

"George Burns is in a restaurant, and there's a kid busing tables, just in from, let's say Nebraska. Recognizes Burns, goes over to his table. 'Excuse me, Mr. Burns, I've admired you all my life,' he says. 'I've just come to Hollywood from Omaha to be an actor, Mr. Burns, and I wonder if there's some advice you'd care to give?' Burns takes a puff on the cigar and—not even looking up—says, *"Take Fountain."*"

This is no split-your-sides laughing kind of story, it's a *corny* story, but because I understood the punch line, A Realization struck me: I'm an *Angelena*, subject to the whims of Pacific coastal heat inversions, San Andreas fault temblors, and—more to the point—subject to the traffic. Subject to the unwanted obsession of shaving minutes off the time I spend in traffic, in my car. Shortcuts are printed money—*gold*—and anyone who drives on Sunset, Hollywood, or Santa Monica Boulevards thinks she's struck the motherlode when she discovers *Fountain* running parallel, in between those three other avenues, and she actually believes nobody else has ever thought of *taking Fountain*, even though every other sentient being in town has made the same discovery years ago.

Every shortcut in Los Angeles was glutted long before I got here, but I spend my journeys—and time before, and after, too—calculating odds.

The only remedy is to avoid the freeways whenever other cars are on them, never travel when it's raining, and never under any circs make an appointment to leave the house at lunchtime or when kindergarten's letting out or there's a Lakers' game or a terrorist alert or some celebrity's on trial for murdering his wife in Santa Monica.

I've pretty much got it down to a system where no matter where I'm going outside my neighborhood I'm going to need an hour in my car to get there. There are a few exceptions, but even they harbor the potential for delay. I can get to the beach and the Pacific Ocean, to Malibu, in half an hour but only if a massive block of siltstone hasn't splattered overnight in the roadway off the rock face of the canyon or if Topanga Creek hasn't made a mess of itself, gorged, like a bulimic, and thrown up. I can get to a back lot at Universal Studios in forty minutes, but only if there are no breakdowns or other minor irritations on the 101. But to get from my house to Beverly Hills or UCLA, USC, LAX, the Burbank Airport or Union Station, I've got to plan on being in my car for at least an hour. There's a bus route a mile and a half from my house that services Ventura Boulevard, and if I were a better human being and lived by my principles vis-à-vis the depletion of this planet's fossil fuels, I would walk the mile and a half to the bus, as legions of day workers do, but what I do, instead, is I try to limit how many times I use my car. Which is why I hadn't used my car this week, hadn't driven since last Friday, four days ago, and why I failed to notice the slow leak in a front tire until I got in the car this morning to go to the Hotel Bel Air for a lunch meeting with my agent and a producer, right on schedule, with what I thought was an hour-plus time to spare, when halfway down my street, I feel the barge tow on the steering. By the time I top the tire up, I'm still on schedule, because I always factor in a five- to ten-minute buffer zone when I plan to wander far (2 or more miles) from home.

And then I hit the 101.

Well, hardly "hit" it. I zip up the ramp into a horizontally stacked parking lot, into a line of steaming metal units coupled end to end like discarded boxcars shunted to a siding, waiting for a train to happen.

And now another Realization dawns:

Jon, my agent at Creative Artists, has exhausted a quantitative amount of accrued goodwill to land this lunch for me with a woman who's the head of a star's production company who claims to have read my work (doubtful) and says she's interested in developing a project based on a novel I've written about the photographer Edward S. Curtis. Most writers who have no film credits to their name (like me), no actual films produced from their screenplays, would probably admit they would have spent the night in the front seat of their car in the parking lot of the Hotel Bel Air to make certain they would be on time for an opportunity like this, unlike me, who gave herself only an hour (and a little +) and who is now going to be very, very *late*.

Or maybe not.

Maybe, as so often happens, this will start to thin for no apparent reason and I can still get there on time. This valley, the San Fernando, holds several million people at this very moment, of which at least a hundred thousand are with me on this highway; stalled. Passengers on plates. 240 billion years ago the west coast of America was somewhere slightly west of what is now Las Vegas and Vegas was the city by a sea. The coastline ran north/northeast from the Mojave Desert past Las Vegas, past our national Nuclear Test Site, into Utah. The great American craton floated uneventfully on the great North American plate, and everything within eyesight from where I sit, here, moldering in traffic, was at the bottom of an ocean, until *wham*. Two tectonic plates collided, pushing up these coastal ranges in crescendo—the Los Padres, Verdugas, Santa Monicas, San Gabriels, San Bernadinos, Panamints—climaxing in the Sierra Nevadas. From where I sit right now looking east toward the Verdugas, the San Andreas fault is ahead of me, its two opposing sides making better surface time than I am. I and my fellow stalled commuters sit on the Pacific Plate, drifting, even while we sit here, two inches a year toward San Francisco. Between us and the San Andreas there are three other major faults—the Elsinore, San Jacinto, and Glen Helen—but it's the San Andreas fault that defines California more than any other natural feature, more than the half domes at Yosemite or the fumaroles above Mt. Shasta or the beaches at Big Sur. San Andreas is right lateral, which means no matter which of its two sides you're on, the other one is moving to the *right*. San Francisco, up the coast to my left four hundred miles, is on the North American plate, along with Fargo, North Dakota; Albany, New York; and Tampa, Florida. L.A. is on the Pacific plate, drifting north. In two hundred million years, L.A. will pass the Golden Gate and Nob Hill, L.A. on the western side, San Fran on the east, which is more than any two seemingly immobile masses will be doing soon in any of the eight lanes on the 101.

And now: I'm very *very* late.

Lunch will start in twenty minutes whether I'm there or not, and there's nothing I can do about it, except to try to wait it out to the next exit and get off the highway onto ordinary (I hope) less congested surface streets.

One of the draws of living in the West is the lure of these dramatic landscapes, the pull of these wide-open spaces evoking narratives of ancient geologic time, narratives of passage, disappearance, death; persistence. Up to my right on the Mulholland ridge above Tarzana, there's a scenic overview where you can park your car and sit on a bench and look out across the whole San Fernando Valley. Seven miles wide, at its widest, and twenty miles long, the valley's like an island surrounded not by water, but by mountains, and I like to sit up on the Mulholland ridge and imagine what it looked like five hundred years ago before the Spanish came. I put my thumb up the way actors playing painters do, to crop the foreground, blot out the bank buildings at Sepulveda, the rides at Universal, the black glass Blue Cross/Blue Shield headquarters in Canoga Park, and I try to imagine what this place looked like before the horse. Before the train. Before the car. That's the game The West invites, the game everybody plays out West: pretending we can see the past, here, in the present. Pretending we can call down the impossible, invalidate the present, and convince ourselves we're in another time, another century. The West—true West—attaches to you like a shadow. I don't think this happens in the East—I don't think the landscape summons an imagined past the way the land does here. I don't think people in Manhattan, Boston or Atlanta turn a corner, see an eighteenth-century graveyard and make an easy leap into imagining the past. In European cities, yes, you can come around a corner and intersect another century, stand in a limestone sanctuary and imagine you are seeing light through stained glass the way it looked six hundred years ago, but in the west, at the cities' edges, there is the very real encroachment of the older Eden, the original one, the land in its unaltered state. You can see it from the windows of your car without leaving L.A. County. Drive out to Red Rock Canyon or the Vasquez Rocks or take a hike up Mt. Calabasas and you're in the wild, in another time, entirely. There are places, here, in the valley, where you can go, where there's not a building or another person within sight. Unlike the crowded basin beyond the mountains to my right, there are streets here that expire into dust beside an old adobe, but everywhere you'll go within the confines of this valley, you will feel its thirst. The mountains block the cool marine air from the coast and pose a permanent rain shadow. Streams form in winter, but they rapidly evaporate in spring and by summer they are rock-strewn baked arroyos. Two stubborn narrow ones join in Canoga Park behind the high school football stands and it is there, in a concrete crib, that the Los Angeles River shapes its unlikely identity. It's nothing, really—in any other town east of the Rockies it would be a joke, the kind of miserable low velocity ditch into which any city with a decent river would toss junk. *Real L.A.* is on the other side of the mountains to my right, and just like the L.A. River I need to find a way through their walls if I'm going to get to Bel Air at all, but because the faults tend north/northeast along the present coast, the coastal ranges follow that direction, slicing L.A. County's loaf into individually prepackaged servings. If you're on the 101 heading east—or *not* heading, as I am—and you want to get off the freeway and take surface streets from the valley side of the Santa Monicas over the hills to the other side, to the *basinette* of the real L.A., you can't just zigzag, you can't just improvise, you have to follow the geology, you have to take either the canyons or the passes, and, from west to east, you have only these six choices:

Take Topanga Canyon.
Take Sepulveda Pass.

Take Beverly Glen, Coldwater or Laurel Canyon.
Or take Cahuenga Pass.

I take Beverly Glen, which means first I have to take the Win-
netka exit to Ventura Boulevard which takes an added fifteen minutes because a Dodge Dart with a half-a-dozen 12-step decals
plastered on it overheats on the exit ramp, its slogans asking *What
Would Jesus Do?* which is not the existential exercise I need right now
because, let's face it, ain't Jesus running *late*, Himself? What would
Jesus *take* is what I want to know, and having called the Hotel Bel
Air once already from the 101 to say I'll be slightly delayed, I now
call again to say I'll be there in ten minutes but when I get to Beverly
Glen I have to downshift into first behind a long slow line of simi-
larly-minded-short-cut-takers and I inch uphill behind a Saturn
with a vanity plate that reads UP4PART. And maybe it's because at
this point I'm already forty minutes late, maybe because at this point
I've blown the possibility of salvaging this meeting at the Hotel Bel
Air, that I entertain the very real possibility of DOING SOMETHING
CRAZY, doing something crazier than sitting in traffic for two hours
for the ridiculous proposition of AUDITIONING, because that's what
this meeting is: another Up 4 Part. Another loony desperate writer
coondoggin' the shiny penny, and maybe it's because in my standard
transmission vintage model PT Cruiser I can either *go uphill* or I can
turn the AC on, *but never both at the same time*, which means I've been
breathing fossil fuel exhaust for the better part of ninety minutes
with the windows down and the sunroof gaping, or maybe it's because there's just something about THE WEST, the CALL OF THE
WILD and the prospect of ANOTHER ARTIST screwing up, that suddenly I want less to know what Jesus would do than what would

Dr. Gonzo do? The question *What would Hunter S. Thompson do?* presents itself as a reasonable fallback strategy as I take the turn into Stone Canyon at 40 mph, leave the keys with some kind of valet posing as a mariachi guy and rush (what's *this?* a *footbridge?* are those *swans?*) through the full faux Alhambra of foliage into the faux provençal dining nook toward the table, breathless, rumpled and apologetic, with my hair all EINSTEINED, giving off its own exhaust, mascara/lipstick smeared and bargain Nordstrom Rack linen/rayon MADE IN INDONESIA jacket rutched across my tits to encounter THEM: two women in Armani, militantly trim and toned.

     ME: So so sorry, I'm so late.

They smile and show their pearly whites. JON, my agent, signals I have lipstick on my teeth. STACEY, the producer for the star, has brought along MICHELLE, a young assistant They have finished eating their chopped greens. A WAITER comes to take my order and to take their plates away. I notice my manuscript lying between them, faceup. I can read the title upside down. THE SHADOW CATCHER. From her briefcase Stacey extracts a phonebook-thick paperback feathered with yellow Post-it notes. I know it well, this book, it's the Taschen paperback edition of Edward S. Curtis's COLLECTED WORKS.

"—*what can I say?*" she says. "EDWARD S. CURTIS. What passion! What personal courage!" She layers her palms on top of the book, as a NUN would, on a BREVIARY, and breathes, *"There's a movie in here!"*

And she wants to turn it loose, I can tell, like an exorcist on call. *That would be a great idea for a movie* is only ever meant to be a compliment. Not only here in Tinseltown but all across America. *It was like a movie* always means something happened, *you saw something happen right in front of you* in an emotionally charged larger-than-life context. *It was like a movie* can only ever mean that you're a camera. It can only ever mean that while you're looking at what's happening in front of you, you've also managed to step back from the experience, you've willed yourself into the position of spectator, you've willed yourself to be detached in the observance of performance. But *There's a movie in here* means the stuff is still a little messy, too messy to be construed as entertainment. Too messy to offer up a possibility for profit, for a lesson or a parable. It's not art. It's life. And if you were Cartier-Bresson you'd move yourself into position, you'd align yourself along the arc of possibility and wait for a decisive moment when life, itself, composes into art. Or, if you're Edward Curtis, you dress the mess to play the part. You disguise the truth to make the image that you want. You find *the movie in there* at any cost.

"Of course ever since we've been attending Sundance—how many years is it now, Michelle, thirteen? fourteen?—there's been a writer in Park City flogging a new Curtis project."

"Mine isn't a new Curtis project," I put in, surprised by what I hear as a little trill of stridency in my voice. "Mine is a novel."

"Well of course it is," she smiles. "Which is why I knew we had to have first look."

She pats my manuscript and I realize, with relief, she hasn't read it. Jon must have brought it with him to the table.

"'The Shadow Catcher.' It's the name the Indians called him, no? The name they gave him when he showed them pictures of themselves?"

"That's the legend, yes."

My voice seems to be coming through a mask.

"Look, I want to be honest with you," I say as a way to help her

17

crib my work "Curtis lived a long, long time. Eighty-four years. He had a very complicated life." I gesture toward THE COLLECTED WORKS. "The time he spent taking photographs of Indians is only one of many chapters in his long and complicated life, and the story that I've written might not be the story that you want."

I look at Jon, and Jon looks pained.

"Curtis is dead," I continue. "His children are all dead. His life has passed into public domain. You could hire someone to write the script you're looking for. You don't need to option my version of his life."

"I'm *paid* for picking winners," she tells me.

She pushes Curtis's self-portrait toward me.

"How could someone who looks like this and risks his life to make gorgeous images of Indians not be perfect for a movie? How tall was he?"

"Six feet."

"Blue eyes?"

I nod.

"As I was telling Jon before you came, we've had our sights on a Curtis project for years—but nothing's been right for us so far. What we're looking for is a story that combines *all* the elements— the outdoors—adventure—romance—plus it's got to have the *do-good* message. No one would ever know the history of these tribes, what they wore and how they lived, if Curtis hadn't risked his life to track them down and make these photographs."

I blink a couple times. I, too, have brought along some books and now I place them on the table.

"I don't know if Jon has told you, but I researched the book for several years before I started writing it. So I've become something of an expert on his life . . ."

"—*the* expert," Jon puts in.

"I started out with admiration toward the body of this work, these stunning photographs, the breadth of their achievement, and toward the man who was responsible for making them. You could say I fell a little bit in love with him."

"Me, too," Stacey confesses.

"Who wouldn't?" her assistant comforts her.

"What's not to love?" Jon poses.

"I thought, as you obviously still do," I continue, "'Gosh, what a hero, what a masterpiece of service to his nation.' Here's a guy, no formal training, no formal education, who builds his first camera from scratch, learns through trial and error, on his own, what was then still considered the *science* of photography, not the *art,* and not only masters the technical difficulties of recording light but turns the processes of capturing it into works that are noble and magnificent and beautiful to behold. A man who, out of the blue, out of a commitment to his nation, sets himself the task of photographing every native tribe west of the Mississippi, every one of them, including the natives of Alaska, before they vanished to dust, before their tribal customs disappeared under the burden of colonization, under the weight of the white man's coming. And then—on top of all of that—miraculously—gets the job done."

"I'm loving this guy more and more," Stacey confides.

"Let me ask you something," I propose. "When do you think these photographs were taken?"

I push one forward.

"This is Red Cloud," I point out. "Revered Sioux warrior. When do you think Curtis made this picture? Or this one," I suggest. "These are Apaches."

Michelle suggests, "Around the Civil War?"

"That seems right," Stacey agrees. "I'd say . . . mid-nineteenth century?"

"*Twentieth*," I emphasize. "Every one of these. Taken, not as you believe, or as you're *led* to believe, when the tribes were roaming the Plains, hunting buffalo, camping by rivers in their tipis, but after they'd been neutralized, confined in high-security encampments, herded onto reservations, deprived of their livelihoods, forced into the manufacture of 'Indian-ized' tourist junk, their children forcibly assimilated into Christian schools. After every one of them was no longer a free individual but a prisoner of war. Curtis didn't risk his life finding them—he paid the Bureau of Indian Affairs a fee to photograph inside the reservations, that he drove to, in most cases, in his *car*. This is a test exposure that he took—"

I push an image toward her. It's a photograph Curtis made of his Ford parked next to a Sioux tipi.

"It's a car next to a tipi . . . so what?" she says.

I push another image forward.

"—this is the image of that location that he published in *The North American Indian*. See the difference? No car."

I show her a print of two Piegan braves seated in their tipi with a prized clock between them; and then I place Curtis's preferred version of that print, the one he published, next to it. The clock has been erased, manipulated in the darkroom.

"Curtis would take one Indian from one tribe, a Piegan, let's say, and dress him up in Assiniboin regalia, and that was fine by him. Dressing Navajos as Siouxes. But if there was any totem of modernity—a car, a clock, a zipper or a waistcoat, Curtis would do everything he could to guarantee it was erased."

"So what's your *point*?"

"—my 'point'? My point is these photographs have been constructed for a purpose. An *artistic* purpose, yes—they're beautiful to look at. But they're lies. They're propaganda."

"Oh come on—look at these faces. These faces don't lie. These faces are beautiful. And they're full of truth . . .

" . . . I see dignity. Humanity. And strength," she adds.

"—and I see something bought and paid for by Big Business. In this case, by Union Pacific. By J.P. Morgan and the railroads. Where do you think Curtis got the money to finance all these photographs? Granted, he tried to raise the funds outside the corporate sphere by appealing first to Teddy Roosevelt and the Smithsonian—"

"Curtis was in touch with Teddy Roosevelt?"

"He photographed him."

"—when T.R. was *president?*"

"Curtis photographed T.R.'s daughter Alice's White House wedding."

"—he was *a wedding photographer*, too?—more and more I love this guy! How well did he know T.R.? Did they talk? Do they have scenes together? Who can we get who's big enough to play 'Teddy Roosevelt'?"

I ignore this and plug on: "When the Smithsonian turned

Curtis's project down, Roosevelt wrote a letter of introduction to J.P. Morgan for him. And they met."

"What a great scene."

"—yes, it was. And Curtis got a lot of mileage from it. According to his version of their meeting, Morgan turned him down at first, but Curtis refused to leave until Morgan promised him the money. Curtis asked for $15,000 a year for six years to put the collected photographs together—more than half a million in today's dollars—and Morgan told him the Bible had cost less, but he finally wrote the check. And that's where I start to question our hero, as a hero. The man who built the transcontinental railroad, the man who *was* Union Pacific, the man who was behind the wholesale slaughter of the Plains buffalo is the man Curtis goes to to finance these portraits of Plains Indians, who depended on the buffalo for their existence. Don't you think that's—oh, I don't know—*suspect?*"

"Who can we get to play J.P. Morgan?" she asks Michelle. "They were *fat*, weren't they. Big men, back then. All those guys . . . Roosevelt and Morgan . . ."

"It was a sign of wealth," Jon puts in. "Even with the women."

"If only there was, like, a *white* James Earl Jones," Michelle says.

"Nicholson could do it," Stacey suggests.

They're so busy seeing movies in their heads I wonder if they've heard a word I've said. "All I want you to understand, before you read the book I've written, before you even spend another day entertaining the idea that Edward Curtis was a saint, or a poet, or a hero, is that his life was long. His life was, as I've said, complicated. And, like every one of us, he was less than perfect. Less than ideal. Certainly not the man he strove so hard to make everyone believe he was. Possibly destructive. Certainly painfully dangerous to any-one who loved him. And never without blame."

"—*oh my god*," Alison recognizes: "You fell out of love with him."

"She did and she didn't," Jon tries to explain.

"—I *did*. And then I didn't."

I push another portrait forward.

"What's this?" Alison asks.

"Our hero. A later version."

"—*yikes*. What happened to him?"

"Life. Eighty-four years is a lot of living. I know you have a ver-sion of him that you're fond of, but all I'm saying is you have to un-derstand that there are several versions of your man out there, as I was disappointed to discover. What I finally had to do was make a kind of map of his whole life, draw a sketch of it, as if it were a landscape—then look down on it, like I was flying over it, so I could see the patterns."

"And what were they?"

"Well, you've got the beginning years over here, the early life. Then there's the middle bit where Curtis meets the woman who will change his life—Clara—marries her, has kids, establishes a studio in Seattle, Washington, as a society portraitist. Then, when he's thirty-two, there's another part: he meets the then Chief of Forestry by pure chance while climbing Mt. Rainier and the next thing you know this guy takes Curtis to the Southwest where he sees his first Plains Indian. Then, for nineteen years, from 1900 to 1919, all Edward does is photograph Indians. He's away from home ninety percent of the time, but pretty nearly every time he comes back, his wife gets pregnant—until he just stops coming home at all. He doesn't even meet his last child until she's eighteen years old. Clara divorces him in 1919—bitter mess; real ugly. Edward is now fifty-one years old. He has a sister who's sided with his wife in the divorce; a brother he hasn't seen since he was six, another brother who's denounced him as a charlatan and thief—he's made his wife an enemy and he barely knows his children. And he's perennially in debt. So he reinvents himself again and comes to Hollywood and lands a job with Cecil B. DeMille as the still photographer for *The Ten Commandments*. By the 1920s he's in debt to Morgan, whose heirs force him to relinquish all his copyrights to American Indian, Inc. He sells off part of the Indian art and jewelry he's acquired, borrows more money and opens two studios here in Hollywood, one in the Biltmore Hotel and one in Glendale, where he slogs away as an average studio photographer for another sixteen years. Then around 1937 he drops out of sight, wandering around

Nevada and California, searching for gold. Down and out, eighty years old, he tries to get the U.S. government to pay him for his work as an ethnologist. Instead, he's condemned by the Secretary of the Interior and denounced as a phony and a fake on the floor of Congress. On October 19, 1952, he drops dead in his daughter's apartment from a heart attack and dies, in L.A. County."

"Wow—he died in '52 . . . he lived that long. That's, like, during Elvis," Michelle blinks.

"Wait, I've got a scene," Stacey says: "It's 1952. We start in the daughter's apartment," she acts out. "California sunshine streaming through Venetian blinds. A TV plays in the corner. An OLD MAN, 84, lifts a slat of the Venetian blind to gaze at traffic on the street outside. A THUNDERBIRD goes by. (50's *right? those* BIG FINS?) A CADILLAC. Followed by a PONTIAC. The names of *Indians*—THUNDERBIRD, CADILLAC, PONTIAC—turned into CARS! Seeing this, the OLD MAN grabs his chest, falls down, has a heart attack and dies. The OLD MAN is actually *Edward Curtis!* Then—FLASHBACK: YOUNG CURTIS (*the handsome one*) on horseback, his CAMERA on a packhorse, on THE PLAINS. TIPIS in the middle distance. He rides in. *What do you think? It's kind of Citizen Kane meets Dances with Wolves.*"

"—*Citizen Kane?*" I repeat.

"—oh: *hey:* oh, my god: isn't there even an Indian reservation that's called ROSEBUD?"

I look at Jon. Jon looks at me. "I'm curious to know how you fell back in love with him enough to write the novel," Jon asks.

"Because of this," I say.

I draw out a Polaroid and lay it on the table.

"What is it?"

"Read the stone."

"—oh my god it's Curtis's grave. You *went* there?"

"I went everywhere I could. I went up to Seattle to find the buildings he and Clara lived in—I went out to the reservations. I went to the Smithsonian, the Morgan Library. Then finally I drove to Forest Lawn one day. And sat down next to him."

"—*our* Forest Lawn?" Alison asks.

"He's buried in Glendale. You should go. Before you make your movie."

"—*why?*"

"Because that's where the story is."

She tilts her head, looks at the photograph, then back at me: "*I need more.*"

"He was an absent husband and a disappearing father," I explain. "A shit to everyone who loved him all his life."

"Geniuses always are."

"Well, you can believe that if you need to."

"—don't *you?*"

"For a long time, I couldn't figure out if there was anything that Edward Curtis ever *loved.*"

"Why did he have to *love* something?"

"Because it makes a better story."

"Well then—he loved taking photographs of Indians."

"—then why did he *stop?*"

"You tell me."

"I have. That's what my book's about."

The room goes suddenly astonishingly *quiet*. It's almost like a stunned reaction to my saying That's what my book's about. It's frightening. You can hear a pin drop. It's as if every sound has been sucked out of the room and then I feel A PRESENCE loom and a beautiful tanned hand falls on Stacey's shoulder. *Don't mean to interrupt, the car is waiting for us,* and there He is. Like a vision. Probably the most beautiful human I have ever seen and Stacey is saying *You know Jon* and Jon is shaking hands with Him and Stacey is saying *And this is Marianne who's going to write the Curtis project for us* and He flashes me a smile and extends his perfect hand in my direction saying *I'm really looking forward to hearing your ideas,* and I lift my hand and slide it into His, look up into His eyes and tell Him, "Ga."

Thousands of women have probably said exactly the same thing to Him since He was twelve so He fields my stupefaction with impeccable grace and then Stacey tells Jon she'll call him to confirm a meeting for next week and she tells me that she's looking forward to reading *The Shadow Catcher* on the weekend, then they're gone and Jon and I are left there all alone, at the table, in His life-altering absence.

"*Ga?*" Jon asks. "—that, and being fifty minutes late," he summarizes. He picks up my Polaroid of the Curtis gravesite. "Worth the trip?"

"Did you know He was going to be here?"

"He's been living in hotels. Since the separation."

"You might have warned me."

"So you'd come on time? Or so you'd come with better hair. I meant *this*. Is-it-worth-the-trip-to-Forest-Lawn? I'm curious what you found there. 'Cause it's not in the novel."

"I thought I owed it to him."

"And, so . . . *what?*—he spoke to you?"

"*They* did."

"The . . . *Indians?*"

"His children."

"I thought they were dead."

"—and buried. Right there. All four of them. Two on either side of him. Not even with their own spouses. It's as if they thought they might finally get his attention. For all eternity."

"They idolized him," he estimates.

"There must have been something wonderful about him, for all four grown-up kids to want to be there."

"My daughters won't want to be buried by *my* side, and I'm pretty wonderful."

"Yeah but, you haven't disappeared."

"—those adventuring types: I've always been suspicious. What are they running *from?* Do any of those guys who discover the North Pole ever have a wife and kids?"

"Sure, but the archetype of THE COWBOY is a loner. Man, a horse, the open country—that's the movie these birds want to make. I could tell them fourteen different ways it's not the story of Curtis's life, they'll still want to make a cowboy movie out of it."

He walks me out and pays the valet and sees me to my car. "Know where you're going?"

"I'm gonna stay on Sunset to the 405."

"I'll call you when I know something," he says. "Take care," he adds.

I start the car, he backs away.

I wave.

And suddenly he signals, STOP.

"On second thought—" he calls out:

"—*take Sepulveda!*"

reds

The 101, which you have to take from the 405 to get to where I live (unless you take Ventura Boulevard), runs North to South from Ventura County toward Los Angeles, but then as it passes through Los Angeles, it doglegs inland in a true West-to-East direction, even though the signs still say 101 North and 101 South. So when I'm driving home from downtown L.A., from anywhere in the basin or from the other side of the hills, I'm always driving WEST, which in the afternoon means I'm driving toward the sun or, to put it another way, into the infrared. Into the western sunset, into the RED of western sky. Sunset where I live is only rarely red—it's generally burnished rose or fatty salmon-colored—but I understand the Newtonian inarguables of Earth's refraction and the truth that: at the close of day the world goes red. This fact of life is even more stunning if you happen to be in one of those places on Earth where the exposed rock is of the Triassic era, a time in Earth's history when it's believed there was more oxygen in the atmosphere than in previous eras, owing to the lack of plant life on the surface. Superoxidation, it's believed, produced the kind of ferric red you see in rocks containing iron in places like Red Rock Canyon, for example. Or Sedona, Arizona. Or the Utah flats. Or around the Solway Firth in

Scotland, for that matter. Red earths, red rocks, the color of dried blood. Earthly redbeds everywhere are a symptom of Triassic time, and anywhere they surface on Earth's skin, as if on a living body, their color is the same: *blood*. It's said that red was the first color humankind could differentiate. I don't know how this could be proven but I suspect it has to do with Newton again and probably with the shape of the human eye as it evolved in the human skull, perhaps being, prismatically, more bullish on the carmine wavelength. I collect these little facts about the color red because my daughter is a redhead; and because my Greek grandmother's maiden name was KOKINOS (the Greek adjective for RED). She, herself, was *not* a redhead, although her twin brother Sam was reported to have been one, which I find confusing. RED is associated with ALARM (no doubt because it's the color of mammalian blood), and it is officially the most alarming color on the current Homeland Security Alert color chart. If I had to choose the human hair color that I find the most beautiful, it would be red because it's frankly stunning and alive and volatile (besides my daughter, Da Vinci was a redhead; so was Jefferson; and so was Curtis), but outside the spectrum of human beauty, I don't particularly like the color. I don't particularly like garnets or rubies (or strawberries for that matter.) I don't wear the color well, having a high complexion, anyway; and I don't even grow red-colored flowers, with the exception of three explosive bougainvilleas that I inherited when I bought my house. I went through a red period in London when I decorated with Moroccan carpets and Turkish kilims, but here in California I don't have a single piece of crimson fabric in the household. So when I come home from the meeting at the Hotel Bel Air and the red light's flashing on my answering machine, it's noticeable right away, even from the doorway. For me to have 9 MESSAGES in a single afternoon is (here it comes:) a *red letter day*:

> 1— "Miss Wiggins? This is Emily Rosen of Sunrise Hospital in Las Vegas, Nevada. My number is 702-731-8112. Please call me back when you get this message. It's an urgent matter. Thank you."

I play it back again, to make sure I've taken down the number right. *Vegas*—where the odds are always stacked against the future and the biggest cons are played. Where identity is mutable. And fortunes bleed into the RED. The antithesis of all Nevada's *ghost* towns—fastest-growing city in the nation. Sound my country makes when she is making her escape:

> 2— "Miss Wiggins, it's Emily Rosen again. 702-731-8112. Sunrise Hospital. Please return my call."
> 3— "Miss Wiggins, Mrs. Rosen again. If you'd call me, please, at—

And suddenly the phone rings. Startling me.

Hello—?

Miss Wiggins?

—yes.

Marianne Wiggins?

—yes.

Miss Wiggins, this is Mrs. Rosen from Sunrise Hospital in Las Vegas, Nevada.

(I recognize her voice.)

I've left several messages for you, already, today.

(I say nothing.)

Miss Wiggins, if I may just confirm: you are the daughter of John Wiggins?

What is this about?

John F. Wiggins?

(I don't answer.)

Born third December nineteen twenty?

(I answer, slowly, but suspiciously: affirmative.)

Miss Wiggins, your father was brought in late this morning in cardiac arrest. He's in our Cardiac ICU at present, but he's still unconscious. I'm sorry.

Well, you should be. My father died more than thirty years ago.

John F. Wiggins, born December 3, 1920, in Quarryville, Pennsylvania? Social Security Number one nine six, one oh, eight two one six? I've got his Nevada driver's license right here in my hand.

If this is a prank, you oughta know I'm reporting this to the police as soon as I hang up—

I assure you, Miss Wiggins, this is not a prank. There was a newspaper article about you in his wallet, which is how—

OK, that's it.

(I hang up.)

And immediately dial 411, ask for the general telephone number of Sunrise Hospital in Las Vegas to compare it to the number this Rosen lady left. The area code and first four digits are the same. I dial the general number, ask for Cardiac ICU.

Cardiac, hello?

Hello. To whom am I speaking, please?

Nurse Furth. To whom am *I* speaking?

Ma'am someone purporting to be from your hospital has been calling my home in Los Angeles all day long, regarding a patient who was brought into your unit this morning? John Wiggins?

I'm not at liberty to divulge patient information over the telephone.

Well, can you tell me if someone called Emily Rosen works there?

Oh yes—she's in Admitting. Are you the daughter we were trying to find earlier?

(I'm too stunned to form an answer.)

I tried to find a number for you earlier, when your dad came in. We've got him stabilized, but I think you'll want to get here a.s.a.p.

Ma'am: my father's *dead*.

Oh god, is that what they told you—? Oh lord no, no, Mr. Wiggins is still unconscious, but—

Mr. Wiggins is *dead*. My father is. *My* Mr. Wiggins. I don't know who your so-called Mr. Wiggins is, but my Mr. Wiggins died in April 1970. So this is some mistake.

Well I apologize, Miss Wiggins. But I don't see how that's possible.

—you *don't*? It's not like JOHN and WIGGINS are low-probability NAMES. Don't you run I.D. checks? Go online. Check the Social Security Death Index. My father's facts are in there. Anyone with reading skills and a computer could have stolen his identity.

Well only if they're *eighty-four years old*.

(She's got a point. *Absurd* as it may sound.)

How old does your guy *look*?

Eighty. Eighty-*ish*. Plus he had a Universal Donor card in his pocket with you listed as his next of kin.

(I stare out my kitchen window at the sunset. And blink a couple times.)

Miss Wiggins—?

Yeah I'm thinking.

Let me transfer you back to Mrs. Rosen so she can run that DMF for you.

(I wait. DMF, I know, stands for *Death Master File*. I know this because I logged onto it, myself, researching Curtis.)

—Miss Wiggins?

(I recognize Rosen's voice.)

I apologize for hanging up on you before, Mrs. Rosen, but I needed to verify your call.

I'm running that DMF check right now—yup. Well golly. Here he is. Just like you said. JOHN F. WIGGINS. Died April 1970. Sorry about that. We don't normally check to see if someone's already *dead* when they come in with valid I.D. and a warm body. Don't know how this happened. I've never *had* a situation quite like this.

Are you going to notify the police? I'd appreciate knowing who this imposter is—how he got his information. You say I'm listed as the next of kin? Was mine the *only* name?

Yep.

—because I have a sister and she should have been listed, too.

Well, *Identity Theft*. There's no explaining how it works. It's everywhere. I don't suppose ...? there's any chance ...?

(*What?*)

That your father had a twin?

No, Mrs. Rosen.

—or that he might still be alive?

None.

—had to ask. —alrighty, then. —let's stay in touch.

(I check the time—eight thirty on the East Coast, in Virginia. I dial my sister, and she answers.)

—hey, little bird (I say.)

—*hey!* I was just thinking about you!

Am I interrupting?

Heck no we're just crashed out in front of the TV.

(It's unusual for me to call her at this hour, during family time, and she intuits something.)

Listen—something weird just happened: I got a call from a hospital in Las Vegas. They say they've got an eighty-year-old man who claims he's daddy.

You're joking.

No. Someone's posing as him. Swear to god. Some eighty-four-year-old with daddy's name and Social Security number ... And the thing is— (We both fall silent. Until J-J asks:)

Why are you doing this?

This isn't *my* idea, J—

Somebody's using his old I.D. So what?

Some *eighty-year-old-man.* I think I oughta go and see.

Thirty years, and you're still—

—don't you ever wonder?

No.

Well I do.

Well you shouldn't.

Don't you ever dream that—I don't know—he went somewhere? —*instead?* I dreamed once he *showed up* and told me he'd been living in another city all this time. It was really strange. I woke up strangely ... confused ... but sorta happy.

(She doesn't answer, but it sounds like she's breathing funny. Then finally she says,) That's a childish fantasy.

I know, but—

Please don't do this, Cis.

—we never saw the body.

Marianne—

Uncle Nick went to identify him. You probably don't remember. And I think Nick took George or Mike or Archie with him. Now *they're* all dead.

—just stop this, will you?

(I stop.)

It's morbid.

(She may be right.)

I mean, *Las Vegas!* (she says, as if *that*, in and of itself, should settle any argument.)

I think I should go find out what this guy's story is (I say.)

(J-J doesn't answer.)

What do you think? (I finally ask.)

You know what I think, (she says.) I think this is all some hoax you're buyin' into. For whatever reason.

You're not curious?

I didn't get the so-called *call.* So I'm not so curious. But you do what you hafta do.

Well, I'm gonna drive to Vegas.

—you're going to *drive?*

I think that's the *point.*

—how far is it?

Five, six hours.

—you're gonna go *alone? Take someone* (she argues. My sister's version of directions.)

"I'll be fine, don't you worry."

"Call when you find out. Call me—promise."

"I promise."

"I love you, Cis."

"I love you back."

But still I want to tell her that for someone as used to chasing shadows for a living, used to searching history's mists to tell a story, how can I refuse this chance to face this *ghost?*

edward and clara

Clara could hear them moving in the room next to hers, on the other side of the thin wall, their morning sounds discreet as dawn, and just as purposeful.

Even in the dark and through the wall she could distinguish between the two of them—the dowager, the slower of the two, coughing up deposits from her lungs, spitting, while the other one, younger and more eager to begin the day's adventure, tiptoes to the chamber pot, delivering the sound of liquid streaming against porcelain. Then she hears the older woman positioning her pot, followed by an almost inaudible hiss and the sharp inglorious smell—even through the wall—of urine.

This business of waking down among the elements still rankled her. It was barely civilized, she thought, this so-called house—a wooden shelter, as makeshift as their pretended family was. Their pretense of putting forth the myth of an extended clan bound by duty and devotion. That myth was as wormy as the floor joins and the crossbeams, but Edward had built it up around him out of nothing, cleared the land and raised the timbers, tarred the roof and seamed walls. It might as well have been a shantytown, she'd thought when she'd first seen it. She might as well be living in a tree. Or in a *tipi.* Half an inch of timber backed by tar black and rough paper was all that stood between her bed, her being, and the untamed Wild. There was a floor and a stone fireplace in what was called the kitchen, but the walls were less a solace than a taunt that they were all an inch away from living like some primitives. All six of them. An inch away from being Indians.

Her known world had collapsed within a single violent instant of her parents' deaths six months ago. Not only had she lost the people she loved most, she had lost the world that had defined her. She was too old to think herself *an orphan,* too habituated to her parents' love to think herself *destitute.* Never, in all her childhood years and childhood fantasies, had she entertained the possibility that she'd end up living in the West, living in the wild, living anywhere at all except within the comforts and the confines of a modern city.

Everything about her education and her guidance by her parents had habituated her to a way of life that had revolved around ideas, around a larger social order, around a daily conversation with the culture that men and women had constructed against odds down through the ages in outposts as far away as Athens, Antioch and Alexandria. Her mother had taught piano theory in the front room of their family home in St. Paul, Minnesota, and performed winter concerts under gaslight chandeliers in the conservatory of the Scandinavian Club. Her father was a portrait painter, a man who had translated the *St. Paul Gazette* into Latin over breakfast for amusement, who had traveled both to Holland and to France to learn the alchemy of paint and gesso. There had been laughter in their lives, music and impromptu joy, puns in foreign languages and the company of people who delighted in the unexpected transport of a Dvořák *scherzo* or stood mesmerized before a canvas of a woman clutching violets in her snow white hand. It had been a shock to learn how close to ruin her parents had maintained the pretense of a comfortable life, how the bright patina of her parents' lives had hidden darker currents—*debt*—how everything, even the piano and the trays of oils and pigments, had been hocked and balanced in thin air on borrowed money, mortgaged to their spent tomorrows. Had she been their sole survivor, Clara would have mustered the required guile and courage to apply herself to modest labor and found herself employment in the city of her birth—that's what her parents' legacy had taught her; that's what her mother would have done. Clara had to her advantage the example of her mother's perseverance as an archetype. While she was alive, her mother, Amelia, had sewn and cooked, performed Chopin *études* backward, laughed and joked and told Greek myths for bedtime stories. Traduced Ariadne, vain Icarus had been Clara's childhood imaginary friends—extensions of her mother's storytelling. Theseus, Prince of Athens, had been her own Prince Charming; Medea, her first knowledge of the ideal of womanhood gone wrong. From her father she had learned different types of tales, painted narratives confined in gilded frames. Her father had told her about paintings he had seen in Europe, icons of religiosity, the archangel Gabriel lighting through a window on a cloud of fire to announce to the young Virgin that she, alone, among All Women, had been elected by God to bear His child. A girl could get intoxicated by such stories. Especially in St. Paul, Minnesota, where happy endings waited through the heavy winters, where the winters were experienced as *weights* of snow, and where the nights were haunted by the untranslatable messages in the music made by trains.

Here—out here in the Territory—the nights were haunted by the banshee notes of loons and the persistent sloughing, like a giant's respiration, of the Puget Sound. Here, her nights were haunted by her memories of happier days and by the horror of her parents' corpses still too vivid in her mind. Had she been their sole survivor she would have stayed in Minnesota to find employment, but since their deaths her duty and concern had been for her younger brother, eleven years her junior, her parents' bonus baby and the center of the family's adoration. *Hercules.* Lullabies had been written for him; paintings painted. He had been doted on and coddled and, unlike his namesake, was more like fresh milk in a loving churn, his nature undisturbed and thick as cream. Hercules: only eight years old, he was as feckless as an egg in an abandoned nest. She couldn't leave him and she couldn't find a way to raise him on her own. Entreaties for help to her parents' patrons and their coterie of artist friends in the days following their deaths amounted to sympathetic but polite *nothings*. Only Ellen Sheriff Curtis, her mother's childhood friend, responded with a concrete, though less-than-perfect, Plan. *Come to Washington Territory,* she had telegraphed.

Train fare enclosed.

Think of us as family.

Despite the invitation's gloss of intimacy, charity was charity, Clara knew—its chain of command ran in one direction, only.

There is no power in receiving, and the possibility that she and Hercules might find themselves indentured to the Curtises was among Clara's several fears about transporting herself and her hapless brother into unknown territory. Washington—a Territory, not a State. A place so backward it couldn't organize its citizenry to vote themselves into the Union. What sort of place was this Port Orchard on the Puget Sound? Was it a town—or a stockade? How far away was the nearest piano, the nearest concert hall? As distracting as these questions were to her, her chief concern about accepting Ellen's offer was Ellen Sheriff, herself, now Ellen Sheriff Curtis. Squat, pale, timid, her mother's friend had always reminded Clara of that ewe in every herd that manages, through her own passive stupidity, to strangle herself in a fence. A tragic character but without the heroism. Maybe that was part of why Amelia had befriended Ellen—again and again through their long friendship, Clara's mother could play fiery Athena to Ellen's tepid Hestia. Or maybe there had been a former fire in Ellen that her marriage had extinguished.

Johnson Curtis had apparently swept Ellen off her feet the way a very bad sneeze can knock a person sideways.

Shiftless, relying on his personal communication with God to get him out of scrapes, Johnson fancied himself an orator, although every *bon mot* he delivered had been spoken previously, by someone else. In the post–Civil War boom era when businesses in St. Paul flourished on the swell of profiteering, Johnson's every venture failed, one after another, until, called by God, he declared himself A PREACHER and took off into the hinterlands of northern Minnesota with his second-born son to preach, administer baptisms, intone last rites and marriage vows to the dubiously devout in exchange for a roof over his head, a bit of bread and perhaps a nip or two of spirits less powerful than God but nonetheless dang strong. He abandoned Ellen in St. Paul with their other three Biblically-named children— Raphael, named for the principal Archangel (and not, as Clara's father hoped, for the Renaissance painter); Asahel, whose name in Hebrew means *Made by God*; and Eva, the Biblical First Woman. The son that Johnson took with him to portage rivers, cook, beg, watch after him and play his servant, had been christened ELIDAD, a name in Hebrew which means *whom God has loved*. The Biblical ELIDAD had been a chief of the tribe of Benjamin and one of the appointed to divide the Promised Land among the tribes. But *Elidad*-the-son-of-Johnson, only twelve years old when his father pressed him into service in the north woods of Minnesota, woke up one morning and rebelled, if not against his servitude, at least against the pretense of his name. Raphael, Asahel, Eva and Elidad Curtis would henceforth be known to their father, mother and the world as Raphael, Asahel, Eva and EDWARD. EDWARD Curtis. Edward *Sheriff* Curtis, in honor of his mother whom Johnson had left behind, penniless and destitute except for the enterprising efforts of Clara's mother, her childhood friend, Amelia. Amelia organized a place for Ellen, Raphael, Asahel and Eva to live; organized lessons for the younger two and an apprenticeship for Raphael; organized piecework with a seamstress for Ellen, organized donations of food, furniture and clothes from Christian charities and her non-believing artist friends. Ellen and her daughter Eva were habitual guests in Clara's family home—most frequently on Sundays when they'd arrive from church just as Clara's parents were beginning to surface from their Saturday nights. "Aunt" Ellen became a fixture in the house—more like a maiden aunt than a contemporary of Amelia's, especially after Johnson and Elidad (now Edward) had been gone more than a year and there was no positive assertion that they were ever coming back.

No one could have been more gracious to Ellen than Amelia in her loyalty and optimism; but charity exacts an attitude of deference, regardless. It exacts a posture. Ellen shrank before their eyes. Especially after Raphael, her oldest child, picked up and lit out for the territory one cold night, taking nothing, leaving nothing but his past behind. No words were exchanged, no gratitude for his Existence, no short or long good-byes. Here one day; and gone the next. A family ghost. Sixteen, he was mourned by Ellen who enlisted Clara's father in a search, but nothing ever turned up to explain where Raphael had gone. Seduced, abducted or kidnapped, he was never heard of again by any of the Curtises. Among them his name—that divine talisman of Johnson's choosing that was supposed to be a blessing—was never spoken. And although Ellen took her son's disappearance hard, and shrank at least an inch beneath the burden of its sorrow, she nearly lost another inch beneath Johnson's next proposal. Maybe running from The Law but certainly running on empty and the surety that only prophets enterprise, Johnson wrote to Ellen to announce that he and Edward were headed West by train to make their fortune.

Where palm trees grow like cotton, he had written.

What a heartbreak, Clara thought.

What an *ass*, her father clarified.

Johnson swore that he had heard on good authority that there was gold in the Yukon and the prospects of that mineral had already left a trail of lucre all along the coast of the Pacific from California to the great Northwest—lumber money, shipbuilding, the fur trade.

For decades now, a new Pacific city in the North had started gaining muscle. *Seattle* had supplied the timber that kept the Asia trade afloat. There was money to be made there, Johnson wrote. He and Edward would find a plot of land and build a house and send for Ellen and the other children within the year.

She had heard it all before.

She had heard it when he left her in Minnesota to go off and join God's War against the South in '62. Heard it when he wandered back, War's demons in his eyes and in his ardor. Heard it when he took their second youngest son with him to vent his ardor on the unsuspecting Minnesota woods.

This wild talk of Johnson's.

Always preaching to her about the blandishments of patience in a woman. About what waited in the future. As if her life on Earth were meant to be a single solitary wait. For what?

He had never even asked where Raphael had gone, or why.

If it hadn't been for Clara's mother, Ellen would have slipped into a long night, but Amelia kept her spirits up and kept her going, and then, miraculously, Johnson started sending letters as he'd never done before. His letters fueled Ellen's and Asahel's and Eva's hopes. Whether falsely or not, it didn't matter, Clara saw: there is no other quality of hope than that it floats a proposition. You can't *un*hope a thing. To hope against a hope is still a form of hoping. Hope is something that's the same thing as its opposite. It's a thing that is the same thing as its shadow.

Seattle.

"So far away. But it must be a *Christian* place . . ." Ellen had attested to Amelia. ". . . if Johnson's there."

"I'm certain that it's very civilized," Clara could remember her mother consoling. "We hear they have the telephone. Very modern. And there's a credible college there. With full female enrollment. Universal suffrage."

Ellen's facial muscles had pinched her mouth as she'd repeated, ". . . *suffer-age?*"

But as the boastful reports had continued to arrive from Johnson by the post it had been revealed that Seattle, itself, the city, the boomtown, was not, precisely, the current locus of the Curtis family's hope. The land that had been purchased—(*God knows how,*

Clara's father had remarked, perhaps enviously)—lay not near the inland channel but off-land, on an outer island, facing not the port nor the shipping lanes nor the city but, well, *water*. Facing the Orient. Or, if you were to draw a straight line: facing Russia. But Edward had cleared this tsarist-facing parcel and Edward had dug the foundation and Edward had quarried the stone for the hearth. Edward had planed the spruce trees and the cedar. Edward had raised the roof beams. Edward—who was in all ways except name Head-of-family—Edward had built them a house.

And out from St. Paul they had gone—Ellen, Eva and Asahel. By train. To the West. The *Northwest*. And Clara and Hercules and her mother and father had all trooped to the station to bid farewell and to watch them depart.

Four days on the iron roads.

Ellen had not lived with Johnson for eight years.

Edward had not seen his mother, sister nor younger brother for the same amount of time. Still, when Ellen, Eva and Asahel descended from the iron horse onto the rickety platform at Tacoma, the reunited family had fallen into one another's arms.

Except Edward.

Who kept his mother at arm's length.

The world at arm's length, for that matter.

Eight years had cost him his youth. Vigilant, serious, silent, the twenty-year-old bore the burden of Johnson on his bones like those Chinese, coolies, he had glimpsed at Western depots, laying iron in the sun and the rain for The Railroad.

Now at last he could welcome these strangers, his family, as his own freeing agent. A way out. A blessed release from the thieving old man.

Asahel, who had stood only a yard high when he'd last seen him, was now an eager young man. Dark and compact like their mother, Edward's brother was not as tall nor as fair-haired as he but they shared a singular trait: they were the *good* sons, the ones who had stayed under steady employment—one to the mother, the other to Johnson.

They were dutiful, decent.

They weren't Raphael.

But Edward was already planning escape. He had built with particular care a room in the house for his parents. A matrimonial room, three times the size of the other two bedrooms, same size as the kitchen. He had bought them, with his own wages, a bed. And a glazed-tile wood-burning stove he bartered off a Norwegian.

Give them a few weeks. Settle them in. Teach Asahel what he needed to know of the region.

Then he'd be off.

On his own.

Come and give us a smile, Ellen had begged him. She seemed shocked at the sight of her husband, half the size of his former self but still gamey, wild-haired and fierce for her flesh. Johnson had clawed through their first night together in the new bed and was dead of paroxysms of ardor and bile the next day.

Martyr, Clara's mother had sighed when she'd learned of his death.

Ass, Clara's father repeated.

The Curtises, now only four, seemed to fall off the map. Washington Territory *was* far away, as far away in her family's imagination as China or Rome. Amelia sent a steady stream of energetic newsy letters because that's the sort of person that Amelia was but

Ellen's replies were grim and slim and never more than one page long. She had, indeed, found a Christian community armed and ready to embrace her out in Washington Territory (Latter Day Saints? Seventh Day Adventists? Amelia couldn't tell the differences among the tribes) and she was entreating a reluctant God to help find Eva a prospective husband. "I imagine Clara has young wolves aplenty huffing at your door," she speculated. "Such a pretty thing." Pretty, yes, Amelia agreed, herself, on reading this. There were wolves, certainly, on Clara's trail but she wasn't interested in them. Her "engagements" were of a different kind—one month the study of Dutch still-life artists, one month the Florentines, another month the history of ancient glass, two months believing she should pursue a career in nursing. There were many St. Paul girls of Clara's age among the people they knew who evidenced this flittiness, an energetic brief commitment to a cause, girls who seemed to bat the air in optional directions as butterflies bat the air to stay alive. They would do this, they would do that—it was fatiguing to observe. But what passed for a joyous exercise, a struggle to be free of conventional constraints and expectations, was really only the final throes of a struggle to the death for most of Clara's contemporaries. *Matrimony* clipped their wings. *Marriage* was to be their grand career. *Childbirth* their creative act. But Clara took her parents' marriage for her own ideal—a lifelong flirtatious conversation, a prolonged engagement—and the young men she had met in St. Paul all seemed to lack the necessary humor, the off-handed heroism required by a life forged between two besotted equals. She would have forgone the equality of a prospective match, the balance in the equation, if there had been some Zeuses at her door disguised as bulls or swans but all she got were eager boys with knobby throats whose idea of a life "in commerce" meant not a life in married harmony, but working at a bank. She wanted what her parents had—the loving touches, the mutual obeisance, the lingering in bed in morning, the open door to friends whose married lives were less than perfect, less ideal than her own parents', to whom everybody turned in times of conjugated crisis. Why should she look beyond her home for happiness when happiness was there? Why should she marry? It seemed neither perverse nor unreasonable that she should choose to stay at home at an age when other girls were courting futures for themselves. And if it took her an extra year or two to determine what was right for her—it would be nursing, she had finally decided—why should she hurry toward decisions that could, ultimately, alter the shape of her entire life? But she should have seen the signs. In hindsight, she should have seen the shadow of a worry on Amelia's face when Clara announced she would seek acceptance at St. Paul's Women's Nursing Academy in September. Of course you must, darling. You *must*, Amelia had enthused. Never asking about cost, as other parents might have done. Waving off discussion of tuition. Letting every talk of money go unspoken.

Clara had enrolled in the Academy in September of the year following the Curtises' departure. Amelia still sent letters but any thought of Ellen and her strange brood and stranger fate had long ago sailed from Clara's sphere of attention until Amelia prompted her to sign a family Christmas card early in December. Write something to Eva, darling. Something heartfelt. She's out in Washington Territory. Unmarried.

Clara had drawn a picture of a snowman.

Beneath, she'd written,

HO peful
HO mespun
HO liday.

Draw a heart around it, Amelia urged. Something cheerful.

Clara had drawn a sun above the figure.

Which would, she knew, never really offer solace to a snowman.

As for their own solace in the approaching Christmas season—
yet again, in hindsight, Clara should have seen the signs. In past
Christmases the fir tree had been brought inside in mid-December,
decked with stars and ornaments her father had painted. In previous
years, every night in the two weeks before Christmas another gift for
Hercules and Clara had appeared, ornately wrapped, beneath the
tree. But at the beginning of this year, in the week of the Epiphany
last January, Clara's father had brought home a massive glass jer-
oboam he had found in the alley behind the Italians' grocery shop.
Christmas jar, he had announced. And what had seemed a strike
against the overstated lavishments of the baby Jesus' birthday was, in
hindsight, the first hint of straitened circumstances in the household. Amelia had continued giving music lessons, increasing them in
number, by demand, from six or eight per week to six or eight per
day, but Clara's father had sold neither a commission for a portrait
nor a civic mural nor a private painting for at least a year, or more.
Not that she had noticed. Why would she have noticed? The family
never talked of money and he was always buoyant in his work, disappearing upstairs to the attic room with the northern-facing dorm-
ers every morning when the light was right. But she should have
noticed. She should have noticed, she later thought, his new preoc-
cupation with what he called the current popular obsession with the

latest fraud. The "art" form of photography. She should have noticed the small stain of rancor when he called it outright cheating. A hoodwinking travesty. Stand in front of a machine and have your "portrait" rendered, he'd disclaimed. Frame it, hang it in your sitting room, in your bastions of industry, *chimpanzees* could execute the skill required, *click*. That *click* required as much skill and artistry as a canvas painted by a monkey.

So her family had collected pennies. Dimes and nickels, too, though mostly pennies, and the jar had slowly filled. It had been exciting, really, watching the mass of coins rise slowly. Hercules would run home, breathless, with a found coin from the street, and he had gone knocking at the Polish widower's next door, asking to perform odd jobs so he would have some small change to contribute. At least four dollars in the jar had been earned by Hercules, himself, and he'd sat staring through the green glass, sometimes, pointing to a dime, a nickel, saying, "That one's mine." It had seemed to make him proud so Clara hadn't stopped to question the reason for the jar. It was *the Christmas jar* and it had sat on the floor in the dining room the whole year and in the second week in December all four of them, like eager children, had emptied it across the Persian rug and counted up the coins. They had found thirty four dollars—thirty four and change—it had seemed a vast amount, and Clara could remember feeling her face flush and noticing how happy they all were. Deducting the cost of the Christmas tree (two dollars) they would receive, each, eight dollars for their Christmas shopping—one gift, each, determined by drawn lots. Clara had stared at the four folded strips of paper hoping her mother or her father—not Hercules—would draw her name. Hercules drew first. Then gave a cheer. "I drew myself!"

"Is that what would make you happy, Hercules?" Amelia had asked.

Yes.

Not really in the spirit of Christmas, though, is it? Clara had objected.

He drew another lot and drew his father's name, and it fell to Clara to chaperone her brother with his money.

They had meant to go, they had meant to take the trolley into town that very week to give themselves time for shopping in the large emporiums, but Clara had had long days of term examinations, and then the week before Christmas day, the only week they had to stroll and look along the major commercial avenue of St. Paul, it had begun to snow. It had begun to snow one afternoon and then it snowed all night. By the evening of the second day the trolley lines were overcome and transportation in the streets outside had come to a full stop. Clara's father built a fire in the front room fireplace and Amelia organized a picnic on a blanket by the fire for their supper. They popped corn and toasted squares of cake, and as the night crept in Amelia raised a hand and told them, *Listen,* and they all grew quiet. The fire snapped and hissed and distorted what she wanted them to hear, so she drew them to the front door and opened it. There was snow up to their knees on the front porch. Nothing moved except the lines and dots of drifting flakes.

Sometimes I dream for it to snow, Amelia said. I *will* it.

She drew a finger to her lips to signal quiet, *Hear* it?

Clara strained to hear a sound through all the silence. Hear what, mother?

The *acoustics.* The whole world's a concert hall.

"Play us something, darling," Clara's father had said, leading her back inside to her piano. He had left the front door open and Clara lingered at the edge of night as the notes rose from her mother's fingers and floated out across the city, an accompanying phenomenon to nature's own.

The snow was followed by a day of freezing cold, the sky a blank slate like a block of sullied ice which pressed into one's lungs and froze people in their tracks as they tried to shovel. Sitting in the downstairs while her mother played that evening, Clara thought she'd heard it, finally, that bafflement of snow, silent, calm and soothing, as if the house were cupped in mittens.

. The next day, the eve of Christmas Eve, the sun had risen strong and stunning, drawing people from their homes where they'd been stranded, avid to start digging out, eager to be witness to the beauty that the storm had wrought. Once he'd cleared a pathway to the street, Clara's father rounded up the sleds and, laughing and delighted by the unexpected balmy turn the weather had taken, the four of them joined others in their neighborhood in a motley parade toward the open land on Finland Hill.

"I brought my money with me," Hercules had confided to her.

"Why did you do that?"

"Two days left to Christmas. There's a chance that we'll find some place open."

And, indeed, they had. A funny little shop on a corner five blocks from their street, where, for whatever reason, none of them had gone before. A lot of work had gone into its presentation on that morning, the sidewalk had been cleared, a banner hung, and it was evident the owner didn't want to lose another day of business in this Christmas week. Fronted by a brick skirt from which a story-high glass window rose, the storefront beckoned with a display of lacquer boxes, silks and rice paper scrolls of the kind generally associated with the China trade, but there were also moroccan leather books and inlaid marble chessboards on the shelves inside.

"I'm going in," Hercules announced.

"We can do it on the way back," Clara reasoned.

"You need to find a present, too," he argued.

True: she hadn't found the gift yet for her mother.

Ten minutes, Amelia shooed them, laughing.

"Don't watch us—turn around!" Hercules insisted.

Inside a funny little man rose up from behind a glass display case, wearing a round felt hat shaped like a can of peaches.

Fresh in, all foreign, he promoted.

We're just looking, Clara told him.

She had cast a glance over her shoulder at her parents standing with their arms around each other in the sunlight dutifully aiming their attention toward the street.

"Shiny gold, some pearls?" the man in the canned hat was asking her, but Clara's attention had been drawn to a specific case. "Are those . . . music boxes?"

Yes, miss.

"Even that one?" She'd pointed to a porcelain enameled box, palm-sized and painted with a single violet on its top.

The man unlocked the case and drew it out. Handing it to her, he prised open the lid and a tinkling phrase began to play, like notes played with a silver spoon on icicles.

Holy cow, just look at that, is that a compass, mister, Dad would sure be pleased to have a compass—

How much is it? Clara asked.

Was ten. For you ... I take eight dollar.

Her heart had skipped but she was careful not to show it.

She cast a glance back at her parents.

"Let me see this compass, mister," Hercules plowed on. "Don't you think Dad could use a compass swell as this one, Clara?"

Don't show it to him, Clara told the man. *Think*, Hercules. Why would Father need a compass? When would Father ever use one? You want to see that compass because it's just the sort of useless thing that *you* would like ...

Outside, just then, Amelia had laughed at something that Clara's father had just said. Clara looked at her again, the way she threw her head back, her laugh ascending upward from her throat, climbing like a chordal scale in harmony, all tinkling light, just like the music box.

I'll take it, Clara had informed the man.

He had nodded, she had smiled.

Her mother had continued laughing, and then there'd been the sound of distant thunder, only brief, too brief, and then the floor had shaken, all the glass had shaken, all the tiny lovely objects on display and then the light had dimmed, then dimmed again, as if one cloud and then another, larger, one had edged across the sun. There had been a single uncomprehending instant when she'd stared into the man's contorted face and then there had been an almost deafening great booming roar, her ears had popped and every surface in the building took the impact of a great unmaking. There had been an eerie light like doom and when she'd turned to look out on the street the world had disappeared behind a wall of snow and ice and there was nothing on the other side of the window but a bafflement of snow a story high and in it, at the height of Clara's head, a single human hand, her mother's, stretched out as if to reach above the octave.

Dumb, Clara had stood for several precious moments before she'd understood that all the snow above them on the building's slanted eaves and roof had fallen, tons of it, like a guillotine on both her parents. *Break the glass* she'd breathed and even before she, herself, could move, Hercules had swung a chair against the plate-glass window and was climbing through the broken shards and solid mass of snow to try to reach his mother's fingers.

The man in the can-shaped hat had run in circles, clutching at his ears, crying out in a strange language Clara hadn't understood— then he had made a beeline for the door, pulled it inward, open, and had faced a solid wall of ice pack from the avalanche. Instinctively, he'd run at it, leading with his shoulder but had hit it with a deadening thud as one would hit a granite mountain. The snow, so innocent and pliable in its particular, had compacted under pressure of its mass like particles of sand beneath the strictures of geology in the Mesozoic Age. Lithified, sandstone can take the form of quartz, and quartz was what the wall of snow looked like. The man in the canned hat had hit it with his fist and his fist had come back bloodied. Then the man had turned and run toward the back room of the shop, still crying in his foreign language, and soon Clara had heard his echoes through the wall of quartzy snow from the outside, distant, very distant and still unintelligible, as if arriving from another continent.

Clara had hauled Hercules, whose knees and hands were raw and bleeding, from the frozen pack of snow, across the shop floor out the back into the morning by the alley door. They'd run around the building through two feet of snow up to the corner where they'd turned to view the wreckage. Where there had been, minutes before, a recognizable storefront, its eaves, its upper stories and its roof, there now was a fresh glacier, sparkling in its novelty, a just-hatched mountain obscuring both the building's lower stories and the side-walk, breaching into the street it had extended like some lavish extra icing, extra scree, and Clara had seen at once the only avenue for res-cue was from inside the shop. Passersby had sent a runner for police, another runner for the nearest fire brigade, and a hardy few had started gouging at the monster with their shovels.

Hercules, Clara had said. She'd knelt down and taken his hands in hers, cupping his raw knuckles, and looked him in the eyes and seen his fear as raw as his hands—he'd been so valiant in his re-sponse, so quick: in that instant a splinter of devotion had lodged in-side her conscience. "Get Mr. Lodz," she'd told him. Mr. Lodz was the widower from Poland who lived next door, the man for whom Hercules had swept the sidewalk and thinned hedges; the European gentleman whom Clara's father had called Solomon of Minnesota. "He won't want to come but he will once you tell him what has hap-pened. Don't be scared of him. Tell him we need help."

Hercules had nodded, staring at her raptly, then he'd handed her a tied bandana from his pocket. Take this. The eight dollars, he had said. Pay someone to get them out.

He'd turned and run toward home, but not before she'd realized he still believed their parents were alive.

She could not remember, later, who it was that she'd enlisted to go back into the shop with her—some passerby, some incidental person who had been nearby when the avalanche occurred, on the street, perhaps, clearing snow, himself, with a shovel in his hands. She could not remember, later, what she'd told him but she got him to accompany her inside and then he, or perhaps she, had called for others to join in the effort. She could not remember things in proper order, later, all the things that had happened in the next four weeks except one vivid memory that stood out from all the rest and kept recurring. It was the moment that defined the next four weeks, the next six months—perhaps, even, the rest of her whole life. She'd been standing in the shop and she had reached across the breach where the window had once been and she had touched Amelia's fingers. And in that instant she had known that she was dead. In that very instant she had watched her mother's fingers blanch from red to blue to waxen yellow and she had drawn her own hand back as if her flesh, still so alive, was in violation of a trust, as if her own hand was the ghostly one. From that moment forward she'd responded only as a specter, as a stranger passing through her own dreams. Lodz had arrived—unshaven, in a black skullcap—with Hercules in tow, and Clara had succumbed to silence, then, succumbed to shock, allowing Lodz to take command and make decisions. So much to do, so many things—and her not knowing how to do them. Somehow, she had no memory how, they had returned home that afternoon and Lodz had asked where Clara's father had kept the family's documents and papers, where he'd kept the bills and the financial records. At some point, perhaps the next day, these things had been found and she remembered sitting with Lodz at the dining table, answering his questions. She remembered Lodz's housekeeper being there, too, cleaning in the kitchen—and other people, faintly familiar, milling through the house, clutching her hands and saying things she hadn't wanted to hear, *can't believe it, so very very sorry, dear.* There had been a man one morning, standing in the front room with a ledger and a pencil, taking items off the mantelpiece, examining them. *My* house, he had snapped at Clara when she'd asked him who he was, before Lodz had arrived and forced him out. Six months they owed in rent, the man had shouted, *six months*, and soon after that Lodz had said she needed to start packing up what few things, what valuables, mementos of her parents, that she and Hercules might want in the future, might want to keep. She had already seen, going through the papers with Lodz, the unanswered letters from St. Paul Women's Nursing Academy demanding payment, among other such demands, so she'd begun to understand the slippery ground that she and Hercules were on, but she was not prepared to learn how desperate their present situation was until Lodz confided, solemnly though gently, that very likely a constable would be arriving soon to force the sale of all of their belongings and evict them. "Take your mother's jewelry," he had said. "Things simple to pack. The furniture, the larger pieces—by law, we're bound to let them seize them. Take the things that they won't notice would be missing." She remembered standing with him on the top floor in her father's studio and Lodz asking, "Are these paintings worth anything, do you know?" When she hadn't answered—being unable to—he'd said, "Well, they're too large for you to take, anyway," and she'd stepped forward to the easel where a portrait of her mother stood and showed him how to take the canvas off its frame and roll it, and together they had rolled all her father's paintings into slender cylinders and Lodz had promised he would keep them safe.

Through this, through the bleak funeral and the setting of the stone, in the background, Hercules had wept. Grief trumps pride, it always does, real grief, the kind you never want to come, the kind that blots out everything, knots the safety rope of hope into a stranglehold and hones whatever happiness is left into a thorn. People in the house, visitors, had heard the weeping emanating from his upstairs room and they had looked at Clara as if she'd been remiss, as if something needed to be done to succor him. Such pain was not a welcome sound. It was discomfiting, it tore at their decorum—a child grieving publicly as only a widow might, in private, wasn't something that the St. Paul crowd was used to, there was something in the sound of Hercules's lament that was too raw, too uncontrolled, too criminal, too much like the sounds of protestation that the ancient gods had raised from men like Oedipus and Orestes and Job, that pagan and Old Testament crying that had dominated man's existence before the muffling of the Christian era. Late at night, early in the morning, Hercules had cried the way Clara had wanted to, herself, with stark abandon. She had sat on his floor, patting on his back, had sat outside his room when he had locked her out, and listened, as one listens to a sermon, to a siren song or to an oracle. To have given oneself over to expression of emotion, that way, remained a thing beyond her reach, and she would think about that kind of abandon as she sat there in the dark, what it must be like to be consumed beyond one's reason by raw feeling. To give in to it. Be shanghaied by it. To have one's ability to reason vanquished by unconsolability, fury, rage—or, even, love. Hercules, by virtue of his grief, had seemed more alive than she had, in those days. But on their final day together in the house, on the day before they would move in, temporarily, with Lodz, Clara had been helping Hercules pack his clothes and he had begun to cry again, his blond head sinking to his chest, his narrow shoulders heaving. *Stop*, she'd whispered. Stop this now. You need to stop it, Hercules. We'll be at Lodz's tomorrow and you can't keep on like this. Not in someone else's house—

To her surprise he'd struck at her, his fist landing on her upper arm. "You're always telling me to *stop*— I could have got them out, I could have saved them but you told me to *stop*—stop and go get Lodz—and when I came back they were *dead*—"

"Don't blame me, Hercules," she'd said, and he'd shaken his head in protestation, and she'd seen that look deep in his eyes, that *terroir* of terror that she'd seen the day their parents had been killed. "It's my fault," he'd begun, "I'm the one who wanted to go in there, I'm the one who said we should go in that stupid place, if it wasn't for me they wouldn't have been standing there—"

She'd taken him into her arms and let him weep—understood its deeper cause for the first time—and she'd rocked him back and forth, as if to exorcise all the unknown hells the dead leave in the living when they disappear into their guiltlessness.

Lodz's house smelled of cabbage and his dead wife's old clothes, and Clara and Hercules were more miserable in the damp spare room behind the pantry than they had ever been before, but at night, although Hercules still wept and had more reason to than ever, Clara could tell that he had tried to hide his misery by covering his body in the musty bedclothes and weeping in stale pillows. After a near interminable week of being at loose ends, despairing over where to turn and what to do, Ellen Curtis's letter had arrived from Washington Territory and even Lodz, ever the pragmatist, declared it a godsend. From what was left after the forced sale of their parents' property, plus a few contributions from well-meaning citizens, Lodz had managed to amass the sum of eighty dollars, which he gave to Clara in an envelope with the ominous advice to "use only as a last resort." And this, he said, handing her two crisp ten-dollar notes, "is from me. One for you and one for Hercules. Buy yourselves something you can treasure. In your new adventure." So she had taken Hercules with her to the Friday market down by the river—part State Fair, part *marché des puces*—where, within ten minutes, Hercules had spent his whole ten dollars on a used suit of clothes, cap, cape, waistcoat, worsted pants and stiff high collar, which he would probably outgrow within the month, but Clara hadn't argued, just to see him smile. For herself, nothing had caught her eye until they came across a naval merchant who had on display an array of brass fittings, spyglasses, oars and seaman's trunks. One of the trunks was tinted a pale yellow with a hand-painted reproduction of a familiar painting on its lid and gold stencils on its sides, the SS *ICARUS*. It was the copy of the painting that had caught her eye, her father had once kept a photogravure of it beside his easel, though this reproduction was far better, rich in color and showing the deft hand of a true artist. "It's Dutch, that is," the merchant said to try to sell her.

"How much do you want for it?"

"Don't you want to see inside?"

"How much?"

He'd made a quick assessment of what he thought Clara could afford and told her, *Seven.*

She would keep her mother's linens in it, and her mother's tea service. And her father's books on the Italian artists. But when she and Hercules had gone to lift it by its handles to carry it away, it proved heavier than it had looked. "The books I let you have *gratis*," the merchant smiled. Because he'd never otherwise get rid of them, Lodz had remarked when Clara showed them to him. "They're in *Dutch.*"

"I think they're pretty," Clara had said. "I like the illustrations. What are they about?"

"How to build a telescope," Lodz laughed. "You and your brother. Like your parents. Heads up in the clouds. Meanwhile feet without no shoesies."

Clara had packed her meager valuables into the new sea chest and bound their other few belongings in cloth and rope and on the last Saturday in January Lodz had seen them off on the Northern Pacific train bound for Tacoma, Washington Territory, on what was known as General Custer's line, the one his 7th Cavalry had ridden between St. Paul and Fort Abraham Lincoln, to which Custer had been assigned to protect the Dakota and Montana Territories from Sitting Bull and his land-happy Sioux.

Lodz had walked them to their seats, told them to speak to "no stranger, never, only train employees," and then, with a surprising show of avuncular emotion, shed a Polish tear when he embraced them. As the train crept forward along the curving track out of St.

Paul's Union Depot, Hercules fogged the window, asking, "Will we see the cemetery from here?" and Clara had closed her eyes. I'm not looking back, she'd told herself.

Not that she'd been able to look forward, either—life with the strange Curtis brood held no happy prospect for her, except the hope that in Asahel, whom she knew slightly, and Edward, whom she didn't know at all, Hercules might find a man, a hero in imagination, more suitable than Lodz to guide him through this present grief toward manhood. She was doing this for Hercules, she told herself. And therefore: for her parents.

They had been seated in the Ladies' car—a polite designation which translated *Women's and Children's Car*, a segregation designed to keep the sexes clear of each other on the four-day journey and to keep impressionable young souls away from the general rowdy company of single males, mineralogists, con artists and roustabouts lighting out from the known states for The Territories. Their car was occupied out of St. Paul by the two of them, a troupe of nuns and a coal-burning potbellied stove in the center aisle to ward off cold. At St. Cloud, Minnesota, the first stop, a family with four children got on, the father going forward to the Men's car when the mother settled in. Ragtag children, too, got on, while the train was stopped, a chorus of them, immigrants from less-favored states in Europe, Clara could tell from their dark hands and dark complexions, selling warm rolls, pickled eggs and heated stones to place beside one's feet. Penny for a hot stone—she and Hercules were close enough, themselves, to that scrambling existence, so she bought two stones from a fierce-looking girl and when she'd opened her small change purse the girl had riveted her with a look that warned, Luck, not moral reason has given you your place in life. Where's your mother? Clara had asked, in retaliation. No mother, the girl answered. Then we're even, Clara tallied, handing her the pennies.

In the middle of the north Midwestern winter, it had grown dark at four o'clock and Clara and Hercules had eaten the food Lodz's housekeeper had packed. A conductor came around with blankets and straw pillows and fed the stove and took orders for their morning meal the next day at the depot in Bismark, Dakota Territory, where they would make a mandatory stop. Clara arranged a bed for Hercules across a row of seats and tucked the heated stone beneath the blanket by his feet. Do not leave this car, she'd whispered, patting him.

Promise. —Clara?

Yes?

This is an adventure.

Yes, it is.

They would have enjoyed themselves.

Yes, they would have.

She'd sat across the aisle from him, her head against the window and she'd stared into the black abyss that was the outside world. No lights. Steam, smoke and cinders were the only signs this night that man existed in these parts: and *noise*, the pounding of the engine felt in every bolt and join along the train's snaking length. She took out the map they'd given with the tickets, figuring they must be somewhere now outside The States, somewhere coming on Dakota Territory, churning on toward Fargo, a non-place, nothing but a place the railroad made, named, like most of all these so-called cities out here—Billings, Livingston—after men who had done nothing in their lives to distinguish themselves but build a railroad. Was that heroic, in the ancient sense? *Another Roman Empire*, her father had remarked about the country's nation-building: who the hell were Mssrs. Fargo, Billings, Livingston compared to Antony and Caesar? Had they any Cleopatras in their beds? Had they ever *heard* of Tragedy? All this land out here—bartered for its mineral rights, its copper and its coal and gold—had Greece been built this way? She knew next to nothing about commerce, about how fortunes were built and made—she knew almost nothing practical in life, in terms of practical, applicable *skill*. She knew how to sew a button. Knew how to tie a tourniquet. How to diagnose a fever. How to *see* a painting, see its harmony and see its flaws. But she couldn't sell a stone to earn a penny. That was something that she needed to discover how to do. Turn a given fact of nature into money. Take something as God-given as the earth, or as her life, and turn it into something like the Louisiana Purchase, a self-generating profit. Dakota Territory, Montana Territory, Idaho Territory—all part of the Louisiana Purchase: all these so-called bounded states of being she'd be passing through: what sort of fictions were these places, except man-made fictions of the profit-driven kind? Were they works of art? Or sovereign nations? They were artificial designations bounded by dictums of greed, and she needed to learn to speak that language if she and Hercules were to survive. She needed to learn how to make a livelihood in order to escape from charity. In Seattle, she had heard, there was a University, even an opera house, but although she'd tried, before they'd left, to find a portrait of the city, a picture of its streets and civic centers, the only picture of Seattle that she'd found at the St. Paul Public Library had been of a sullen timber port, logs jamming in the foreground, tall ships crowding the shoreline of what appeared to be a backwater fishing village overshadowed by tremendous pines.

Seattle.

She'd repeated the syllables in her mind, *see at tall*, lingering on each sound, wondering what railroad tycoon had inspired the town's name and what country he had come from with a name like that, Seattle, and then she realized that the rhythm of her thoughts was the rhythm of the train and that the troupe of nuns was singing in that rhythm, too. Well, not singing, actually, humming, harmonizing with their mouths closed, a fifth, a third, a seventh, Clara saw her mother's fingers lifting off the keys to play those chords and the hallowed beauty of the music caught her by surprise, so unexpected. Other music flooded over her, memories of Chopin, Schumann and Amelia playing, always, her mother playing the piano, and the loss of that, the loss of all that beauty overwhelmed her, almost religiously. She'd plucked the embroidered handkerchief from her sleeve cuff and had dabbed her eyes, glancing across the aisle to see if Hercules was watching her. His blond head lay peaceful on the pillow, as his body rocked in rhythm to the rails. Sound asleep. Like any normal boy his age. Miraculously not weeping.

She must have slept, herself, sitting straight up, because what she'd remembered next was waking to the tinkling of soprano bells. Each nun had one, and as light rose behind the mountains outside the window, and the day had dawned, the nuns began to pray among themselves, each one ringing her own tiny bell for punctuation. The train had slowed.

The train had slowed and then the whole long thing had groaned to a shape-shifting halt, steam escaping like a demon soul from each extinguished part. Bismark. The Dakota Territory.

The nuns had gathered themselves up, birds lifting from a field, and Clara had not known what to do next, nor what was expected of her. She'd been acting on the fly for weeks, learning as she'd gone along, *aware* that she'd been learning, a first sign of being an adult. No one had informed her there would be a stop along the line where she'd be required to detrain. No one had forewarned her that their parents were going to die. Each casual happenstance since their deaths, therefore, put her on alert as portent for the worst. She had boarded at St. Paul in the belief that the railroad car she rode in was a closed set of circumstances, a closed paragraph, that the train tracks were a story line delivering her, premeditatively, from one point in her life into another. No one had told her there would be the odd depot, the unexpected staging place, along the line, requiring improvisation.

She followed the nuns into the aisle, down the iron steps to the platform, clutching Hercules with one hand and the other on the drawstring purse with eighty dollars inside, hidden in her bodice— and good thing, too: because what they encountered at the Bismark depot was a scene designed to part her from her money. There was a barbershop for men, a "hotel" for the ladies where they could rent a room for a few hours to have a bath and change their traveling clothes. There was a smoking room (again, for men), a restaurant, a saloon (for men), two waiting rooms (one for men and one for women), a dispensary, a chapel and—as the *pièce de résistance*—there were Indians.

Rising from a vastness too empty to comprehend, Bismarck depot appeared to her to be a masterpiece of cunning engineering. It was *big*. It offered one the illusion of a small but self-sustaining city. Landing at its threshold, being forced to grasp it in the forefront of the larger picture, pumped its size, inflated it and its importance, drew the disoriented passengers into its seductive promise of warm food, hot water and the blandishments of a known, cosmetically civilized and appealing world.

Clara had been too naïve to know how to order breakfast from the conductor the night before, so she and Hercules stood, immobile on the platform in the morning sun, while their fellow passengers filed past them with confidence into the beckoning maw of man-made comfort.

The depot, she reckoned—this artificial place—was meant to provide amenities the train, itself, was lacking. Passengers were required to detrain to be entertained and lulled into a sense of bought-and-paid-for engineered adventure. Time was displayed as it existed locally and elsewhere: there were clocks hanging on the depot walls heralding the current times in Chicago, San Francisco, New York, London, Paris and Oslo, as if to grant to each detraining soul a sense of kinship with a larger world when, in fact, they had been sidelined on the godforsaken tracks of a godforsaken nowhere. She was there with Hercules and she was responsible for him and she suddenly thought of their father traveling alone to Europe in his youth—to Paris and to Florence—imagined him detraining in a foreign landscape surrounded by the unfamiliar sights and sounds of latent possibilities. He would not have *hesitated*, she imagined. He would not have hoarded eighty dollars in a drawstring purse. "Let's find ourselves some breakfast, Hercules," she then and there resolved.

An albino buffalo, yellowed as an old piano ivory, mounted on the restaurant wall, looked down on them, along with heads of elk and bear and deer and several full-sized giant rodents standing upright on their hind legs. She smiled as Hercules read the entire menu to her as if it were a sequel in a boy's adventure. A young woman no older than herself poured cups of fragrant coffee for them and Clara, still emboldened by the image of her father travel-ing to Europe on his own, asked her, "Do you live out here?"

"Sure do. There's a dormitory for us right behind the depot."

"Us," Clara realized, were the dozen young women serving ta-bles.

"But there's nothing out here."

"And plenty of it!" the young woman laughed. "Three trains a day. We can't get lonely. Plus we get to meet some real nice people."

"You work for the railroad?"

"Sure do. Northern Pacific."

"And they pay you?"

"Of course they do."

"How much?" A question she would never have thought to ask a month ago.

"Enough to set aside. Plus we get to ride the line for free. I'm ridin' out to San Francisco on my next time off."

"You should work here, Clara," Hercules volunteered.

"Then who'd look after you?"

"I could live here with you and shoot buffalo—"

"Where you two headin'?" the young woman asked.

"Washington Territory."

"What takes you way out there?"

"Our parents died," Hercules piped up. Dry-eyed. It was the first time Clara had heard him speak the words. "Can I have anything I want to have for breakfast even if it costs too much?" he then had asked.

She would not be spendthrift but she would not deny them common pleasures. Just this once Hercules could order buffalo steak and flapjacks if he wanted and she could treat herself to fresh

Dakota trout and eggs. There were jobs for girls like her, out here, jobs that didn't seem much worse than factory jobs in Minnesota, working for the granaries. She would find employment in Seattle, even if she could not afford to finish her abbreviated education, and she would "set aside" and save just like these young women in the railroad depot. Meanwhile she would draw her greatest pleasure from the simplest things—a glass of water and fried eggs, her brother licking maple syrup from his fingers—because it had occurred to her while sitting there that everyone she would encounter in her life from now on would be a stranger. Except, of course, for the distant Curtises.

"You're the only person that I know in the whole world," Hercules had said just then. Then asked, "Do you think they see us?"

"Who, Hercules?"

"Mother and father."

"I don't know."

"Sometimes I think they're watching me. I hope they are. I think they'd like it here. I think they would be proud of us."

"I don't think the dead have eyes, Hercules."

He looked up at the albino buffalo, then down at his buffalo steak. "There are other ways of seeing than with eyes," he'd said. "Sometimes you see things in your thoughts."

"I don't think the dead have thoughts," she'd told him.

"I need to think they do," he stated.

Minutes later, when they walked outside again, they found the platform lined with Indians.

Clara had seen the occasional Indian from northern Minnesota on the streets of St. Paul, but she had never seen human creatures such as these, people as weathered as old timber, who seemed never to have sheltered from the elements, whose hardscrabble poverty showed in their eyes and teeth and fingernails and feet. "Are they real?" Hercules had asked.

"Of course they're real."

"No, I mean are they real Indians?"

"Yes."

"Are they going to kill us?"

"No."

"What are they doing, then?"

"Trying to make money."

"Why?"

The Indians—she couldn't tell, sometimes, if one was male or female—sat on the ground, their backs against the depot wall, their pathetic wares spread out for sale on woven rugs before them. Hercules clung to her arm and she had to tell him not to stare as they walked the full length of the platform and then back again. But it

was hard to keep one's gaze away from these strange people. None spoke, few moved, and in their silence they seemed to her more like the taxidermy, the trophies on the walls inside the restaurant, than like fellow thinking creatures. They sat rigid on their dirty rugs, not really trying to sell the things they'd laid before them—items constructed of the most elemental things: straw, feathers, clay and animal carcasses. Some of the passengers lined up to have their pictures taken with a "chief," a solemn stony figure in a feathered headdress and a vest made out of bones. But most of their fellow passengers handled the baskets and the pots and put them down again, dismissively. Some weighed the silver trinkets in their hands, necklaces and rings inset with blue-green stones, ill-formed and clumsy, Clara thought, she could imagine no modern woman of her mother's style and taste deigning to wear such heavy, decorative things. The Indians, themselves, seemed not to care that nothing sold, seemed not to understand the elements of commerce. They seemed, oddly, in a state of non-existence, having arrived on the platform from godknowswhere in order to enact a play in which they were the scenery, nothing else. "What happened to them?" Hercules had asked. "They look so sad. They look like someone's died. I think they're sadder than I am."

A good sign, Clara had thought: that he could imagine sadness greater than his own. Art, their father had frequently told them, was exactly that: to make art is to realize another's sadness within, realize the hidden sadness in other people's lives, to feel sad with and for a stranger. Hercules had pressed his nose against the carriage window as the train had lurched to life, inching forward from the Bismarck depot. And still the Indians had not moved. He had watched them solemnly and then, in a gesture understood by any human, he had

raised his hand and waved farewell to them. Whose sadness were the Indians imagining, Clara wondered: whom, among the dead, did they miss, were there ancestors who, among the dead, they needed to believe were watching them, as Hercules believed their parents were? Their faces registered a state of emptiness, perhaps from looking at this too vast canvas for too long. As the train developed steam and speed the country rolled past in undifferentiated magnitude, she could see, to the horizon. How could a soul survive out here, she thought, without a mirror, without a printed word, without a line connecting one to mankind's history, mankind's self-perpetuating sadness? We're not made for open spaces, she considered, they humiliate and humble us and make us search for God in granite niches. All this open territory—so important to the men back East—for what? To join the coasts. Join two halves of coastline. Connect us sea to sea. Control the money in both pockets. Was it *beautiful*, or *scenic*, all this? It was *terrifying*, she had thought, and as the day wore on, she slept, then woke, then slept again. Waking, she was suddenly obsessed with finding someone in the landscape, anyone, a moving figure, proof that humanity outside the train existed.

Night fell and they'd stopped at Billings, and at Butte, Montana Territory, and then, opening her eyes in morning, she'd thought she'd seen a shadow racing on the rising plain and realized she was looking at a running bear, infuriated by the train. The cold increased and they'd been suddenly surrounded by snow and mountains, curtains of gray rock shimmering with ice at arm's length, it had seemed, from the carriage windows. They had moved to seats closer to the central stove and Clara had rented extra blankets from the conductor and had heated and reheated the stones beside the stove to warm their feet. They ate thick sandwiches of rough brown bread and salty beef purchased from a squaw in Sandpoint, Idaho Territory, where they'd laid over half a day while the train took on carloads of sand for traction through the icy inclines. She'd slept some more and then, when she thought the stiffness in her lower back and neck and shoulders had become too hardened to be relieved, the conductor had announced Tacoma depot *next*.

They hadn't had a proper wash for days but with a little spit and elbow grease she'd polished Hercules's face and hands and buttoned him all up in his second-hand suit and run her fingers through her auburn hair and tied Amelia's lambskin and velvet bonnet on her head. She could see them, the Curtises—Eva, Asahel and Ellen— standing by a buckboard next to the rickety platform, looking, she had thought, as expectant, worried and confused as she herself was feeling. But then a swell of gratitude went through her, the train came to a halt, releasing its steam, and Hercules was at the door and down the steps and into Asahel's welcoming embrace before she had been able to stop him.

Her descent had been more cautious.

Perhaps, even then, she had been unknowingly anticipating Edward, searching for his face, even though she'd never met him.

There was Eva, pale and thin and tight-lipped. And Asahel, brown eyes brimming with excitement, grinning ear to ear. And Ellen, who had taken one astonished look at Clara, touched her throat and gasped *Amelia!* and collapsed onto the platform like a sack of old potatoes.

Clara was by her side immediately, her one semester of nursing education rising to the fore, cradling the downed woman's head in one hand, feeling for a pulse with her other. "Has she been ill?" she'd asked of Eva and Eva, biting on her lip and looking paralyzed, had shaken her head. Clara had taken a vial of *sal ammoniac* from her traveling bag, broken it in half and waved the fumes near Ellen's nostrils.

"Oh, *Amelia*," the older woman said again, coming to, "they told me you were dead."

"It's Clara, mother," Eva scolded. "*Clara.*"

"Amelia, dear, dear friend," Ellen said again, patting Clara's hand, "I'm so happy that you're here."

When Lodz had first seen Amelia's portrait that Clara's father had painted, he'd said, "Except for the dark hair, this is real you. You have her face, you know?" so the bonnet, clearly, was at the root of Ellen's daft confusion, and although Clara told her, "Aunt Ellen, it's me—it's *Clara*," Ellen still clutched at her and whispered, "So relieved to see you, dear. You'll know what to do, Amelia. You always do, praise God."

They managed Ellen into a sitting position, then slowly to her feet, as she all the while held onto Clara, looking up at her with a dreamy expression that was frankly creepy, and Clara had begun to suspect the older woman might not be quite right in the head, a pos-sibility that struck fear in her over what kind of tenuous security she'd wagered for herself and Hercules. Asahel organized their bag-gage and before long they were all seated in the buckboard and Clara, up front, next to Asahel, had the first opportunity to assess her new locality. It was sparse, for one thing, the Tacoma station, minimal and impermanent, hardly worthy of the designation End of the Line. It was a timber building built more like a religious camp-ground structure than a masterpiece of railroading. If you were rid-ing Northern Pacific rails then this was where you were when you and it ran out of steam, and it was pretty paltry, she had to say, con-forming to no image she had expected—specifically: there appeared to be no town. There appeared to be no end-of-journey *place*, no respite from the wilderness she'd been looking at for these past days: no destination. Rain, but not-rain, a sort of visible and particulate wet air, like the inside of a cloud, raindrops held in time, sustained and not falling, misted on her face, her clothes, and lent the atmos-phere a filtered presence, a gray light, as if one were living in a shad-owy past. "Not so cold," she'd finally said to Asahel. Always safe, in start-up conversation, to talk about the weather.

"Haven't been here all that long myself, but winter's pretty mild they tell me," he agreed, "compared to what you've been through. On your journey here, I mean." They happened to glance at each other, then, accidentally, and there was warmth and under-standing in his eyes. Something else, too, something of a greater meaning or of a greater heat, which she was too exhausted to start to try to translate.

"I was sorry to learn about your parents, Clara," he said. "They were fine people, always good to us when we had no one else."

"And I'm sorry, too," she'd said, "about your father."

"Oh," he shrugged. "You know, I hardly knew him. I have more memories of your father than of my own." And there was that shadow, again, in his eyes, when he looked at her, that she couldn't decode.

"Is it far?" she'd asked, staring ahead. "To the—"

"Fifteen miles. Then a ferry."

"And will we see Seattle?"

"Seattle? Gosh, no. Why do you ask?"

"Curious. What's it like? Have you been there?"

He started to laugh. "No reason for me to. No time."

"And Edward," she'd faltered, trying to mask her disappointment. "Where is he?"

"Edward?" He pointed with the horsewhip over his shoulder. "Edward's up there, for all I know."

In her confusion Clara thought he had meant heaven. She'd thought for one awful moment that he meant Edward was dead.

"Mt. Rainier," he pointed again, and behind him, over his shoulder, Clara saw the mountain for the first time, majestic and snow-capped, dominating the distance.

"He's—?" she stammered.

"—on the mountain," he confirmed.

"But—*why?*"

He'd laughed again, warm and welcoming, like his eyes. "Well, when he comes down, ask him yourself."

The fact that the elder Curtis, the head of the household, had contrived not to be present for their arrival did not bode well, she'd thought. What if they weren't welcome? What if Ellen, off her head, had forgotten to inform him?

"Edward goes away," Asahel said, by way of explanation. "Then he comes back. You'll see. Edward always comes back. He always does. Edward always comes back home."

Clara might have dozed, sitting up, or else the densely forested countryside looked the same mile after mile because she seemed to lose track of time. Even the choppy ferry ride couldn't invigorate her sense of dread and fatigue, and she was grateful to Asahel for taking charge of Hercules as she stood, gripping the rail of the boat, searching the trailing fog, as previous sailors must have done, for symptoms of a recognizable life.

And then they were there. Although what "there" was was hardly recognizable. Asahel drew the horse to a halt and helped his mother and sister from the back and began to unload the buckboard as Hercules ran toward the barn and Clara sat, unable to move, staring at what was before her.

Surrounded by green-black fir trees on three sides, this was a clearing, of sorts, a cleared rectangle in the middle of a pine tree forest, the narrow dirt road leading into a cul-de-sac with the house, if you could call it that, to the right side, the barn to the left and a sheer drop of land straight ahead where, between the pine trees, she could see the Puget Sound and hear it lapping on the shore, below. The earth in the foreground, between the barn and the house, was tamped bare and muddy and paved in places with crushed oyster shells. There was a timber rack next to the barn on which some kind of flesh was curing in rows and an overpowering aroma led her to conclude it must be fish. There was a garden, badly kept, between the house and the coastal promontory, staked for vines but overrun with chickens. There was a hand pump in the center of the bare ground between the house and barn, beside a water trough where a tomcat sat licking at its testicles, and beside the porch steps to the house, wrapped in blankets the same color as the fog, there stood two Indians.

Ellen was already shooing at them, "Go away. No make-ee business today. Edward no here. Go, *go*—" while Asahel helped Clara down from the buckboard, meeting her expression of alarm with the explanation, "Friends of Edward's. He finds work for them." Then Hercules came running from the barn, exclaiming, "Clara! They have horses here!" and Clara was trying to calm his excitement as they went up the porch steps past the Indians into what she supposed was meant to be a kitchen.

The floor was some kind of uneven stone, there was a hearth, a stove, a copper basin, hanging pots and brooms, a long pine table with two benches, shelves lined with mismatched plates and tin enamelware, and two glass-fronted highboys painted pink and yellow. "Come, Amelia, come," Ellen beckoned and led Clara from the kitchen toward a narrow passageway that led to other rooms. Clara followed her into the first room on the left, larger than expected, nearly the size of the kitchen, with a glazed tile stove in one corner and a matrimonial-size bed in the center of the floor. "You take this room, Amelia," Ellen said, gathering up what few personal belongings there were from the bureau and the hat rack. "I'll move in with Eva."

"—no, mother, *no*," Eva urged, appearing in the room, taking Ellen by the arms to stop her and entreating Clara with her eyes. "—*please*," she whimpered.

"Oh, no, we'll be fine. I never liked it in here, not after that first night. Amelia needs this larger room for all of her nice things."

Eva turned to Clara. "Tell her you are *not Amelia*," she begged, her eyes blazing, and although Clara understood her despair at having to share her privacy, at her age, with her dotty mother, a purely selfish impulse rose within her. She could see herself living in a room this size, alone, filling it with her own thoughts and memories, making of it a refuge from this strange place and this strange family, and, involuntarily, her gaze flitted to the door to see if there was a lock on the inside. There was. "Aunt Ellen," she said, only halfheartedly, "you must let Eva have a room of her own. And you must stop calling me Amelia."

"Well, what should I call you, dear?"

"Clara."

"Don't be silly, dear." She continued gathering her pile of things. "Eva, tell your brother to bring Amelia's trunk in here."

Eva glared at Clara. "It's not fair," she said.

"Don't expect me to talk sense into her if you can't," Clara answered, which set the record straight. "Now show me the rest of the house so I can figure all this out."

As her mother had done with the disarray of Ellen's life back in St. Paul, so Clara would do in these new circumstances, with Asahel's and Edward's commission and approval, of course, as she believed that both of them had grown into responsible young men, capable of solving problems for themselves. But on the distaff side, the day-to-day and largely female running of the house, Clara had assumed hierarchical supremacy from the moment Ellen fainted on the railroad platform. She and Eva held a delicate truce, Eva chafing in her supportive role but still pleased to exercise her exclusive right to play the helpless ingenue. It became a predictable split among the six of them (counting Hercules), a division of daily life and daily labor along gender lines. Even without Edward present on the compound, his influence was felt in the way he'd organized the structures, organized the buildings. The house was built around the kitchen and the sleeping rooms for, originally, the oldest and the youngest members of the family. The barn was built around himself. The barn was where the tools were stored, the horses and the mule were stabled—and it was where Edward, and, subsequently, Asahel, retreated every night to hunker down among the leather and the steel and the smell of animals to sleep *as men*. And that was where Hercules, from the first day, as soon as he had seen the cowboy-like bunkhouse rooms beside the stalls and stacks of hay, had wanted to be at night. With the animals. And with the men. With Asahel, who assured her it was civilized out there, proper sheets and blankets on the beds, but Clara said she'd have to see it. She would see it, first, before she gave permission. "'No Girls Allowed,'" Hercules had told her, "there's a sign up on the wall."

"I'm not a girl, I am your guardian," Clara had reminded him.

"He *cries*, sometimes, at night," she'd confessed to Asahel, so he'd let her in. And it was wonderful, far better than the window-less room allotted to him at the dark end of the narrow passage-way in the house. "If I hear him crying," Asahel had told her, "I will come and get you." He had moved to touch her hand with his, but then retracted it. So it had happened, from the first day, that Hercules had been adopted into the all-male brotherhood of the barn, and Clara had unpacked her *Icarus* trunk, her father's paint-ings and her mother's embroidered linens in the room that had been built by Edward to consummate the future happiness and solace of his parents. On her first night there, she'd realized that the house, with this arrangement, was occupied, solely, by women and that if there should be an unexpected occurrence in the dark, an intruder or a bear or fire or a snake, there was no man inside to help. She'd unpacked Amelia's tea set and placed it, ceremoniously and showily, on the center shelf of one of the highboys in the kitchen, and then she'd unpacked Amelia's sewing basket and placed the razor-sharp steel scissors defensively beneath her pillow. Then on the third night there, before she'd accustomed herself to the natural terrifying sounds that a strange house makes, she'd been woken from a dead sleep by the noise of something moving in the kitchen. She'd closed her fingers on the scissors and had sat up, stopping her breathing so she could listen better. And there it was: a vocative murmuring, like a dove, perhaps, or an owl, and then the scraping of a chair leg or the bench across the stone floor, and then a precise and chilling clinking noise, one she knew inarguably, from experience, as the sound of a fine china cup striking a fine china saucer.

Not really thinking what she'd do if there were an actual intruder, Clara had made her way into the passageway in the dark, her bare feet stinging on the cold stone floor, her hand around the scissors, holding them as if their double blades were a single-edged knife, and was surprised to see the fluid shadows of a lantern's light playing on the floor in front of her, coming from the kitchen. Still not weighing the consequences she burst upon the scene, scissors raised above her head, to discover the two Indians at tea, sitting at the long pine table with her mother's cups and saucers in their hands, a jug of whiskey between them and, to her right, a red-headed man, tall, his suspenders down around his waist, standing at the copper basin, shirtless, shaving. He'd turned to her, his razor in his hand, his face and beard half lathered, and all she would remember would be the color of his eyes, a blue more honed, more steely and more deadly than the weapons both of them were holding. *Edward*, she had realized.

He neither moved nor said a word but his gaze, steady and unwavering, bored into her, showing no emotion, as if he were a pane of glass passively returning her reflection, and she suddenly realized she must look a fright, like a woman from a madhouse, her linen shift open at the neck, her hair in disarray around her shoulders. She brought the scissors down to her side and took a small step backward, uncomfortable in his gaze and suddenly aware that not only he but all of them, the Indians, too, were staring at her. *I'm Clara. I heard a noise*, she wanted to say, but couldn't, her heart suddenly too large in her chest for her to catch her breath. She took another tiny step, lifting her feet from the cold stone to warm them, and her eyes involuntarily left Edward's and fell once more on the Indians. She parted her lips, once more trying to speak, and turned back to Edward, the unspoken thought, she knew, flashing in her eyes: *They're using my mother's china.*

You're using my house, his challenged.

"I'm sorry," she finally spoke, and turned and fled.

It was not the initial encounter with him that she had anticipated; and he was not the man she had expected—although, truth be told, she'd formed no image in her mind, nor any preconsidered judgment about Edward, save that he would most likely be a version of his brother, and that he had had the foresight, perhaps romantic, but most certainly optimistic, to build a room for his parents that was the most civilized, beautiful room in this largely uncivilized, not beautiful house. When she'd been unpacking her *Icarus* trunk, pinning her father's paintings to the walls and rearranging the sparse furniture, she'd noticed details in the making of the room—a heart drawn in the mortar between beams, the initials "ESC" carved in wood—that had made her stop to consider just what kind of man this Edward was. She had thought he would be kind—easy to break into a smile, like Asahel. She had thought she would like him, without even trying. And he her—again, like Asahel. She had not considered that he might be cold or unfeeling or that he wouldn't like her and what that would mean. What does it mean when a man doesn't speak, when he holds himself bound in silence like those first Indians she'd seen selling badly made trinkets at the depot in Bismarck? She would seek him out in the morning, she had determined—seek him out and solicit a welcome or, at least, a new introduction. And though that helped her to sleep, she didn't sleep well, knowing that he and the unnamed Indians were a small distance away, and near dawn it didn't take more than a brief tap on her door to wake her: it was Eva. "Mother's sick," she told her through the door. Clara pulled on a shawl and followed her to where Ellen lay in the next room on her side in bed, her knees drawn up. "*Pain*," she uttered. Her face was gray.

"Where?" Clara asked, and Ellen had pointed low on her back. Clara placed a hand on Ellen's head, then felt along her jaw beneath her ears, prised her legs down and felt along her abdomen, rolled her over and pressed along her back, then accidentally bumped against Eva, standing next to her. "She doesn't have a fever," Clara whispered. "But where's the nearest doctor if we need one?"

"Brisbane Island," Eva told her.

"None over here?"

"Only for the animals."

"Aunt Ellen, what kind of pain is it?" Clara asked. "Sharp or dull?"

"Sharp as the devil's tooth, Amelia."

"Did you urinate this morning?"

"Did I *what*—?"

Clara slid the chamber pot from beneath the bed, swirled the contents and offered Eva a whiff. Then she showed Eva how to administer a mustard pack to Ellen's lower back and she made Ellen drink a beaker of water while she watched.

"She has to drink a beaker every hour," Clara instructed Eva. "She's passing a kidney stone."

Eva squeezed Clara's hand. "Thank you," she said.

"Edward's back," Clara mentioned.

"I know."

"How do you know?"

"When he's here he draws two pails of water in the morning from the pump out in the yard and leaves them for us on the porch."

"And when he's not here?"

"I have to draw the pails myself."

"What else do you do?"

"I'm sorry—?"

"Around here."

"I do all the cooking. And the laundry. And the cleaning."

"But then how do you—how does the household—how do we make money?"

"Couple days a week, Asahel and Edward job out at the sawmill."

"And that's enough?"

"For what?"

"Enough to pay for everything we need?"

"Well, look around. Does it look like we need much?"

Later that morning, when she and Eva had been in the kitchen cleaning vegetables, Clara took the subject up again. "What about a school? Hercules needs schooling."

"Christian school on Brisbane, I believe."

"None over here?"

"Nothing that I've heard of."

"But there must be children?"

"Plenty."

"Well where do they all learn?"

"To read, you mean?"

"To read, to write—"

"I never thought about it. I don't know."

"Maybe we could teach them."

"You and me?"

"Why not? Teachers are *paid*."

"Well, we couldn't just start, now, could we? Wouldn't we have to ask someone?"

"I don't know. Is there a mayor or—is there any kind of government?"

"There's the ministry. I suppose we could ask the reverend—"

"Anything besides the ministry?"

"The sawmill."

"Do they hire women?"

"Have you ever *seen* a sawmill?"

Edward entered from outside without a word and poured himself a cup of coffee from the pot steaming on the stove. He was wearing doeskin pants the color of the core of the potato Clara was peeling, a starched blue denim shirt, a silk neckerchief the color of spring lilac and a rust-colored leather broad-brimmed hat. He was, she realized with surprise, altogether the most striking man she'd ever seen.

Eva stood and smoothed her skirt, silent and attendant on her brother. Then Edward turned and, looking only at his sister, asked, "How is our Mother?"

"Better."

"Good."

"Less pain."

"Excellent."

"Clara has ascertained it is a kidney stone."

Awkward silence.

Then Eva prompted, "You've met Clara. Clara, this is Edward. Edward, Clara."

And to her own amazement, Clara stood.

He stared at her, still not speaking a word, his eyes so blue above the denim shirt she thought her heart would burst. She cleared her throat. "I—my brother and I want to thank you, Edward, for—"

"Express to Mother my concern," he addressed Eva, interrupting.

"I will," Eva had replied.

And he was gone, bounding down the porch steps in a single jump, racing across the open compound in long, urgent strides as if he were the only Greek at Marathon—disappearing into the barn. That was the way that he appeared to Clara through the following weeks and months—running, always running, on the move and in a hurry to escape, to be *somewhere else*, to disappear, to light out, to be gone. He never took his meals with them and only rarely came inside the house for longer than a brief, perfunctory but daily visit. Several times he disappeared for a week at a time and Asahel would let her know, Gone again, but he'll be back. You'll see. He always comes back home.

As the winter wore on and the rains increased, she began to feel more trapped in the aimlessness that was the Curtises' communal life. Isolation, too, began to take its toll. Except for the two Indians who came several times a week looking for work from Edward, visits from anyone were rare, and except for the buckboard ride every Sunday to the Baptist Missionary church house on the island, Clara and the Curtis women had nowhere else to go. Clara had struck out on foot with Hercules looking for a neighbor or a place where people gathered, a general store or a trading post but between the Curtis homestead and the sawmill there were only two other houses, each a mile apart and occupied by kind but largely backward and illiterate Russians. She went several times with Eva and Ellen to the Baptist Missionary ministry, hoping to meet other men and women of some education and social purpose, even if only driven by their missionary zeal, and she had tried to inaugurate a few acquaintanceships that foundered swiftly on her inability to commit her soul to their beliefs. There was a school, but it was a Sunday school, lessons administered by the reverend's wife, and Clara soon found herself solely responsible, and underprepared, for Hercules's education. The books she'd brought with her were those curious and intricately illustrated books in Dutch, French and Italian she had acquired with the *Icarus* trunk and some of her father's former volumes on the art of painting, for which Hercules exhibited no evidence of inherited skill. His skills, it developed, first to her disapproval, and then with her slow acceptance, were in the outdoor life, a husbandry of animals both large and small, following Asahel and Edward through their chores, growing stronger, more robust with every passing month, even as she grew more pale, despairing and alone. Her initial attempts at kinship with Eva reached a level of polite ease but never ignited into a bond of shared ambition. Eva's ultimate desire in life, Clara had determined, was to be a wife, a wife and then a mother, to continue her present routine, an existence that was distinguished by its service to others, and Clara had watched her flirt shyly but convincingly with every unmarried man at the Sunday services. Asahel, alone, afforded Clara the opportunity for conversation beyond the mere exchange of pleasantries and domestic business, but there were not enough leisure minutes in the day to accommodate shared discourse. They were always working, it became clear to her, at something that would never have a lasting meaning or lasting effect. Her life, their lives, seemed to be being abraded by the daily drudgery, diminishing away. She had never known such physical labor, nor guessed the price that it exacted on the mind, not only was her body taxed in ways she'd never experienced before, but her ability to engage in playful thought was fleeting. Her skin grew rough, her mind grew dull, her hope grew dim, and the only happiness she knew was in watching Hercules radiate the natural joy of his existence. Work was what defined each day—tending the stove, heating water, carrying the chamber pots to the outhouse, cleaning them, cooking, slaughtering a chicken, cleaning it—and work, the labor of it, was what drove her into dreamless sleep each night. Then one day in late March a false spring broke from the coastal winter gloom, the sky was clear of clouds from early morning and the sun shone in a bright and faultless sky. Clara decided to hang laundry on a line stretched between two fir trees beside the house and as she was wrestling a wet bedsheet through the mangle, Edward suddenly appeared in the yard with a leather ball and kicked it high into the air.

Hercules, followed by Asahel, ran to retrieve it, and a game of kick-and-catch ensued among them. Clara heard them call to one another back and forth as she stretched the bedsheet on the line and pinned it. Then she heard Hercules begin to laugh—it was a sound as bright and sunny as the day—and she peeked around the sheet to watch. Hercules was running with the ball while Edward and Asahel ran after him, dodging and faking, and all the while Hercules was laughing, laughing as if sadness had never touched his life, as if he were a tiny child again and innocent of death's swift thoroughness. She wondered briefly if he would have ever been so happy in St. Paul, if their parents hadn't died, and she was suddenly overcome by a grief so sudden and weighty that it knocked the air out of her chest and shook her shoulders as she cried. She hadn't cried this way when her parents had died and now she cried as much for the loss of them as for the loss of her former self. She hung onto the sheet so she wouldn't fall but her pity for herself bent her over and she couldn't catch her breath between her sobs. It was as if she'd saved up all the grief of the last months for this moment and she couldn't bring herself under control—nevertheless, she was aware that the leather ball had suddenly bounced past her and when she turned to look, wiping at the tears flooding her vision, there stood Edward only inches from her, staring at her with those blue eyes. Again, he didn't speak. But as another wave of weeping overwhelmed her he stepped to her and pulled her head onto his chest and held her tightly in his arms. She could feel the whole length of his body pressing against hers, and she could smell him. There was a vein pulsing in his neck where his shirt was open and she watched it for a few beats then put her lips to it and closed her eyes.

A few seconds later she was calm and she felt him lessen his hold on her, and then he backed away. Asahel was there, a look of quiet desperation in his eyes, and then Hercules was running past her with the ball and both Edward and Asahel ran after him.

So, in the end, it was love that saved her.

Un-named, unrecognized, at first; and certainly, for a long time, unrequited.

The feeling came unexpectedly and unannounced—an unheralded quickening in the air around her, an excitement of the mind, and, unmistakably, she began to look forward, rather than to dread, each new day. She began to look forward to what each new day might bring—a glimpse of him, or an encounter, a look, perhaps a word. She began to recover a sense of well-being, a sense of purpose, even if it was only to engage in a fantasy of doing something that would make him stop and notice her or saying something that would make him smile. But in the same week of their embrace Edward had disappeared again and she was left to daydream and to draw ungrounded and wildly optimistic assumptions. When he returned he barely noticed her, which only fueled what she now acknowledged had become a full-fledged infatuation. It wasn't *him*, she told herself. It wasn't specifically for *him* that she pined, but for the embrace, that moment when, surrounded by another's arms, her body had seemed less of a burden, had, in fact, seemed light. But then she'd see him and she'd realize her obsession was not an abstract passion like an artist's, like her father's passion for his work, but that it was a lover's passion for the object of desire, for the object of her love. She was in love, and she had no one in whom to confide, no one from whom to seek advice and counsel, so she sought her mother in her mind, her mother's ghost, her mother, who would have no doubt approved enthusiastically, encouraging her along the most reckless and outrageous path. He had embraced her, hadn't he? And that stood for something, didn't it? Despite his silence and his distance. But his silence and his distance stood for something, too, she knew. Stood for something far more certain and established in the man than any rare signal of emotion. Still her inclination to delude herself was too attractive: to know the physical embraces that her parents must have known, to breathe the scent of someone's skin and feel his pulse against her lips—that was a seductive, even necessary, self-delusion. If it had happened once, surely it would come her way again. It would have to.

But it didn't.

Edward stayed to himself, a revered but inaccessible cipher on the family's periphery, until one day in May when he rode into the compound with a large contraption wrapped in blankets and strapped onto the back of the buckboard. The Curtis women came out on the porch, followed by Clara, as Asahel and Hercules helped Edward grapple the mystery item to the ground and unwrap it.

"What are we supposed t' do with *that?*" Ellen asked derisively.

"*Enjoy* it, Mother."

"Well what *is* it?"

"A bathtub, I believe," Eva suggested.

And not any ordinary tub for bathing, Clara saw. Shaped like a dancing slipper, high in the back, curved and snug at the front, it was hammered from a single sheet of copper which made it lightweight and portable, bright as a penny.

"Where did you get this from, brother?" Asahel teased. "From that house of fancy women?"

Edward colored. "*Language*, Asahel," he scolded.

"Well I'm not havin' it in the house," Ellen maintained.

"Fine, we'll keep it out here, then," Edward told her.

"Don't see why you go wastin' your money on what we don't need," Ellen complained. "We got tubs already. Two of 'em." Heavy, nickel buckets you had to stand in, Clara thought, next to the stove where you heated the water. And then struggle to carry the whole mess outside to dump it when you were done.

"It's too pretty," Ellen went on. "The Lord cautions against ostentation," she reminded her son. "What were you thinking?"

Edward touched the back of the tub with his palm and let it glissade down the curved and smooth lip. "That it might bring pleasure to someone," he said, his blue gaze fixed on Clara for what she thought was noticeably too long, while her heart lurched, before he and Asahel carried the tub onto the porch. There it stayed, for a month, unused by anyone, although Clara wiped it clean every day, reliving, in her mind, the way he had looked at her when he spoke the word, pleasure. *Aren't you tempted?* Eva asked her, sneaking up behind her one day while she was polishing the tub with a soft rag.

Clara faced her, her color high, and almost said, *It's mine.*

"I'm tempted," Eva admitted. "Let's fill her up and—"

"You'll do nothing of the kind," Ellen had snapped. "You tell her, Amelia, she'll listen to *you*. God is watching what you do, Eva. He's counseling your future husband."

Clara rolled her eyes as if she were conspiring with Eva, but she had determined in that moment that she would find a way to claim the tub's first bath, one way or another. Because the pleasure was intended to be hers. And then, as if fortune, or what Ellen would have deemed to be God, were smiling on her, her opportunity arrived a few weeks later in the form of the Baptist Missionaries' annual week-long summer retreat. Ellen was going, of course, as was Eva;

and to her surprise, Hercules had asked to go as well, because their farrier was a member of the sect and had offered Hercules instruction in the craft if he were to join them for the week. *Please*, Hercules had wheedled in his most charming way.

"They want your soul," she tried to scare him.

"Oh I know that," he told her, smiling. "It's learning *a trade*," he bartered, playing on her greater fear that both of them might never break the bonds of living off charity.

"All right," she acquiesced. When Hercules heard hoofbeats he thought of horses. She thought of unicorns or zebras, and she was secretly thinking of the baths that she could have, when everyone was gone.

Asahel would drive them in the buckboard, and no one knew where Edward was nor when he would return, and as the day of their departure dawned Clara was kept awake by the realization that she'd be alone on the compound for the first time and, strangely, this awareness left her feeling more excited than alarmed. She'd come to know the two Indians by their names, Mopoc and Modoc, and she had come to deal with them through sign language and through pictures that she drew, whenever the two of them came looking for work when Edward was away. They were harmless, she had learned, dimwitted and a bit slow to grasp her well-designed instructions, but they were, in the end, useful to the household. Once a week, usually on Sundays because they knew the other women, with whom they didn't want to deal, would be away at their Sunday services, the Indians would wait by the barn for Clara to come to tell them what she wanted for the week. Squirrel? No squirrel. She hated cooking squirrel—they were tedious to clean, there was no meat and what meat there was was gamey. Yet every week they brought her squirrels. *No rabbits,* she would tell them and draw a picture of a rabbit, draw a strong black line through it to mean *no* rabbits yet week after week they brought her rabbit carcasses on poles until she understood that the line that she'd been drawing through her rabbit picture translated *kill* to the two Indians. So she'd learned to draw, then shake her head. Draw—show the picture—shake her head. And they would shake their heads. And still they brought her squirrels and rabbits when what she wanted them to hunt was boar, wild turkey or a deer, something she could salt and cure for more than just one meal. The butcher wagon came with its salt beef, dried pork and bacon twice a month, but she would rather give the household money to the Indians who brought her better quality and were, to be honest, cheaper. She was lying in the dark on the bed Edward had bought for his parents, thinking about what kind of picture she could draw to make Mopoc and Modoc understand she did not need the usual ration of meat this week because the others would be going away, when, in the room next to her own, she heard Eva stirring, heard her through the thin wall using the chamber pot, and Clara was on her feet, the anticipation of this day of independence culminating in the sudden thrill that it was here. She dressed silently and quickly, listening first to Eva's movements then to the movements of Ellen—the hiss of her urination—and then, in her bare feet, carrying her stockings and her shoes, she tiptoed through the kitchen. Light was barely rising in the east, the birds were stirring in the realm of thinning shadows and the air was sweet with pine and the clean brine of Puget Sound as she sat down on a porch step to pull on her stockings, then stopped, noticing the two pails sitting there, filled with fresh pumped water. *Edward,* she understood. She stepped into her shoes without lacing them and stood. And there he was, energetic shadow, coming round the corner of the house, bending down to pick up something from the yard.

Edward, she said aloud, bringing him upright, holding something in his hand. He took one step forward, stopped, then took another as if to bring her into sharper focus. She tried to see his eyes, if he was smiling, but his face was hidden by his hat. How's the roof? he asked.

"The roof," she repeated, and he pointed, upward, so she looked up.

"Any leaks?" he asked.

Dumbly, she shook her head.

"I'm finding shingles in the yard," he said and held out a cedar shake to testify. "Big wind last week."

She nodded, in agreement.

"Day is young," he said and then he took off at a trot into the woods toward the cliff and the distant sound of water. "Will you not take breakfast with us . . . Edward?" she called out, just as a lantern light began to shine from the small window in the barn. She went back up the steps with the two pails of water and lit the lantern in the kitchen and, tucking in her hair and pinching both her cheeks in case he should return, set to work, starting a flame beneath the kettle, measuring out the flour, lard and water to make bread and biscuits. By the time the first low rays of sun sliced the air between the trees outside, she had four loaves cooling on the basket trays, the table set and a fresh chicken on the boil for the travelers' lunch.

"What are you going to do, all by yourself?" Eva asked, appearing crisp, dressed for the journey. "You should change your mind and come with us," she urged. "There will be bachelors there and you might meet someone."

"Is that all you want, then, Eva? To meet someone?"

"Don't *you*?"

It was still only seven thirty in the morning when Clara finally waved them off, standing in the yard in the bright sun as the buckboard pulled away, Hercules standing in the back signaling farewell with his arms as if about to fly. And then as soon as they were out of sight the Indians appeared. Like liquid, Clara thought. The way her father had once showed her about aquatint, the way it spreads into the paper—the way a liquid, once it's spilled, flows into an empty space. That's the way they seemed to move—Edward, too, she realized—waiting for their moment and then taking shape before one's eyes, as if from the air, like shadows. They waited while she went inside to get her charcoal and a piece of paper, as was her custom, but when she handed them the sheet of paper there was nothing drawn on it. They looked at her, their eyes like wax. She made a gesture to communicate *nothing*, crossing her arms in front of her then spreading them wide open while shaking her head—and still they looked at her, their blank expressions impossible to interpret. "Nothing, understand?" she said aloud. "Everyone has gone away. No meat, no fish this week." I may as well be talking to two fence posts, she thought—their faces registered neither comprehension nor emotion nor intelligence and she was reminded yet again of the Indians she and Hercules had seen on the train platform in Dakota Territory, those Indians whose faces gave no hint of inner life, of hope or of humanity. Those Indians had seemed to her not to care whether they sold their wares or not, but these two, Mopoc and Modoc, showed up every week like clockwork willing, if not eager, to barter services for money. She thought, too, of the children selling heated stones for pennies on the railroad, remembered the feeling she had

had when she'd thought how close she and Hercules had come to being reduced to that condition, to that state of near penury, one step away from outright begging. She could give these two a dime to make them go away but she remembered the chafe of charity, the rash it left on one's own dignity, the irritation on the back of one's own neck as one bowed her head in gratitude. These Indians wanted *work*. They wanted work for the same reason that she did and to send them away with charity's coin in their hand or, worse, empty-handed, would be to rupture the chain of responsibility. She didn't like these Indians but she had entered into a tacit contract with them and if she were the first to break with that understanding then who knew what they might do or what might happen next, so, while they watched her without moving, she drew a picture on the piece of paper. If they were going to hunt for her today, then she wanted them to bring back something big. She drew a buffalo.

It was perhaps an act of mockery she realized, too late—there was no reason that these two Pacific Northwest tribesmen would have ever seen or heard of an American bison, but when they looked at the drawing she could see a shift in their expressions, not so much a movement in their eyes as a darkening.

"Bear," one of them said, gravely.

"No bear," she said—she did not want bear meat with its stench and hair and grease. *Buffalo*, she said.

The word seemed to toll a knell between the two of them. They seemed to have stopped breathing and drawn themselves up even taller where they stood, already straight and dignified as regimental sergeants. They were dressed today, as they always were whenever she had seen them, in white men's clothes, rough woven shirts with buttons, workmen's pants dyed indigo, cheap leather boots, and one would not have guessed their Skokomish or Twana affiliation save for their hair which was black and thick and straight and long, and for the skin of their faces which looked like expensive glove leather, and for the fact that one of them wore a feather behind his ear and the other wore a feather in his rolled-up shirt cuff and both of them wore leather thongs around their necks braided around shells and ocean-polished sea glass. But now something hung between them in the air, between them and her, an intimation of who they were when they weren't hiding behind cultural masks, or fear or mockery or stoicism, who they were when they spoke their minds and hearts, who they were when not seen through a white woman's prism. One of them unshouldered his rifle and the other took the piece of paper she had drawn on from her and then held out his hand for the piece of charcoal. Clara gave it to him. The two Indians exchanged a glance between them and then the one with the charcoal drew a swift thick violent line through the figure of the buffalo then threw the drawing and the charcoal on the ground. Both of them looked at her with what she thought might have been dark understanding, but then, again, might have been cold pity, then they turned away from her and disappeared, as if in a silent march, into the woods.

She retrieved the sheet of paper from the ground and crumpled it inside her fist, walking toward the house. She had never seen a buffalo, except in taxidermy. Did they still exist? Maybe they, like unicorns, were animals less missed for what they might have been, alive, than what they are as myths. She stopped and smoothed the sheet of paper out and looked at it—pretty close, she thought, a credible rendition. She could draw, her father had taught her, and who were they to throw her drawing on the ground? Had she insulted them? Why should she care? They and their ilk had still been drawing stick figures and unenlightened geometrics five hundred years after Cimabue and Giotto; four hundred years after the Italian Renaissance in painting. How could anyone ever try to build a bridge across a chasm of perception between two kinds of people, two tribes, as wide as that? She crumpled the paper again, suspecting that, within hours, the two Indians would, once again, deliver squirrels.

On the porch she paused in admiration of the gleaming tub, perfect in its artistry and execution, and *Now or never*, she determined. There was the matter of the kitchen, of the cleaning up from breakfast, which she dispatched not only with efficiency but with a sort of womanly insouciance: she was going to do something that she'd secretly desired for some time: she was going to spoil herself, indulge in pleasure: she was going to have a *bath*.

It wasn't easy. The tub was light to lift but ridiculously commodious, almost knocking her and it headlong down the steps as she tried to reckon with it. Finally she slid a blanket under it and dragged it to a spot not too far from the kitchen and the stove where she would have to heat the water, a place right near the house beneath the laundry lines between two trees where she draped bedsheets in a square to hide herself. With two kettles on the boil at once, she was determined to fill it to the brim, to have a *soak* not just a rinse or what was called a skinny-dip, and while the kettles boiled she went searching through her mother's things inside the *Icarus* trunk for the precious rectangle of authentic French thrice-milled lavender soap. Can there ever be too much of a good thing? she wondered, after so many days of nothing good at all? She draped a clean night shift over one of the laundry lines then closed the bedsheets-as-curtains all around the copper tub, steaming with hot water, and undressed. She tied up her hair, unwrapped the soap, lifted one leg over the lip, and then the other, and slipped in. The lowering, she understood, was ceremonial. Then, after lowering, there was extension, the moment when she unfurled her legs and the hot water lapped her throat and her whole body floated. Clara put her head back on the high curve of the tub and closed her eyes and began to lather herself in suspended sightlessness. She lathered her legs, her stomach and her breasts, her arms, her face and then she submerged herself entirely in the water and when she surfaced she opened her eyes and saw Edward high above her, floating so to speak, standing in bright light, staring at her from the roof. No more than thirty feet away, he was standing on the roof of the house with a hammer in his hand, staring down on her between the sheets protecting her from view on all sides except from above and for a brief moment their eyes locked, Clara's gaze holding his own blue, and then, without a thought, she stood so he would see her, naked, dripping wet.

A rifle shot rang out just then from the woods and before Clara could understand what was happening, Edward turned toward the noise of the rifle shot, slipped, and somersaulted off the roof. She heard his body land and then there was a moment of terrible silence before she pulled her shift over her wet body and ran to him.

He lay with his torso twisted, his arms above his head, legs bent away from his hips. Kneeling next to him she could see his chest rise only slightly with a slow breath. She untied the bandana at his neck and found the pulse, the same throbbing she had touched with her lips, then she looked for bleeding and found none. His eyes were closed and when she lifted his eyelid his blue focus was rolled back in his skull. *Edward*, she said. She tapped his cheek and repeated his name then got to her feet and ran to the alarm on the porch, a triangle-shaped piece of hollow iron that she hit over and over again with an iron pipe, the clamor sending birds in a riot from the trees. She rang 'til she counted sixty, then she ran back to Edward. Asahel had once said the alarm could be heard all the way to the sawmill and she planned to ring it every ten minutes until someone came because from the look of his limbs she feared he had broken some bones and she was wary of moving him on her own. She cradled one of his hands and gently unfurled each finger, feeling for breaks. Whole paragraphs of written instructions for accident victims from her nursing textbooks ran through her thoughts and she determined the first order of business was to restore his consciousness, if she could, so he could respond to his injuries, respond to the pain in his body and tell her where it was. She knew she still had *sal ammoniac* in her traveling kit and as she stood up to go get it, she saw Mopoc and Modoc on a tear from the woods. They were at Edward's side in a matter of seconds. He fell from the roof, she began to explain. "I need to bring him around, so stay with him while I go get—" They had dropped to their knees beside Edward's body and Mopoc, or Modoc, held his head while the other one extracted a small drawstring bag from his belt and drew out a wad of vegetable matter, a tightly-rolled leaf. Clara sank to her knees beside him to watch as he carefully unrolled the leaf and then instantly all three of them recoiled from a stench. Clara leaned in to look at the source, her hand clapped over her mouth, vision glazed with salt tears. The cause of the caustic aroma appeared to be some sort of small organ, rotting and fetid, a fish heart, perhaps, or a liver, full of pus and disgusting, but all it took was two passes of it beneath Edward's nose and his eyes opened and he sprang awake. Edward, can you speak? Clara asked him. He stared straight ahead. "Edward, you've had a fall. You may be injured. I need you to lie very still. Do you understand me?"

Still he stared, didn't speak.

"If you can speak, I need you to tell me what year it is."

A shadow passed through his eyes as if he had reason to fear or distrust her and she could feel both of the Indians searching her face for a reason. What year is it, Edward? she asked again, fully recalling Paragraph Two of her textbook: ASCERTAINING MENTAL FUNC-TION AFTER REGAINING CONSCIOUSNESS.

"1889," Edward said, and his speech wasn't slurred.

"Very good. And what is the name of your brother?"

"Which one?"

Clara smiled. She had forgotten Edward had two brothers, and the fact that he was remembering what she hadn't recalled was a good sign.

"Raphael. And Asahel," he said. "And your brother's name is Hercules."

"Excellent. Now I want you to follow the tip of my finger with your eyes." He did, and so did the Indians, after which she asked him, "Are you in pain?"

He nodded briefly, glancing sideways at the Indians.

"Right hip."

She touched him there. She could see from the angle of his legs and from the lack of blood that he might have landed on his but-tocks.

"How bad is the pain?"

It was not a question, she realized once she'd asked it, that he would ever answer.

"I fear you might have broken some bones in the fall, Edward," she repeated, "and I'm not skilled enough to diagnose or treat that condition so I need you to ask these gentlemen to go at once and fetch a doctor. Can you do that?"

Edward looked at the two Indians and nodded. They stood up.

"Wait," Clara said. She looked at them, then back at Edward. "They understand English?" She looked at them again. "But you never do as I instruct," she marveled.

"They take no orders from a woman," Edward said.

Clara stood. "Before you go you need to help me move him. Off the ground into the house," she instructed. "We'll use those sheets hanging over there." They nodded and went to the laundry line, returning with the sheets, onto which the three of them gently rolled him, mindful not to cause him extra pain, but doing so, she could see, despite their care. He made fists and a line of perspiration glistened on his forehead but he made no sound of protest. They lifted him inside the sheets and Clara led the way into her bedroom, turning back her mother's hand-embroidered Belgian linen bedcover so they could lay him down. Clara drew aside the Indian who had had the fish innards and asked him, "Have you any remedy for pain?"

Again, by his masked response, she had the feeling she had asked another unanswerable question, that, although there might be some solution either she was not entitled to it or something else boycotted the reply. "Have you anything to help him?" she rephrased.

"Edward brave," the Indian told her, as if she doubted it. "We go now," he said.

"If you don't know how to find a doctor, then find Asahel and tell him."

"We know what to do."

They left and she was alone with Edward in the house he'd

built. He stared straight ahead. "What place is this?" he asked.

She sat near him on the bed and looked at him carefully, afraid that he might be lapsing into insentience again.

"This is the house you built," she said, starting, very slowly, to straighten one of his legs and then begin to massage it, very lightly, with both her hands, feeling for alignment in his bones.

"I've never seen this room," he argued.

"You have," she told him, continuing to work to straighten both his legs. "Your initials are right over there, carved in that beam, see them? 'E.S.C.'"

"No, this is different."

"How?"

"This is not the room I know. Something is different. The walls. They're white."

"I painted them."

"These pictures."

"Those are my father's paintings." She unlaced his shoes and prised them off, keenly observing him for any register of pain.

"I tell you," he said, still looking around, "I would not recognize this room as a place that I have seen before. Except the ceiling. I recognize the ceiling."

"I'm going to have to cut you out of these pants, Edward—"

"No."

"—to see where there is bruising."

"You will not cut these pants."

She removed his stockings and asked him to wriggle his toes. He did, in silence. The pants, she said. She laid a hand on one of his shins. It hadn't escaped her notice that the pants were doeskin, nor had she failed to note how soft—almost sensual—they were.

"No cutting," he repeated. "There's a drawstring," he proposed and started to untie the knot at his waist.

"No, don't move," she said, "I'll do it. You lie still." She unslipped the knot and slid the waistband open. She had never seen a pair of pants designed like these.

"They're hand sewn," he said.

"I can see that," she replied and began to shimmy the fabric down around his hips. He looked away, toward a corner of the room as his naked body was exposed. "Whose sea chest is that?"

"Mine," she answered—then, noticing the blossom of discoloration on his hip, said, "Here it is." She touched his skin. "This is where you landed . . ." She slid the pants over his thighs and knees and feet, then held them up to look at them, hardly aware that he lay exposed. The pants were extremely light but what made them extraordinary in her eyes was that they were lined on the inside, top to bottom, with aged royal blue silk taffeta, the smoothest taffeta she'd ever felt, as if from a deceased contessa's dowry.

"I made them myself," he said. "To my own specifications. Took a month. Very practical. Lightweight, water resistant, but still sturdy."

And *pretty*, she assessed. She folded them, then turned back to examining the point of impact on his body. Again, Edward looked away when she touched him. Roll this way, she signaled and helped him roll to the side that hadn't been bruised.

"Where did you learn this?"

"Learn what?"

"What you're doing."

"I don't really know what I'm doing . . ."

He looked at her sharply, as if she had crossed him. "You do. I can tell."

She rolled him back over. Let's take your shirt off, she said, and as they struggled him out of his sleeves she told him, "Before my parents were killed. In St. Paul. I studied nursing. It's what I wanted to do in my life."

"Women want that?"

"—want what?"

"Something to do in their lives."

"—well of course."

"Not the women I know."

"—and how many is that, Edward? —two?"

He almost smiled. \

"Three. Counting you."

Now roll onto your stomach, she told him. "I'll help you."

Nothing back here, she reported. No bruising, no marks. "Other than *here*," she said, cupping his hip, "are you in pain anywhere else?"

He shook his head. Shaken up, is all, he said. He began to shiver. She positioned pillows behind him and coaxed him to relax, drawing one of Amelia's linen sheets over him, topped with a damask featherbed and she watched his long expressive fingers assess the expensive counterpane. She tucked the bed linens around him and said, I have an idea. "Stones," she told him. "Heated stones. They'll draw your attention away from the pain. It's a trick I learned on the train when—" He gripped her hand—forcefully, then made it tender—as if he waited to make these physical gestures toward her only when she least expected them. Or when he least expected them. Or when he no longer had any control over himself. *Thank you*, he said. He caressed her fingers with his own. "If you hadn't been there—" His blue eyes nearly floored her.

"But," she started to say. " . . . I'm the reason that you fell."

"What do you mean?" She colored. "Oh, *that*." He released her hand. "You're not to blame. The gunshot startled me."

So intimate and yet not intimate at all. Clara did not know how to interpret most of everything he said to her, or did, so she fell back to the safe practice of nursing him. "Are you hungry? I boiled a chicken this morning and there's broth—"

"*Broth*," he said the word as if beginning to recite a prayer.

"I'll bring you some. And heat the stones—"

He gripped her hand again. Is that you? He nodded toward the portrait of Amelia pinned up on the wall.

That's my mother, Clara said. Painted by my father.

"He painted all of these?"

She nodded.

"And he made a living from it?"

He let go of her hand in another of his abrupt transitions.

"He made a life," she said. "A very happy one."

"A life," he repeated.

She touched his arm. Will you be all right on your own while I go into the kitchen?

If you give me something to do.

—to do, she said. She looked around.

I must be doing something, he explained.

Of course you must, she understood, going to the *Icarus* chest and extracting several books. "These ought to keep you busy. — Dutch? —or, no, here—this one was my father's. In Italian, but there are pictures—"

She went to the kitchen, refreshed the fire in the stove and set about making a tray of bread and soft-boiled eggs and broth to take to him. She caught a shadow of herself reflected in a pane of glass of

the cabinet and it brought her up short, the shadow of herself, looking like a hospital intern, cotton shift hanging off one shoulder, hair
unkempt.

When she returned carrying the tray she found him tossed back
on the pillows, arm across his forehead, shading his eyes, as if he had
just survived an agony. He said, "There's a chance that I've been
blind my whole life."

Well that's possible, she told him, "but I doubt it. Sit up, Edward. Have some food."

He gripped the book she'd given him. Where did this come
from? he asked.

"My father brought it back from Florence." *Italy*, she added. She
set the tray down, rolled back the bedsheets and placed a heated
stone on his right hip and another on his thigh. Then she covered
him again and set the tray beside him. There was service on the tray
for one. Aren't you eating? he asked.

She fed him bread dipped first in egg and then in broth. "Do you
feel the stones?"

He nodded.

"We need your mother here to pray to God—forgive me—that
you haven't shattered your pelvis, Edward," she told him. "Here, I'll
show you—" She dug in the *Icarus* chest until she came up with a
heavy tome with the words ANATOMIE/DAS SKELETT etched in gold
on its green leather. She sat on the edge of the bed, turning pages.
Beautiful book, Edward said. He ran his fingers down its padded
edge. "Handsomely made. I thought only Bibles were as beautiful as
this."

"Lodz thought I was a fool for taking all of these—Lodz was our neighbor—he thought I was irresponsible taking all these books in foreign languages I can't even read but how could I resist? They were so pretty—" She realized she was talking far too much, although from the way he stared at her he didn't seem to mind. She found a page in the German anatomy book where there was a drawing of the human pelvis and she held it up for him to see. I don't think you've damaged the ball and socket, here, she said, "or else we'd see it, I'd feel the dislocation beneath your skin . . . but this pan-like bone," she pointed, "you can see how it's a single piece and it can shatter, crack, just like a plate and we wouldn't see the damage with our naked eye."

"And a doctor would?"

"He could diagnose it, yes. Through manipulation."

She turned the page to a drawing of the human spine attached to the pelvic girdle, legs and feet. They looked at it together. It's intricate, she noted. "I could make it worse by pulling or stretching any of these bones the wrong way."

"And if I've cracked this part?" He pointed to the girdle.

"It will mend."

"On its own?"

"If you don't move it."

"Do you know everything?"

She colored.

I want to know as much as you, he said. "Tell me more." To her surprise he dipped a piece of bread in broth and held it to her mouth and she ate it from his fingers. "Tell me who was Lodz. Tell me about the paintings on these walls and why you have these books. Teach me about *this* one—" He held out the Italian book and tried to read its title, "*Gli Capolavori della*—"

"'Masterpieces of Early Italian Renaissance,'" she translated. She met his uncomprehending stare. "What do you want to know?"

"I want to know when they were painted. Who painted them. How they were painted. Where I can go to see them. I want to know about *this* one—" He turned to a page.

"Oh, *Giotto* . . . my father liked him, too. He learned a lot from him." *

"They met?"

"—lord, no. Giotto was painting in the thirteen hundreds . . . I mean my father learned a lot from looking at his paintings."

"Looking at them."

"You can learn a lot from looking, Edward."

"Yes I know but first you have to put yourself in front of something, don't you? You have to know that it exists. I didn't know that these existed. I can't '*look*' unless I'm seeing. First I have to *see* a thing. And only then can I begin to *look*. What's this hand supposed to be that's hanging in the sky?"

What do you think it is?

Again, his uncomprehending look.

"Understand, paintings of this era were *religious* paintings, undertaken for religious purposes, usually to illustrate a lesson, narrate a tale or humanize a figure from the Scriptures—Christ, for instance, or the saints or the disciples. What distinguishes Giotto from painters before him is his use of human gesture—the way he captures the emotions in a few strokes, here, around the eyes, his preference for human profile over the full face—"

Profile, Edward repeated. "But then he paints a figure facing away from those who view it. Facing *backwards*. Why do that?"

"Same question my father asked—that everybody asks the first time that we see it. That's my father's self-portrait over there—" She pointed to a painting on the wall of a man in the foreground standing at a window, looking out, his back turned at the viewer.

"There's no reflection in the window," Edward noted. "How can you tell that the figure in the painting is your father?"

"Those of us who knew him could—his shoulders, neck. This painting used to be in a frame and the framed picture used to hang on the first landing on the stairs in our house and as soon as I was old enough to reach it I used to take the painting off the wall and

turn it around, look at the back, to try to see what the man in the painting was staring at, what he saw, where he was looking. That's the point of drawing figures in this way. To conjure up the mystery of where they're looking. The dark back of what they're seeing. The dark back of time. Everything, perhaps, that ever existed, that may still exist, somewhere in time, beyond or below the horizon, beyond that place we all see on the railroad tracks, you know, when they appear to come together. The vanishing point. Logic tells us that those iron railroad tracks will never come together, never really meet, and yet our eyes tell us the opposite, they inform the optical illusion that things—lines—come together at the visual horizon. We *know* they don't, and yet we *see* they do. And this simple fact of illusionary lines coming together seems so obvious to us, to our modern eye, to anyone who's traveled down a long straight road or walked out onto the center of a railroad track, and yet five hundred years ago Giotto and his contemporaries couldn't master it—they hadn't discovered this perspective and its simple rules of rendering a landscape in the third dimension. You see how he does it with the human figure—here, this woman and this Madonna—how he drapes the head, shows the face *behind* the fabric to accentuate the *depth* within the eyes. He could do it with the human face and human figure, but he hadn't figured out how to keep his buildings, these city houses, from floating off the canvas—see them, here? —the way these walls seem to collide? —the way one building belongs to a dimension that the other ones don't share? That's why in 1346 you have this disembodied hand—the hand of God, really—hanging in the ether, disdimensionalized, whereas a century and a half later, in this sketch of Michelangelo's for instance, you have a full-bodied God leaning down from Heaven, in perspective, touching Man. Enormous rebirth of knowledge and technique in a single century—compare these little flames Giotto paints above the heads of saints—they look like wildfires—to the subtlety of saintliness Duccio or Da Vinci can elicit."

He was staring at her, looking not just seeing.

I'm talking too much she said, realizing she was almost giddy, light-headed, with this rush of words and their relief from loneliness.

"But then my father—"

"—what was his name?"

"Haarald. Haarald Phillips. When we talked about those figures facing *inward* toward the canvas—how unknowable and mysterious they are—father said perhaps Giotto painted them that way to depict the route of possibility. Not, as I thought, that they are looking at the past, but that they are looking at the other side of time, the time of possibilities, the time of things that *might* have happened but did not. The *bright* back of time, not the dark one. The *bright* one, of hope. Not the one of shadows. The back of time that is all futures. Endless possibilities. Not only the remembered past."

He was still staring at her, his head against the pillow and despite his stillness and his rapt attention she noticed a taut muscle in his cheek, a pencil line of white above his upper lip where the blood was drawn away. She took his hand and he clasped hers needily. "You have to tell me where the pain is, Edward. Pain is nothing to be denied. It's your body speaking. It's a language."

Almost imperceptibly he shook his head.

"The doctor will have laudanum, at the very least."

"No. No opium. You must give me your word—"

"I can't watch you suffer."

"I would watch you struggle. If you asked me to. If our roles were reversed."

"I don't know that I could ask someone to do that. When there is something else that can be done."

More, he said.

"—more broth?" He had drained the bowl.

"More talk. Keep talking. Tell me everything you know. The painting on the sea chest. Did your father paint it?"

She forced herself to worry less and entertain him more. "Not my father's style—can't you see the difference? This painting on the sea chest is a figurative one, realistic. My father's style is moody, more impressionistic. But this was one of his favorite paintings, the original, this is a copy, of course, a rather good one, except for the second-rate colors that were used. Could be that is why I purchased it, because my father was so fond of the original—I've forgotten the Dutch artist's name—or perhaps he was Flemish—sixteenth century, nevertheless, and you can see that by then the Europeans had answered the quandaries posed by the subject of perspective because this painting—it's called *Icarus,* that much I remember—here you see the plowman in the foreground, his figure proportionally larger than the distant ship behind him, even though no human, naturally, is larger than a ship—"

"What does 'Icarus' mean?"

"—I'm sorry?"

"Icarus. What does it mean? What language is it?"

"Greek. I don't know that the name *means* anything. Like 'John.' Or 'Edward.'"

"Icarus is a person's name?"

"Yes, this is Icarus here, in the right hand corner of the painting with his legs sticking up from where he's fallen in the water."

His steady look.

"The boy who flew too close to the sun?"

Uncomprehending.

"The Greek myth," Clara said.

"Yes, go on. I've heard of them. Legends from the ancient past."

"Legends, yes, but legends only now. At the time that they were told they were believed to be as factual and truthful as this text-book." She held up the ANATOMIE.

"What happened to them?"

"The Greeks?"

"The myths."

"People stopped believing in the truth of them."

"Ah. Because they were not true, at heart."

"People stopped believing in the magic of them, then."

"How does that happen?"

"—loss of faith? I suppose most often one kind of faith replaces another. It's not faith that is transformed, but the object of it."

"Then what did the Greeks believe in when they lost faith in myths?"

"Other myths, I suppose. Christianity. *These* . . ." She held up the pages of the saints in Giotto's paintings.

"Tell me the myth of Icarus," he said, "so I can decide if I'll believe it."

"Not a good myth to start with, Edward, for someone who's just fallen off a roof . . ."

She told him the myth, which could be recited in its full in four brief sentences and then he asked her how the *Icarus* sea chest had come into her possession and she told him that, too, about the money from Lodz and who Lodz was and how she and Hercules had gone to the market to shop and she'd bought the chest with all the books inside and how Hercules had spent his full ten dollars on a suit of clothes that he'd already outgrown.

"The suit was handsome?"

"He was very pleased with it."

"I would have done the same. You're laughing?"

"He's a boy, Edward—a boy of eight—and you're a man. I think you would not have squandered your entire fortune on a suit of clothes that you were destined to outgrow."

"Oh but as most men from a meager background I am attracted to fine things, fine clothes." He ran his hand along the counterpane again, in contemplation of its weave. "Your family must have been, at some time, wealthy, I suspect."

"Wealthy, no. Had they been wealthy I would not be here. Existing on your family's charity. Living from a sea chest."

"Wealthy enough to buy your education, though. You are well educated, I observe."

"If I appear that way it is because my primary education derived from my parents' company. They were greatly learned people. Far better schooled than I."

"So you see the root cause of my disability. Given the company that I was made to keep as a small boy."

"You mean your father—"

"But I taught myself to read. *The Leatherstocking Tales*. Do you know these books?"

"Fenimore Cooper," Clara vaguely recalled.

"*The Deerstalker. The Pathfinder.* Oh they're magnificent. *The Last of the Mohicans.* I've read them all. You must read them. You must make them necessary reading. I'll lend them to you. In fact, in honor of your taking time to share your books from your sea chest with me, I'm going to call you Scout. That's what Hawk-eye, the Pathfinder, is—a scout. And that's what you'll be for me. My Scout. That's going to be my name for you."

As he'd yet to address her by any name, especially her own, Clara accepted this false baptism with reluctant gratitude.

"Are there any books in that sea chest, Scout, that you could read to me—in English?"

"English, yes, aye, aye, sir, let's just see—" She went hunting again, among the books and mementos. "—I brought along some favorite novels of my parents, here we are—" She stood up holding several volumes. "Louisa May Alcott, no, that won't do—"

"A woman writer?"

"—even worse, Edward. A woman writer writing one called *Little Women*—"

He looked, almost on cue, newly pained.

"—Henry James . . . I think not . . . here we are—one of my

125

father's favorites . . . make yourself comfortable, Edward, you are in for a treat . . ." She rearranged the pillows around his head, removed the tray, tested the heat from the stones, then settled in beside him on the bed. "Chapter the First," she read, "in which

> *'The Author gives some account of himself and family—His*
> *first inducements to travel—He is shipwrecked and swims for*
> *his life—Gets safe on shore*
> *in the country of Lilliput—Is made a prisoner*
> *and carried up the country.'"*

"What is the title of this adventure, Scout?"

"*Gulliver's Travels*. Irish. But in English nonetheless . . ."

She read without a pause for what must have been at least an hour before she felt him doze beside her. She sat still and watched him sleep for several moments then she slid silently from the bed leaving the book beside him on the pillow. She changed quickly from the shift into a skirt and blouson in anticipation of the physician's arrival, then she left the room, keeping the door ajar. She lit the flame beneath the kettle and set out a tea service to refresh the physician, then considered finding a nightshirt or clean clothes for Edward. Enough time had elapsed for the Indians to have reached someone for help, she thought, as she crossed the open ground between the house and the barn, pausing only slightly to wonder at the wood aroma in the air—not fresh timber, exactly, more like the smell of a cold hearth. The light was strangely eerie, as if a storm were coming, though the sky was still. She entered the barn by the door to the bunkhouse where Hercules and Asahel slept at night and then she realized she hadn't visited these quarters in months.

There were two beds, neatly made up—and a closed door, leading to further rooms that she had never visited, and as soon as she opened the door she knew she had entered on Edward's presence, into the room where Edward dreamed and slept. *Side chapel,* she immediately thought. On those few occasions when she had entered into one of St. Paul's cathedrals she had been struck by the asceticism of the side chapels, the niches, those unadorned recesses washed in reverential light where people went to be alone, with God. That's what Edward's room was like, a sanctuary pressed into service by unrelenting solitude. Everything was *placed,* as if on an altar: nothing was superfluous. There was a bed, a chest of drawers, a straight-back chair, a writing table. Nothing on the walls, no windows. There was something very masculine about the look and feel of it, its readiness for duty, its spartan abnegation of unnecessary frill. On the writing table, an oil lamp with a box of sulphur matches, a dictionary, a jar of ink and a single pen. A stone, riddled through with veins of green. A small gold nugget. On the chest of drawers, standing side by side, the collected *Leatherstocking Tales,* a cheap edition, pages foxed and marked in Edward's hand in pencil. She slid the top drawer of the chest open to discover cotton shirts, three of them, starched and pressed and folded, and a pair of silk pyjamas, black, of the kind you saw on Chinamen, with braided toggles on the top and a drawstring waist on bottom, same as Edward's doeskin pants. The middle and the bottom drawers were empty. Why would Edward build a house, she wondered, an entire edifice to house his family, and then decide to live apart? It made no sense to her. In a corner of the room his carved, polished walking stick stood against the wall next to a canvas knapsack in which she found a pair of laundered stockings and his razor. She took these, the walking stick, a shirt and the pyjamas, and was about to leave when she noticed a slanted cubby door plumb with the wall, into which a grown adult would have to duck to enter. Thinking it a closet where Edward might have kept his boots and shoes and other clothing she unlatched the door and pulled it open and found herself facing a two-storey-like stall, faced with cedar, entirely dark—a darkroom—but for a seam of light coming from the ceiling which she realized must be the outline of a window in the roof. Groping, she found a cord and pulled it and a thick black shade snapped back to reveal not a cubby nor a closet but a large well-organized meticulous workroom, half the size of her father's attic studio on the top floor of the St. Paul house. "No one is as organized in his work as a sailor has to be," her father had once told her, "for him it's life-or-death. Everything must have a place and everything must *be* in place. Shipshape. Like a painter's palette. Everything is organized. Every color separate. Everything at hand when needed. I could do it in the dark, you see? Work my palette with my eyes closed. Sail it. Like a captain in a good ship on the sea. That's what my palette is: my ship." So was the room that she was standing in, a sort of regulated vessel. Shipshape. Ordered. Rows of corked brown bottles organized by size labeled AMMONIUM IRON OXALATE, FORMALDEHYDE, FERRIC AMMONIUM CITRATE, POTASSIUM FERRICYANIDE. There were empty beakers, crude brushes, more like spatulas, with flattened edges, a jar marked WATER (RAIN). There were hinged-back wooden boxes and rectangles of glass and a sheaf of thick dense paper, still she was slow to fathom what it all amounted to until she saw the pictures on the wall. Until she saw the camera.

Photography, the object of her father's scorn.

How often had she heard him rail against its fakery, its allusions to the standards of high art? Any idiot could do it, he had said—by which he'd meant that any idiot smart enough to master the mechanics of the process could pretend to be a portrait artist—but no idiot had produced the images before her. *Cyan*—"Prussian blue"—a color on her father's palette, a living light that vibrated in the eye—that was the color of these images, the color that saturated them. She couldn't tell—she didn't have the visual vocabulary to inform her eye—whether the cyan images had been laid on the surface of the paper or whether they existed *in* it, so inextricably did the color seem to *be* the image, and when she reached to touch one—an image of a man, possibly Modoc or Mopoc, sitting in a bark boat among reeds on a large body of water, most likely Puget Sound—she was surprised to discover by its touch that it was linen, and her mind went back to Edward's assessing hand on her mother's counterpane. She did not know—how could she?—that what she was looking at was the result of a chemical process, oxidation, like tarnish on a ring, and that the illusion of the Prussian blue inhabiting the fibers of the linen was as real as iron transmogrifying, iron becoming something else: as real as *rust*. She saw she was looking at an alchemy she'd never seen in quite this form before—a kind of magic she was slow to understand. There was something here, she slowly realized, looking all around at the photographs he'd pinned up on the wall—a decisive way of looking at the world with an aesthetic that rendered what was seen and what was real somehow more fragile and more beautiful than the way it must have looked outside the camera's eye. There were landscapes he had captured no doubt on the heights of Mt. Rainier, of the treacherously raked volcanic scarps draped in snow and ice from a breathtaking altitude above the clouds hovering among the lower valleys, and she suddenly knew that not only was she looking at a real view of a real place that she would never have the stamina nor strength to capture for herself, but that Edward had climbed there with a camera on his back, *this* camera, this boxy incommodious contraption right in front of her that was as difficult to heft—she tried to lift it—as a crate of roosting hens. Was painting ever arduous? Certainly on the scale of Giotto's murals or the painted ceilings in Italian churches, but nothing her father ever did, none of his canvases, suggested this degree of physicality or any sense of a physical exertion underpinning the image's emotional affect. Edward had *been there* she couldn't help but realize. That was something unique to photography, that a photograph elicited—that sense of being there—that painting more or less finessed. You could paint from your imagination—her father frequently had—but in order to produce a photograph you had to put yourself within a visual range, you had to be there and that locus carried with it its own intimacy. The photographer was acting for you with his eyes, acting as your own eyes would. It was a contract between the artist and the viewer that few painters could make and it was deeply personal, she saw, because she could not look at any photograph of Edward's without thinking about Edward, himself, about the man behind the camera, about how and why he had positioned himself where he had. What he did when he made photographs was an adventure, she saw, it was adventurous—as well as beautiful—and what she learned looking at his photographs made her feel even more thrilled to know him, thrilled to have his company, to be called his Scout.

She closed the blind to his darkroom, closed the cubby door and exited the barn into the eerie filtered light she'd noticed before.

Crossing the yard she heard hoofbeats and turned to find Asahel in the compound on horseback at a gallop with no buckboard behind him, nor, it would appear, a doctor. He dismounted and gripped her by the shoulders, his eyes begging the question to which she had to answer, he's alive.

"Will he walk—?"

"I don't know. Where's the doctor?"

"Clara, don't you know?"

"—know what?"

He turned her by her shoulders to face the sky over the trees to the east. A solitary ash, twirling on the current like a feather, fell before her eyes. Behind it the sky was smeared as if by charcoal.

"Seattle's burning," Asahel said.

"—Seattle?"

"The city is on fire."

A memory of St. Paul with its brick and limestone monuments came to her mind.

"A city cannot burn," she said.

"The waterfront, the piers, all made of wood—everyone for miles around has gone to help. Every doctor . . ."

She blinked. More ash fell around them, gray and black, like fatal pollen.

"—Hercules?" she sought.

"—he's well taken care of, they're turning the campground into a mission for evacuees. I'm off, myself, by boat, to help, as soon as I see Edward—"

He started for the barn.

"We carried him in here," Clara corrected, pointing toward the house. "To my room. He may still be sleeping."

"—Edward? —sleeping in daylight?"

A spark of understanding arced between them: it was unlike the man they knew to squander time.

"Pain," Clara explained.

She waited in the kitchen while Asahel went to see his brother but he was back within the minute. "No point in waking him," he said. He took her hand. "You two will be all right—?"

She nodded, though she didn't meet his eyes.

"The Indians—?" she asked.

"They took to their canoes with the others of their tribe as soon as they saw smoke. Everyone, it seems, is rowing to Seattle to give aid."

He gripped her shoulders again and she felt with dread that he might kiss her but instead he held his breath then let her go.

"Do you want my rifle?"

"Why—?" And then, "Certainly not."

He seemed to entertain the idea to embrace her one more time but then he left, mounting the horse with less bravado than his brother might have, she couldn't help herself from thinking, then he rode away.

She returned to Edward.

"Who was here?" he asked her, waking.

"Asahel. Seattle is on fire."

He struggled to sit up.

"Show me," he said.

"Too soon," Clara intervened.

"I need to walk."

"I know you do. I know it, Edward," she said, smoothing the sheets around his legs. "But not now. We'll do it slowly."

He stopped her hands from fussing and pressed them to his thigh.

"—pain?" she asked.

"—better when you press, like this—" He renewed the pressure on her hands.

"Roll over . . ." She pulled the sheet away and leaned the full weight of her body on her hands on his hip.

He sighed.

"That's better, Scout."

He turned and looked at her across his shoulder.

"—promise me we'll try to walk tomorrow?"

She nodded.

"Those poor people."

"—who?"

"—in Seattle. You should see the way some of them live. Cheek by jowl."

"I thought it was a wealthy city. Newly minted money."

"What city is *only* wealthy—?"

She was reminded, briefly, of the novels her mother had made her read written by Dickens and the Frenchman, Balzac.

"I would never want to die by fire," Edward said.

"What makes you think anyone is dying in Seattle?"

"I just told you." Then on second thought he added, "Maybe there is no good way to die."

"Together."

"—what?"

She was thinking of her parents. "With the one you love," she said.

"I would rather die alone."

"—why?"

He looked at her again.

"Do you want someone to watch you die?"

She helped him into the pyjama top—

("Where did you find this—?"

"I went to your room.")

—and then she helped him urinate into the chamber pot from a sitting position on the edge of the bed, each physical transaction being almost technical between them until she said, "I saw your photographs," and he grabbed her hand.

"I didn't invite you."

"You didn't *not* invite me, Edward."

"They are not for others' eyes."

"Well, too late. I saw them."

She pressed him back against the pillows, straightening his spine, until he was at an angle with the least amount of pressure on his hip.

"Why are they blue?"

"I can't afford to purchase silver." On her look he said, "The prints you saw are called cyanotypes. Poor man's proofs. A non-silver process. Using iron. And cyanide. Developed by the sun. From glass plate negatives," he told her. She had no idea what he was talking about but he gripped her hand again. "Your father was an artist, you must tell me what you think."

"I think they're beautiful," she said. "And brave."

"So I'll ask again: do you think there is a living to be made from this?"

"—a living?"

"Livelihood."

"A life, perhaps, Edward. Certainly, a life."

"Lives are what we have right now. I want something more."

She almost answered *So do I* but the way he looked at her already sealed the pact between them of mutual, if still unspoken, ambition. How do you make the life you want? she wondered. Talent, her father used to say, is more abundant than you think. You have to have the temperament to tolerate hard work. You have to flirt with luck. You have to take the chances that most people wouldn't take.

"I'm not certain that making a wage should be your foremost consideration in entertaining the prospect of a life in art," she told him. "Traditionally, artists are not wealthy men. The people who commission them are."

"Then how do I attract these wealthy people? The ones who will commission me?"

"Establish in a city, Edward. In Seattle. *No one* is going to find you here."

"I don't want to be another of those men you see, traveling house to house, 'Your portrait, Miss, on tin for a few pennies . . . ' I don't want to spend my life immortalizing babies, brides and corpses."

"—then what *do* you want?"

His gaze left her, went inward. "I don't even know if the photographs I make are passable," he fretted. "Within the range of the profession. Or even, for that matter, pleasing."

She realized that she couldn't offer him advice, that she didn't understand the process of photography, that it differed in every way conceivable from what she knew about techniques involved in painting, except for one: both forms existed on a flat plane distorted by illusion to suggest a third dimension. What her father *couldn't* do—why he'd failed to gain commissions in those final years—was the portrait work of strangers. His portrait of Amelia evoked a strong sense of her beauty, an inspired likeness, but even with someone he loved he had not been able to seize upon that look that was her very essence, to capture her soul. As his work had matured toward impressionism he had lost his sure hand at straightforward drawing, lost his earlier enthusiasm for the literal translation of a portrait painter's art and the truth was he wasn't any good at rendering a likeness, setting up a mirrored image of a stranger's soul. So, "Learn to make a portrait, Edward," was the only thing that she could think to tell him. "Whether you want to or not. Whether you want to be that salesman at the train depot selling tintypes for pennies, learn to take the sort of photographs that speak the truth about their subjects. The sort of photographs that people travel with, keep in their pockets, the kind they'd never dream of parting with or leaving behind. Practice on me—I'm used to sitting for my father—or practice on yourself..."

"You speak your mind, don't you, Scout? A rare find in a woman."

"—then ask yourself how you would render *that*, that quality about me, in a photograph."

For the second time, he almost smiled.

"I must see to chores—" she said.

"—don't go."

"—well if I don't you and I will have no supper and the chickens and the mule will starve."

She placed *Gulliver's Travels* in his hands and stacked more books from the *Icarus* chest beside him. In a short while she had fed and watered all the animals, peeled potatoes, rolled a dough and placed a green apple cobbler in the oven. The sky outside burned over Seattle, and by the time supper was ready it was a bright light in the darkening canopy. They ate boiled potatoes, roasted ramps and smoked fish off trays in the bedroom while she read to him from the Swift novel, and then for dessert she served the green apple cobbler with clotted cream and a splash of rough apple brandy she'd been fermenting in a jug. She asked him to explain the photographic process to her and she had to lengthen wicks in both the lanterns several times as they talked into the night until, perhaps as a result of the apple brandy, she could no longer suppress her yawns. She stood.

"—where are you going?"

"I'll sleep in Eva's room. The walls are thin—well you know that, you built them—just call out if—"

"Sleep here."

He patted the bedsheet beside him.

She looked around, involuntarily, as if someone else were watching.

"Edward, I—"

And then, extraordinarily, he smiled, although that, too, may have been the apple brandy.

That first night they touched only a few times, Edward reaching for her hand to press against his hip after she had turned the lantern down, but she was so afraid of the unknown, of a stranger in the bed, that for a long while in the dark she barely breathed. She was surprised, then, to discover at the dawn her face pressed to his back and her arm across his chest, his fingers intertwined with hers. And then, as she lay watching, she felt him come awake, lift their arms together and kiss her hand.

"I'm going to walk today. You promised."

"I promised we would *try*."

But Edward wasn't one for trying anything without succeeding. Even before he would allow her to make breakfast he insisted on trying to stand but she succeeded in advising him against it without first trying to put pressure on his leg and hip from a prone position. There was no further inflammation nor discoloration when she examined him and the first thing she asked him to do was to try to bend his knee into his chest—"*Slowly*," she cautioned—then she worked his bended knee in slow rotation. When this caused him some discomfort she advised staying off his feet for several more days but as she stood before the stove a while later, making biscuits, Edward hobbled in using his walking stick.

"You are a damn fool, Edward Curtis," she warned him.

"—but a walking one."

His face bled of color and she saw his leading arm begin to shake.

"—I'll need your help if I'm to stay up any longer . . ." and as he almost fell she caught his sudden weight against her shoulder and guided him back down the hall and back to bed. All through that second day he exercised at intervals, frequently with her support, and by suppertime he was standing on his own, if only for brief moments, without the walking stick. She read to him, they talked, he told her how he'd first become impassioned with photography. "Ten years ago, now, and Mr. Curtis and I were on the circuit up in northern Minnesota—"

"—Mr. Curtis?" she asked and he explained, "The Reverend," and she understood he meant his father. "We were in a cabin there one night where a child was dying and the Reverend was attending to the child's soul in the back room and I was in the front room with an old man, the father or the grandfather of the dying infant. I had taught myself to read by then but my skills were rough and my understanding of a range of words was fairly narrow, limited to Scripture readings and the meager conversation Reverend and I would make between the two of us. But I could read and I was always hungering for books, seeking to improve myself. And there on the supper table in the front room of this cabin was a newspaper gazette, already fairly old and yellowed and the old man saw me looking at it and signaled, Go ahead. It was called *The Illustrated Christian Weekly*, published in New York and I remember it cost six cents and how this family came to be in its possession I will never know because they were well and truly isolated from the world in a way that makes our island living here seem like the quick pulse of civilization. On the cover of the *Christian Weekly* was an assemblage of what appeared to be drawings—*gravures*—made from photographs of geysers on the Yellowstone Reservation taken by a man called William Henry Jackson. I remember the paper was dated Saturday the 30th November, 1872, and that I didn't know what the word *geyser* was, nor how to say it. Inside the paper there was an article written by William Henry Jackson, himself, and I learned that he had joined the Geological and Geographic Survey of the Territories in 1870 when he was still a young man, traveling with two 20 x 24-inch cameras and three hundred glass plates. And because of his photographs of the Yellowstone region, Congress had established that part of the United States as a national reservation, a park, signed into law that year by President Grant. And I decided then and there that's what *I* wanted to do."

"—sign things into law?"

"—change the course of history with a camera."

"—then how did you learn?"

"I wrote letters to camera clubs, posted them from towns and forts we visited, sometimes waiting more than a year for a response. I started asking questions and I taught myself. A lot of what it takes, photography, is understanding chemistry and simple industry, the same as manufacturing or brewing. And believe me I am still a raw recruit. I have a lot to learn. There are many in the field whose advances and techniques leave me far behind them, in the dark."

She remembered her father talking to her mother about ways he had been trying to improve himself, techniques he was struggling with so as not merely to mimic others of his profession, but to set a standard against which others might seek to improve themselves.

"—a *self*-made man," she said.

"What man is *not* self made? At the end of that night, after the Reverend had delivered his blessings on the dying child and stood about expecting recompense, the old man in the front room told him, 'I'll let your calf here keep the paper and we'll call it even.' When the Reverend found out he had gone away with a *Christian Weekly* that sold for only six pennies, he beat me with it. Then he burned it. Which was the worse offense."

That night they slept in a more intimate, though chaste, proximity and at a certain moment on the morning of their third day alone together Clara was standing at the water pump in the center of the compound and found herself looking around and wishing, Were it always such. Only two of them. Without the others. Except for Hercules. Except for worrying about her brother's welfare she could tolerate this life in the wild with all its hardships as long as she could be alone with Edward. And when she turned to carry the two pails of water to the house Edward was standing on the porch, leaning on the walking stick. "I feel useless," he said when she approached. "I need something to do." He pushed aside a thin dusting of ash with his bare foot before sitting on the step and looking at the still smoky sky. "Have we finished all the volumes in your magic *Icarus* chest?"

At the bottom of the chest, under a lace and velvet ball gown of Amelia's, Clara found two objects from her father's studio she had forgotten that she'd packed.

"Two treasures," she teased Edward, holding them behind her back. "I want you to have them." She sat next to him on the smooth pine porch step in a pool of sultry light from the occluded sun. "First, these . . ." She handed him two L-shaped pieces of thin wood, thin as yardsticks, each arm of the Ls nine inches long and joined at the cornice with a bright hinge. The wood, light enough to float, was varnished to a russet sheen and inlaid with kaleidoscopic circles, opalescent as the scales of fish.

"What are they?" Edward asked.

"My father made them."

"They're beautiful. —but what *are* they?"

She held the two L-shaped pieces at right angles to each other. "Viewing frame," she said.

She slid the two pieces up and down along their axes. "Here, look through the center. At the barn. You can change the dimensions of the frame to form your focus . . ."

Edward took the pieces in his hands and held them up before his eyes and framed her face in them, then, holding them apart, said, "But I can't accept these."

"You must. They were designed for use. I'll never use them, and you will."

"What are these bright circles in the wood?"

"Butterfly wings."

Their fingers brushed as they both reached to touch an inlay.

"Father made them on his trip to Florence. He studied all kinds of strange techniques there. That's where he bought this . . ." She handed him a book.

"*Il Libro dell'Arte*," he read. "Italian?"

"Open it . . ."

Inside, on each page, handwritten between the printed lines in a bold brownish-red ink, was her father's own translation.

"It's a craftsman's handbook by Cennino Cennini—15th century. Here, look—" She turned the pages for him:

"HOW YOU SHOULD GIVE THE SYSTEM OF LIGHTING,

LIGHTS OR SHADE, TO YOUR FIGURES, ENDOWING

THEM WITH A SYSTEM OF RELIEF."

They read her father's translation together: "*Always follow the dominant lighting; and make it your careful duty to analyze it, and follow it through, because, if it failed in this respect, your work would be lacking in relief, and would come out a shallow thing, of little mastery.*"

"—is that what it says? —'of little mastery'?" He took the book in his hands and laid his palms across the pages. "I shall treasure this. Thank you, Scout." He leaned toward her and for the briefest flicker passed his lips across her cheek.

He stayed on his feet most of the day, taking practice walks around the yard, and by suppertime it was clear to her that he was

142

on his way to full recovery. They took their evening meal at the table in the kitchen and after he had finished his piece of custard pie and a mug of sweetened tea he said, "I think that I deserve some rest." Leaning on his walking stick, he stood, while Clara remained seated, stock still, thinking he would leave her there and retreat to his own bed in the barn. But he started down the hall, saying, "—coming?" and she followed him, carrying the lantern. She watched him undress and then undressed, herself, down to her undergarments. He got into bed and sat upright against the pillow and started playing with the viewing frame again, looking through the square the two sides made, focusing views of things around him. "I think this is my favorite toy," he said as she slipped into the bed beside him. He framed her face and she turned her head to profile so her features were backlighted by the lantern.

"That day you were in the tub," he said.

She angled her head more elegantly so she could look him in the eye. The lantern highlighted her hair, a burnished corona.

"Why did you stand up?"

She stared at him.

"So you would look at me. So you would see me."

"—see you . . . how?"

"The way I am."

He put down the viewing frame and studied her.

"Show me," he instructed.

Moving carefully, almost afraid to fall, fearful of disturbing what she intuited was a fatal balance, she stood, walked several paces toward the wall so he could see the full length of her body, turned to face him and slipped off her remaining underclothes.

"Turn around," he told her.

She turned her back to him.

"Lift up your hair," he said.

She raised her hair with one arm and stood waiting, facing away from him, facing the wall, facing into that non-participatory space that figures turned away in pictures face.

"Don't move," he said.

She stood for him, staring forward at the wall, until his silence started to feel strange and his unseen gaze on her created not a shared experience but a partition. She began to want to look back, to meet his eyes, to play an active, not a passive, part in what he saw, so she glanced over her shoulder and saw that he had framed her body in the viewing frame. She stood regarding him and in the shadow of the lantern on his face saw for the first time a different sort of animation rising in his eyes. "Come here," he said, and as she moved to him she became aware of something in his body, in the way he held himself. When she climbed beneath the sheets she saw his excited sex, a third party in the bed.

"Show me how to do this," he asked her.

"Edward, I don't know—"

"You know everything," he said.

Her instinct was to kiss him, press her breasts against his chest and press her body to him, but when she tilted her face to meet his lips he rolled her over, rolled her to her side, her back once more to him and then he pushed her top leg forward and she felt his sex pushing at her, felt him fumble himself forward through the narrow place between her thighs and then she felt the pain of his insertion. She made a small knob of the sheet inside her fist and bit down on it as he pressed forward, deeper, into her. He began to rock against her as she closed her eyes and then in a juttering spasm he fell still, his ragged breath against her back. She had thought that love would be an open confrontation, face to face, that love would be between the eyes, not like this, the way two animals would do it. She didn't speak, although she wanted to, she didn't move, she merely breathed and waited for some gentle sign from him. After a while she felt that part of him that was inside her diminish, then she felt a bath of liquid on her legs and Edward rolled from her onto his back. She raised herself onto her elbows and looked at him. His arm was crooked across his forehead, casting his eyes in shadow, hiding them from her. She said his name. "Sleep," he told her, and she put the lantern out.

She thought she heard him rise while it was still dark and she thought she'd said his name again and that he'd told her to go back to sleep again, but she may have only dreamed it. When she woke gray light filtered through the only window, shadowing the outlines of the pictures on the walls and at the instant that she started to remember where she was and what had happened she knew at once that he was gone. She sat up and listened. There was no sign of him. His walking stick was nowhere in the room.

She stood up and was immediately leveled to her knees by pain, clutching at the bed for balance. Somewhere deep inside her pelvis was a thorn that made it hard to stand and as she knelt, trying to overcome it, she saw that she had bled across the sheet during the night. Her thighs were caked with blood and as she rose she reached for her black poplin skirt to dress in and to hide her stain. Over the skirt she pulled her shift and then she walked, one stiff step at a time, to the door.

He was not in the kitchen.

Nor was he in the yard.

She hesitated briefly, deciding whether to draw water to make coffee for their breakfast or to go and find him in the barn.

But his room was empty. His knapsack was not there. Neither was the camera in the other room and in the barn a single stall door stood ajar where the mule had been set free. Through the fresh ash on the ground outside the barn she could see the mule's tracks leading toward the yard, a line of round depressions from the walking stick beside them. She followed their trace down the rutted track until it met the road. One direction led to the sawmill and the other to the inner coastline and the ferry and she stood and watched the tracks turn sharply toward the route to water where they disappeared to a single vanishing point in the distance. However far away the two edges of the road might seem to converge into the illusion of disappearance, Edward was beyond that point by now, she knew, outside the picture. How far could he go in his condition? He could not walk far—for a day, she told herself—perhaps only for the morning—so her best mode of conduct would be to carry on, prepare for his return as if nothing out of the ordinary had transpired. Except that something out of the ordinary *had* transpired and she was both confused and disappointed by it and ashamed of her compliance. If he had kissed her, if he had said good-bye, if he had ever said her name—she started turning over *ifs* as she sat at the kitchen table, waiting. In a rash of energy she stripped the bed and washed herself despite the pain from a basin of cold water and dressed herself to follow in his tracks but then had second thoughts. What would she say to him? He had left her on the morning after what was reputed to be love, reputed to be sacred between a married couple, between a husband and a wife.

She sat through the dwindling light and lit only a single lantern turned down low when she realized it had grown too dark to see her hands. At the moonrise she brought blankets and a pillow to the porch and made a basic pallet on the boards, but didn't sleep. The moon, gibbous, was the color of her blood.

Northwest Pacific moisture woke her at the dawn, the damp seeping in to chill her bones and she rose, her limbs and back as stiff as corn husks, and began to feel a low-burning anger tempering her mind and body, firing her action. She went through the day accomplishing the chores, rearranging the position of the bed in the bedroom so that it appeared restored or reinvented and no longer reminded her of what had taken place there. Still, after a bleak supper of cold potatoes standing at the window in the kitchen, looking out, when she had tried to retire to the bedroom for the night she found no comfort in the bed that had been bought for one generation of Curtis men and had accommodated another generation of them—where one had died and another had failed to live up to her expectations—and she passed a second night outside on the porch.

When she woke she knew her time within the Curtis family was nearing its completion. She sat up, looked at the new day, hugged her knees to her chest and looked at the ragged compound and its moldering barn and told herself, as Edward must have told himself the morning he had left her, *I need to be quit of here.* Even when, or if, Edward returned what future was there here, for them, for her, with the old woman and her pallid daughter in the room next door, the endless chores, the evaporating dreams of his and hers from week to week? But then she remembered moments when her heart had thrilled at what he'd said, the way he'd looked, his courage and his photographs. When he comes back, she started to rehearse, and if he tells me why he left and if he tells me he is sorry to have gone with no parting word or explanation, then . . .

But he did not come back. The buckboard bearing Hercules, Eva, Ellen and Asahel returned that afternoon, Asahel telling her from behind the reins even before dismounting, "I'm sorry, Clara, I could find no doctor who would leave Seattle, owing to the fire—how is Edward?"

"Edward's gone."

He could see that grief had had its way on her, her eyes were sunken, her face gray, as if she hadn't slept, and he thought his brother dead until Clara asked him, "Did you see him on the road? He took the mule, the camera. Asahel, he's hardly fit enough—"

"Hear that, mother? Your son is cured—we have rushed back for nothing . . ."

Yes, nothing, Clara thought you've rushed back to your home, your lives. To nothing. She avoided conversation with the women and stood with Hercules as he unhitched the horses.

"Did you see the fire, Clara?"

"Only in the sky."

"—it was *enormous*. So bright you could see each building from across the water. Sparks like firecrackers falling in the harbor, then they'd fizz and pop and there would be this *ghost*, scary shape of steam shooting from the water like the spirit rising."

"—*spirit rising*, Hercules?"

He gave her a canny look.

"They're Baptists, Clara, and they talk that way. And the best part—you know who the heroes were that day? The horses."

She followed him, leading both the dray mares to water in the corral beside the barn.

"The horses drove the water wagons right up to the burning houses and the fire men, the men who put out fires, they put gunneysacks over the horses' heads and leather blinders on their eyes so they couldn't see and then the horses went right up to where the flames were because they're trained to be obedient . . ."

"You like horses," she affirmed, smiling at him.

"I *love* them. Mr. Silva gave me a book about the role of horses in the history of the world—"

"—Mr. Silva?"

"—the farrier. And you probably don't know this but it's really *horses* that have saved the world. Especially America. Did you know there were no horses here until the Spanish brought them? They were looking for gold, the Spanish people were, so they brought horses on their ships. Can you imagine that?"

She smiled. "No. I barely can."

"—horses on a ship, I mean *a hundred* of them. And the boat was only, well, from *here* to *here.* The only boat I've been on was that ferry that we took, but, still, I can't imagine what it must have been like, way back then, to cross an ocean in a wooden boat with hundreds of these animals on deck . . ." He smoothed the silver hairs of the mare's neck. "Are you feeling all right, Clara?"

"Better for the sight of you."

"You don't look your usual."

She tilted her head and asked him, "What's my usual?"

He shrugged and petted his favorite animal. "Like a horse," he said.

"—I beg your pardon!"

"—you know. Noble. And intelligent."

"I love you, Hercules."

"Well you have to. You're my sister."

He would be just fine without her for a while, she sensed, for the time it would take her to secure a job and housing for them in Seattle—but, still, the pleasure of his company and the towline of her duty to him kept her wavering in her decision through the next few days. That, and the fact that in some recess of her mind she still believed that she had forged an understanding and a bond with Edward. He would come back and they would continue to grow closer, in both mind and body. Or so she hoped.

But he did not come back and his not-coming-back became more than a constant ache, a wound that wouldn't heal: it became the truth she had to live with, the truth about the man. He would always *go*, she realized, like that idealized photographer he'd read about when he was ten or twelve in the *Christian Weekly*, the one who had gone out to map the West with nothing but a camera and a mule. Like Hercules with horses, Edward had found his first romantic love at a young age and nothing in his adult life was going to stand between himself and that first love—not his family—not a woman—not her—and she understood that, now, and, in fact, drew courage from it.

If he could go, then she could, too.

At the end of the week, she sought a private conversation with Asahel. "I'm going to Seattle," she told him.

"Clara, the fire's out—"

"I'm not going for the fire."

"The city is in turmoil, wait a while and then we'll go—"

"I'm going there to look for work. To live. To make a livelihood."

His brown eyes swelled with color. "Have we not been good to you?"

"Can you drive me to the ferry in the morning?"

His lips parted but he couldn't speak.

"Don't do this," he finally said. "What about Hercules?"

"I'll come back and get him when I'm settled. Meanwhile you'll look after him. He's happy here."

She told the lies she needed to tell to Ellen and to Eva and she said what truth she needed to say to Hercules. And as farewell he handed her a book. "*The History of the Horse*," he told her. "You'll learn from it."

She put on the traveling suit she hadn't worn for more than half a year, the one she'd worn on the train ride west, she closed the *Icarus* chest and packed a small valise and put on a hat and gloves. She had seventy seven dollars left of the eighty dollars Lodz had given to her and she gave five of them to Hercules, telling him, Don't spend it all on clothes. She hugged her brother, climbed onto the buckboard next to Asahel, waved good-bye to the Curtis women and set her eyes on the road ahead. Asahel drove in silence, for which she was grateful.

"It's not far," he finally said.

"No," she agreed.

"I could be there within hours. If you would ever need me to."

She made no response.

On a stretch of open road, with the proximity of the harbor in the air, they saw a single figure in the distance, with a mule, approaching. The man, bearded, was limping slightly and leaning on a walking stick.

"Speed up," Clara said.

Asahel held tightly on the reins.

"Speed *up*," Clara said again.

As they drew nearer to the figure in the road it was clear to both of them that the man they were approaching was Edward and that he, in turn, had recognized them.

Clara seized the whip from Asahel and beat the horses once, then twice, into a gallop, overtaking Edward in the road and speeding past him, before Asahel had the chance to grapple tack and team from her and bring them to a stop.

"—he's my *brother*," he objected.

"Then get *down*," she told him, taking the reins from him and pushing him onto the ground. She was standing in the buckboard with both leathers in one hand, whipping with the other, when she heard the shout behind her—

"—Scout!"

She urged the horses forward, his voice ringing in her ears—

"—Scout!"

And then, unmistakably—

"—*Clara!*"

She stopped. The road ahead, its vanishing point, beckoned to her like the dark back of time, like the unknown space a figure in a painting faces when it turns its back upon the present, turns its back upon the viewer, on their shared experience. Behind her, someone whom she knew she loved was calling out her name. Behind her, his blue eyes.

And so she turned.

lights out for the territory

We turn, we are a turning tribe—born into, borne by rotation—earth propelling us around its axis once a day, like a revolving door, while gravity deceives us into thinking that the sky is moving, we are standing still.

When Edward Curtis died he had gone around the sun eighty-four times, eighty-four revolutions—my father, fifty-three. Another trip around the sun—another turning—is what we're really celebrating when we celebrate an anniversary—another journey of 574,380,400 miles. In his lifetime my father journeyed thirty billion miles through space, without noting it—Curtis, almost fifty billion.

Those are major road trips, when you think about it.

Which puts this haul to Vegas in perspective: just a little run around the neighborhood.

Driving east on the 101 toward Pasadena, skirting through the San Fernando Valley, I'm still on former mission land, acres deeded to the Mission San Fernando *rancho* for growing olives, grapes, corn, wheat and melons. After Glendale, the land rises toward the San Gabriels where the native Tongva, a language clan of the Shoshone, were indentured to the Mission San Gabriel in the eighteenth century, and thereafter called the *Gabrieleno* tribe. East from here, all the way to Death Valley, the native language was Shoshone, and AZUSA is the first town on the highway to bear a shadow Shoshone name.

The American road is an Indian nation.

FIREBIRD. CHEROKEE. MUSTANG. WINNEBAGO.

Is there any other country in the world that appropriates the names of clans for cars?

If you think you've recently been the victim of IDENTITY THEFT, *please press "one,"* a voice advises me every time I call my bank, but no one bats an eye at you in your Jeep COMANCHE or your Chevy CHEYENNE.

You can drive clear across the country without being questioned about your Chevy TAHOE or APACHE.

In your TIOGA.

Your CONESTOGA wagon.

I guess I fell in love with being on the road from being in the front seat of the car with my father, late at night, on road trips from Pennsylvania to Virginia.

I don't think children can identify loneliness in others.

Although lonely, themselves, sometimes, I don't think children have the depth of experience to recognize loneliness as a state of being that exists in others.

I don't think we, as adults, are especially aware of loneliness in others, either, unless that person is obviously *alone*, sitting on a bench, sitting at a remove, picking idly through trash on a street corner, staring from a window.

When loneliness exists inside a family, it havens its own silence. Families breed loneliness that's disguised as shyness, or as boredom; or as *sleep*.

Families are designed to be the social antidote to solitude, so to learn to search for signs of loneliness inside a family goes against our instincts.

We're not taught to look for loneliness, so it passes, like a shadow, over dinners, over evenings watching the TV, between married couples, between parents and their children,

The silence that was probably a kind of dull ache in my father emanated to me on those car rides as a kind of comfort.

He was very good behind the wheel, very capable and uncomplaining, and that communicated to me as a confidence that we were safe, cocooned in a closed environment, he and I up front, mom and J-J in the back, moving through the known and unknown, navigating life together. If there was a social concern over the impulse to manufacture bigger cars and build more roads, those issues were not filtering into the daily news one received as a young girl growing up in 50's America. *To drive* was an innocent pursuit. To drive long distances was an adventure. The superhighways—six lanes, eight lanes, the Interstates—were still on drawing boards, so we progressed behind two cones of light down two- or four-lane roads through corn, cotton and tobacco fields, scrubby, cluttered Maryland woods, towns with church steeples and village greens, Fredericksburg, Baltimore, Washington and Richmond. The cities were allegro movements in the symphony; the fields and farms andantes. The night had rhythm. The towns *approached*, you could sense a town's encroachment through the clearings in the woods, outbuildings would materialize, the town's corona would glow above it in the sky, the distances between the barns would quicken, houses would construct a chorus line. Whether it was dark or light there was specificity in every shadow. And because it was that specific passage along Route 1 through Maryland and northern Virginia, as we drove south we drove into American history, too. I could name the battlefields in order, north to south. There's no other country on Earth that has so many battlefields as road side attractions. If you have a mind to do so you can follow Washington as he evaded or pursued the British through the declared independent colonies or you can stop and scan the twilight's last gleaming over the same harbor waters as Francis Scott Key or follow Lee and Jackson and the Army of the Potomac into boggy marshes over clay pits onto the higher granite ramparts overlooking Richmond.

How my mother's parents came to settle in a place between the James and Appomattox Rivers in the tidewater delta of Virginia from their separate Aegean islands of Skopelos and Limnos was embedded in conflicting legends, different versions of one family's history, but their separate acts of reinvention, taken some time between the two world wars, certified the fact that their only daughter Mary was not only Greek, she was a Southerner.

Which is to say that life with her was, by turns, life with Vivien Leigh playing Scarlett O'Hara *and* Vivien Leigh as Clytemnestra.

Landscape shaped her: the farther north my mother went, the more *Scarlett* she seemed; the farther south, the Greek-er.

She would get into the backseat of the car in Lancaster, Pennsylvania, go to sleep and emerge six or seven hours later in Hopewell, Virginia, a different version of herself. Maybe that's what going back to the place of your birth always does to someone, but I used to think that sleeping all the way through *Mary*land must have exacted an effect on her—she must have traded Marys there, one Mary for another, in that land of all those Marys.

The journey her parents made in their migratory flight from Greece seemed to have depleted their travel genes because they neither one went back to Greece, nor did Mary, nor did she tolerate any kind of journey well. The road put her right out. Ten minutes into a road trip, Mary was snoring—loud and full of drama, even in her sleep. If we stopped at a traffic light or a stop sign, the halt would never interrupt her rhythm, but every time we made a left-hand turn, her snoring stopped abruptly, then picked up again after a minute. Through a city, through Baltimore or Washington, for example, John could keep her quiet for a full ten or fifteen minutes by executing a series of sinistrally directed detours, but eventually we'd hit a stretch of open road and the snoring would start up again. If it got too loud, John would hum or start to whistle, sometimes sing, and the breathing from the backseat, though still heavy and deep, would be peaceful.

The drive had all these syncopations, then—the percussion of the asphalt road, the alternating rhythms of the landscape braiding, like convergent channels of a river, through divergent threads of time, history into the present moment; and the sounds of Mary snoring. *Repetition* was a rhythm, too: the more we traveled this same road, the more memories we had of ourselves in this landscape. We were doubling, multiplying as we went—especially John and Mary, going back and forth along a road they'd traveled for years, ever since they were married. Maybe that's why Mary slept—so her past would stay, as new. So she wouldn't have to see it all, again; watch it change, before her eyes—see the changes in the landscape. But John searched as he drove—I learned that from him, a kind of leaning forward at the wheel, trying to imagine whatever was out there, trying to inhabit what he could or could not see out in the distance. It was the future he was searching—that's the mechanics of the road: the horizon line *awaits*, a destination, where you're going. It's the line of possibility. For John, driving south from Pennsylvania meant driving toward his own remembered past and the pasts of others in his family; transacting with his ghosts. It was a journey through both now, and then. The North, the South. All the Johns, and all the Marys (in and out of *Mary*land). Only Mary and Joseph surpass the coupled names of John and Mary as clichés in American Christendom. They're the Dick and Jane of married couples. John and Mary. See Spot run. Run, John. And marry Mary.

My father first went south because he had to—drafted at the start of World War II, he was posted to Ft. Lee, Virginia, where he met my mother, who was working at the commissary. I don't know how he made that initial trip—by bus, or train—but he must have grasped the coincidence that his paternal grandfather, John Wiggins, the man in whose memory he had been named, had been conscripted into serving his own nation, The Union, and had donned its dark blue uniform and marched south into Maryland, into Virginia, where in 1865 a piece of Confederate lead lodged in his head and he bled out, perhaps in the very woods we passed. Two John Wigginses—two wars—two conscripted journeys from Pennsylvania to Virginia. That original John Wiggins's Certificate of Discharge from Company E of the 179th Regiment of the Pennsylvania Volunteers in the War Between the States hangs in a place of pride in my California home, and it's as much a work of art as any of my daughter's fine art photographs. The penmanship alone is thrilling—to say nothing of the latent narrative the facts suggest. There he was—the first John Wiggins—in the final year of a brutal war, wounded within months of its termination, discharged because of injury, turfed out at Alexandria, Virginia, and paid in full on August 5, 1865. How I came to be in possession of this document—

how my father came to be, before me—seems to me a kind of blessed wonder, a small miracle. It might have passed, unnoticed, into history's dustbin, but it didn't. Its survival, intact, its materiality, is a result of fragile circumstance, *the fact that it exists* is a surprise. When I moved to California from London, my possessions followed me by ship, through the Panama Canal—eighty-six cartons of books, their pages looking sadly foxed and faded in their new surroundings under southern California light. It was only in unpacking that I noticed spots of mildew inside the glass of the framed Certificate of Discharge. Recently I finally got around to cleaning it. I hadn't held the document, itself, since I found it among my father's things, several days after we buried him. I had forgotten what that feels like, the touch of century-old paper, like a weathered buckskin to the hand. The paper—its crispness reduced by age to velvet—has life. Even if nothing were written on it, it would breathe of something, have spirit—the way a fossil does. The size and color of my great-grandfather's Certificate of Discharge from the Civil War reminds me of that sketch by Leonardo in the Queen's Gallery in London—same size, same sandstone color, same sketching-in depiction of a larger landscape, same miniaturization of an overview of life. When I stare at it I have the sense of looking at a kind of panorama of his life, as if this were a map of him. A map of part of him. On the back of the document on its shadow side, the side I hadn't seen for all the years that it was framed, is another map, of sorts, a printed form entitled OATH OF IDENTITY, left blank. Its print runs perpendicular to the print on the other side, and it takes up only one third of the page, the suggestion being that it will form a kind of title page when the document is folded into thirds, the way certain legal summonses today fold up into themselves inside a single slim blue outer page. I believe the reason the OATH OF IDENTITY is blank is because my great grandfather must already have been known to the discharging officer or supplied that officer with some sort of irrefutable proof—possibly a photograph—that he was, in fact, the selfsame John Wiggins that he claimed to be. The only other piece of my great-grandfather's map I own is, in fact, a photograph that's come down to me on trust. By which I mean—I have no proof it's him, only a verbal family legend that the people in this photograph are, indeed, the people I've been told they are—John Wiggins and his scrappy little soulmate *Mary*. *Another* John & Mary. And although this earlier John Wiggins bears no ancestral resemblance to the later John, my father—(except for those very deep-set eyes)— and although he assembles himself like a Puritanical pill, *she* looks like a whole buckboard o' *fun*. *Mary Book* was her name—(and how

nice for a writer to claim a Book on one limb of the family tree). He's got his heels locked, hands locked in readiness for prayer. She's got that one foot inchin' forward, that one hand on her hip, that jutting elbow and those tinted glasses. *Mammy Yokum*, yes! indeedy; thin piss yoked to vinegar. This is the sum of what I know of her, this picture. And that she birthed at least four children. Details of women's lives are usually only tangential in historical records, reflecting attachments to men and the labors of maternity. When I was teaching myself to use internet genealogy sites to write the Edward Curtis novel, I used my own family as the prototype and tried to find all I could about this John and this Mary because Curtis's own father was my great-grandfather's contemporary and had fought beside him in the Civil War. After trial and error I stumbled on this John and this Mary in the 1900 U.S. census, where there was nothing much to learn about my great-grandmother, not even her maiden name, and where John's occupation is listed as FARMER, which is only a mere part of how he occupied himself, if family legend is to be believed. Family legend, as it came to me, is that John took a rebel bullet to the head after which he *saw God*, returned to Pennsylvania and started preaching his own fellowship, founding his own church. This may or may not be true but for the purpose of the Curtis novel it proved providentially insightful because by the time Edward was born in February 1868, his own father, Johnson Asahel Curtis, also had returned home from the Civil War, on a veteran's disability, to become *a minister*. I had to wonder—how many of them were there, these ministering farm boys who joined up, went off, saw the South, saw death and then subsequently thereafter *saw God?* There's something of the WAKAN TANKA, The Great Mystery, in war's power to make braves of boys and wise men of certain braves. But if war makes the argument for peace for some, it makes the argument for sanctioned killing for far more and for every two men like John and Johnson Curtis who left the battlefield as proselytes promoting the word of God according to the Bible, there were hundreds more who left the battlefield better trained for the burgeoning killing fields out West. Whereas my great-grandfather had a reputed genius for threatening to invoke a wrathful God against transgressions that included imbibing fermented beverages, desiring universal suffrage and utilizing the lascivious comforts of indoor plumbing, Johnson Curtis appears to have been a sort of semi-pious parish journeyman, not particularly inspired by good works and The Good Book, but on the side of angels, on the whole, for want of someone of a finer cloth way the hell out there where the Curtises resided in Whitewater, Wisconsin. In 1874 he landed the job of circuit preacher for a region in the upper Minnesota lake country and took young Edward, then age six, with him on his rounds performing marriages and baptisms and, of course, last rites and funerals. Johnson's health was never good after the war and he depended on his young son to manage the more arduous labors of their travels—harnessing the horses, rowing the canoe, foraging for food and wood and making camp. I've thought a lot about that young boy Edward—how the physically adept boy foreshadowed the physically courageous man. He was an engine of activity, as a man, running up Mt. Rainier, kayaking the Inuit coast, dogging Lewis and Clark's trail down the Columbia. He was Huck Finn and Tom Sawyer rolled into one and what he lacked in formal schooling he made up for in raw strength and adaptive cunning. Legend has it that he built his first camera when he was twelve years old from a partial lens his father brought home from the Civil War—but how a complex and sophisticated piece of glass landed in Johnson Curtis's forlorn Union Army bindle begs anybody's guess. The story sounds like vintage Curtis, the kind of tale he loved to tell about himself when he was hustling his prospective buyers back East on the lecture circuit. He may always have had that mid-westerner's braggadocio when he was in the company of Roosevelt and Harriman and Morgan, but on his own on horseback, scouting a location, he was in his element, physically at ease and physically commanding.

Physically beautiful.

As much as my father *yearned* toward landscape, looked at it with yearning in his eyes, he never put himself into it, engaged with it physically, until the very end—which made the circumstances of his death all that more shocking. You wouldn't have thought he had the strength, the sheer ability to do what he finally did. But when I think of Curtis on the land, Curtis in the landscape, I can believe that he could tackle anything, that he had, from the very early years, a natural physical agility, a natural balance in the world.

Like the stereotypical male *Indian*.

Like Huck Finn.

I can imagine him saying to himself, as Huck does, "*Well I reckon I got to* light out for the territory *ahead of the rest because Aunt Sally she's going to adopt me and civilize me and I can't stand it. I been there before.*"

Curtis lit out in a big way—so did my father—though it's impossible to know for sure if they were running *from* or running *to*.

That's the potency of lighting out, of journeying: the *from* and *to* are both in play.

Until you stop. Until you *stop*, the journey is the only rationale.

Huck never says where or what he's bound for, he just needs *to go*. Make tracks. Get outta Dodge. Hit the highway. Avoid, elude, escape *Aunt Sally*. We all have our own Aunt Sally—call her loveless marriage. Call her thankless job. Call her parenthood. Domestic mess. Daily reminder of debt and obligation.

Tedium.

Routine.

The great promise here is that if we load the TV in the truck and move just three states over we can start anew.

Tie the cash cow to the Conestoga and set out across the Plains and Rockies.

Sell mama's stuff and drive all night to Vegas.

Try to count the miles some Americans rack up on a single family tree, I dare you. Not every family lights out as spectacularly as Curtis's—or my own Greek grandparents all the way from the Aegean to Virginia—but most families have at least one member who takes off. Throws in the towel and swears take *that*, Aunt Sal. *Laissez-faire* and *laissez-passer* constitute the air we breathe. It's in the Constitution, the *pursuit* of. Hell, it's written. It's our right. Hell *yes*, drive all night to Vegas. Hell *yes*, join the circus. And in the nineteenth century they were *giving* land away, out here. The railroads were. Homesteading Acts arose in every western state connected by a railroad to the East, so in 1887 Johnson Curtis bit the apple, got the travel bug again and convinced himself that all he needed to restore his health was the purer climate of a Pacific kind. He boarded a Northern Pacific train in Minneapolis with Edward and headed out for Portland, Oregon, then north to Puget Sound, where he purchased land for $3.00 an acre on which he had been told palm trees swayed all the way from Mt. Rainier to the Pacific Ocean. Edward was then nineteen years old and had been serving as his father's shadow body, his ailing father's body double, since he was old enough to wield an axe, chop wood, say grace and talk to people. He had never had a childhood in the modern sense—rural children in the nineteenth century worked as soon as they could walk—so by the time he came west by train in the summer of that year, Edward had his own array of resident Aunt Sallys. Filial obligation. Family duty. His own self-imposed yardstick measure of his manhood. He was a man, already, at nineteen; but if any place can redefine a person's sense of self it's our American West. If Great Britain in the eighteenth and nineteenth centuries had had our land equivalent, she would have put far fewer boys to sea.

Not that a frontier mentality makes a better corps of citizens—even today there are places out here that don't have to fake, as Vegas does, that they've never seen the likes of Aunt Sally. There are places so removed from any civilizing germ that when you enter them for the first time you lose your own perspective, drop, like Alice down the rabbit hole, into a history so much deeper than your own that your existence is too meager to make any mark in the historical record. The first time I drove out here on my own the land began to suck me under as if it were quicksand and the sky came down and whomped me. I'd come over to Canada from London on a job and I got the bright idea to drive south from Regina, Saskatchewan, to the Oglala Sioux Reservation at Pine Ridge in South Dakota, because Curtis had been there and because I needed to see an American Indian reservation for myself if I was going to write about him and the people that he photographed. On a map the drive looks like a simple thing to do because you can run your finger down the page from Regina in Saskatchewan, through Montana, straight through North and most of South Dakota to Pine Ridge on a perfect north/south plumb line. But on any given map of land the one thing you don't see is sky. I started out from Regina as the sky was lightening in pre-dawn and in about a half an hour I had left the civilizing confines of that western Canadian railroad town and was out on open land, looking south at a flat unbroken foreground toward unseen Montana just beyond the straight line of the horizon. The sky was crystal, clean, a deceptive non-menacing blue but it was crowding in, encroaching everywhere, flooding on the land and toward my throat, level to my neck, and if I couldn't keep my head beneath it I would cut loose from the steering wheel and spin untethered into obliterating space. All around me there was nothing but uninterrupted space for as far as I could see, this single thread of road tethering me to what I knew, to where I'd been, where I was going. I pulled off the road to catch my breath and calm my heart from racing. I was the only human being on the scene. The only *being*, period. Except for a sky so vigilant and present it assumed all Being all itself, capital *be*. I got out and walked around the car and opened the passenger-side door and sat down in the door well and put my head between my knees. I am fairly robust, pride myself in my adaptability to foreign places, but for the first time in my life *place* was threatening to make me sick. Wind was an element of sky as it tore over the earth, no impediment to slow it down, to stand against its shapelessness and say THIS IS YOUR LIMIT. This is where you stop; and start. This is what you are. Be it for good or evil we are referential creatures, we need defining points, civilizing points of reference, and existence without antecedents panics us. Panicked me, at least. I realized I was having an unprecedented attack—a kind of agoraphobia. Fear of open spaces. I stood up and kicked around the grass beside the road, tried to find an insect or any living critter, any living thing, but there was nothing out there. Nothing. Not even birdsong. Not even a single bird to follow in the sky. I tried taking full deep breaths, then clambered up the trunk and stood on the roof of the car. What was it Archimedes boasted—? *Give me a place to stand and I will move the Earth.* If I was higher, I could see a longer distance, I figured. See a human, maybe. See a barn. See *something*. Something to enforce the myth of *I*, the myth of who I thought I was that day, the myth of *day*, itself; the recurring human myth of *time*. If you're going to light out, there has to be a something you are lighting from. *From's* a given; from's a certain. *To* is out there, in our minds, uncertain. No one can promise us a *to*. No one ever gives a certain future to us in our hands, that we can hold. If they allege that they can guarantee the future—if we believe they can—they are charlatans and we are party to their lies. And when you stand there in a place as immense as our own continental west with not another creature in your sight for miles and miles and miles around, you realize you are standing in the jaws of your existence. That the journey that you make through time—where you light out to—is the only meaning you can claim. Our lives are our individual claims on the combined experience—our lives are not our names or our professions—and somewhere there's a big rig driver who may or may not have ever told the story of how he was hauling ass one morning years ago south out of Canada toward Montana when out in the middle of nowhere there was this woman standing on the rooftop of her car waving a giant crazy *Hell-o!!* at him as he barreled by, so he opened up the air horn and boomed her one, and how she hung back but kept behind him for at least an hour, 'til he turned off on Route 2 toward the West. By then, the geology had changed, Montana's seismology had kicked in, there were other intermittent passing vehicles and train tracks beside the road to ease my panic, but what I remember most about that big rig coming up behind me is that I hadn't heard it coming, what with all the wind, until it was on top of me and how I turned around and gave the driver a thumbs-up to let him know I didn't need assistance and how he set that air horn off out there in the middle of the continent.

How the sound bent, as it passed.

It sounded like a train.

And it made me feel safe.

Even now, in the dark, on my way to Vegas, I keep the window down, hoping I will hear one in the distance. Hear a train. And see one. In the dark they're scary, moving toward you, that impending headlight hanging in the distance, seeming not to move, until you figure out oh, there must be *train tracks* over there. In the daylight driving east on this route I see them all the time, usually seeing the first one here, in the Cajon Pass, where the land rises to a sudden 5,000 feet from sea level where the Pacific Plate whacked into the American one. The San Andreas fault runs through here, as do two pipelines, four power lines, Route 15, itself, Route 66, and three separate rail lines. In the daylight I can catch a Burlington Northern Santa Fe toiling uphill here on two engines, dragging several dozen containers from China and Taiwan reading COSCO and HAN JIN into the inland empire from their point of entry at Long Beach or the Port of Los Angeles. Tonight the pass is a necklace of descending headlights trailing toward me, but in daylight this climb is a thriller, the drama of colliding plates strewn across the surface in huge blocks of Pelona schist as big as ship containers, as if the earth, itself, had engineered a train wreck. Here at the Cajon Pass I always feel I've really left Los Angeles—after this, the land feels like The West. After this comes the Victorville plateau. After this, it's Barstow; and the desert. In daylight I like to stop in Barstow, not because, as the sign proclaims on Main Street, it's the CROSSROADS OF OPPORTUNITY, but because, unlike Las Vegas and a lot of other newly manufactured western towns, Barstow has a past. Barstow has a history. It has ghosts. And many many miles of tracks. It takes its name—like Seligman and Kingman, Arizona, do—from a train man, and Burlington Northern Santa Fe still operates its main RR Classification Yard there. Route 66 is the Main Street, now both alarmingly tough and despairingly shabby, and there's a railroad museum tucked beside the tracks, but the real roadside attraction in Barstow is the surviving Fred Harvey House built into the depot. Curtis was back and forth through Barstow

on his way into the desert to photograph the Mojave, Walapai and Havasupai tribes, and he must have stood beside the tracks in front of the Harvey House a dozen times. The restaurant's a National Historic site now, not open to the public, but I like to stand there and look through the windows. There were a lot of days, writing this novel about Curtis, when I couldn't understand him, couldn't bring what I knew about him, his self-generated myth, the few true scattered facts, into a coherent whole. I'd think about jettisoning the project altogether on those days, to take up the heroic tale of Fred Harvey, instead, who seemed like a genuinely nice guy and whose business had as large an impact on Western tribes as Curtis's. The Harvey Houses were like missions on the Santa Fe Railroad's *camino real*—familiar places in the wild, places where travelers could disembark in desolate and unknown territory and feel immediately *at home*. It was Fred Harvey's brainstorm to feature Indians along the tracks, in front of Harvey Houses, sitting non-threateningly on blankets, selling baskets and turquoise trinkets to the passengers as they stopped along the way in Lamy, Albuquerque, Phoenix, Flagstaff and the Grand Canyon. Fred would feed you Blue Point oysters, iceberg lettuce and vanilla ice cream at some one-hundred-degrees-in-the-shade outpost in Arizona or New Mexico, courtesy of his contract with the Santa Fe to take delivery of refrigerated goods for free, and you would practically expire on the spot not from the heat but from the miracle. Then Fred's Harvey Girls would lead you out into the blasting sun and point you toward some Indians sitting on the platforms—point you toward some Zuni beadwork or a handy Hopi feathered head-dress or an Apache bow-and-arrow set which would look *so good* hanging on your wall back in Cambridge, Skokie or the Bronx. It was Fred Harvey's idea to transform people on train journeys into consuming entities, into packets of consumption: Johns and Marys into *tourists*. Nothing wrong with tour-ism, I'm a tourist here, myself, I stop and poke around a lot when I'm en route because I think that's the point of travel. I picked up the habit of stopping to investigate roadside attractions from my father on those early trips. I once followed a sign back in Virginia to a little white way-side building by a scenic pine wood where Stonewall Jackson had died. There was no one there (again) but me. And a sign with a green button on it that read PRESS TO LEARN. The voice of a U.S. National Parks Ranger came out of a hidden speaker when I pressed the button and told me the story of how Stonewall Jackson had been shot accidentally by a member of his own corps, brought to this little cabin where his arm had been amputated, where his wife had been summoned and where he had taken his last breath. I stood there with the talking hidden speaker until the recording of the ranger's voice stopped, and then, when it stopped, the world was suddenly much quieter than it had been all that morning. From that silence, right there, there was delivered to me, whole, a story I called "Stonewall Jackson's Wife," and the whole story arrived, start to finish, the way a train arrives; connected, in a logical sequence; complete, in and of itself. That's the only time in my life a story has produced itself for me like that out of a road-side attraction, but: you never know. I've stopped at a lot of road-side attractions, and it's the same as waiting for a photograph to assemble: you just never know when, or where, or how, or if the thing will happen. Nine times out of ten—no: nine hundred and ninety-nine times out of a thousand—no miracle occurs, no eigh-teen wheeler thunders past you on the road, blasting out a noise that reminds you of the sound your nation makes: but, still, I stop because it's worth the gamble.

Maybe I stop because my father used to.

Certainly he's the reason I'm enamored of a passing train, be-cause as well as taking those road trips back and forth between our home in Pennsylvania and my mother's parents' home in Virginia, my father used to take me on drives from our home in the suburbs of Lancaster out into the county to the church his grandfather had founded and to the farmland where he had been born, and we used to stop at all the railroad crossings to watch trains.

On those journeys we were alone, the two of us, there was no Mary in the backseat asleep because my mother didn't like my father's family's church, it went against her own Greek Orthodox re-ligion, where there were priests who wore embroidered robes and chanted in a minor key instead of a preacher with a turkey neck in a drab suit fulminating against sin.

Stopped at the railroad crossings I counted cars—it was my job.

Lancaster had the largest stockyards east of Chicago in those days so a lot of cars were cattle cars. Some of the cars were full of coal. None of them read HAN JIN.

Those county journeys of my father's were habitual, part of how he thought and lived. Most certainly they were how he lit out, if only for a couple hours, from his loneliness and from his marriage.

Even after I left home I believed they were a form of rescue to him, maybe even a form of meditation so it came as no particular surprise one day after I was married and a mother, myself, living in New York, when Mary called to tell me, "I don't think John came home last night."

She wasn't sure.

That was the way things were between them.

Uncertain.

"The boys called from the store, he hasn't been there yet, to open." It was noon, and for as long as I could remember John had left the house at six o'clock each morning to open up the store for his employees.

"Has he done this before?" I asked her.

Again she wasn't sure.

"How can I help you, mom? I'm three hundred miles away."

"I need someone to tell me what to do."

"Well, if he hasn't done this before, then something might have happened to him. I think you should call the police."

"I can't do that."

"It's only a phone call. You can do it."

"*You* do it."

"You're going to have to do this, mom. In case there's been an accident."

"If there'd been an accident someone would have called by now."

"They'll want to know what kind of car he drives."

"Oh god."

"They might ask if you were arguing. Let them ask. Just answer calmly. They're not judging you. It's what they're trained to do."

"—*police*, for godsake. Do I have to—?"

Somehow, she did. The fact that he was missing moved up the chain of command: State *troopers* they were called, back in Pennsylvania. Out here the State guys are the CHP—California Highway Patrol—and much to my amazement one of them has set a flamingo-colored flare off up ahead of me in my lane on Route 15 and is signaling the east-bound traffic to pull over for a chat beside the road.

I watch the drivers of the two cars in front of me have brief exchanges with the uniform, then proceed ahead with caution, slowly.

"Officer," I greet him.

"Ma'am." His flashlight beam sweeps over me. "I have to ask you to go it slow the next few miles. We got sheep loose on the highway."

"—*sheep*," I marvel. In this age of terrorism. "You need help rounding them up?"

The flashlight beam holds my eyes, then sweeps over to where his car is parked, blocking a gaping hole in the wire fence. "You're the first to ask," he says. "If you don't mind putting your car where mine is it would free me up 'til we get some backup—"

The last time I was out among sheep was years ago in Wales, which was enough to convince me that creatures with that much space between their eyes make a wholly appropriate sound to describe their cognitive spatial dilemma.

It's a toss, which are smarter: sheep or flounder.

I pull up behind the CHP cruiser, block the hole with my car as he drives away, turn the engine off, roll down all the windows. High desert air. Another roadside attraction. Sheep like to *light out for the territory*, too, I guess. You build a potential escapee every minute that you build a fence. And a fence might make good neighbors but not when it separates two parts of a self. When I first started charting the parts of Curtis that he had left behind, I figured that the panorama he saw from the train ride he had made out West with his father was what had set him off in search of American Indians. I thought it was wide open space that he had longed to light out to. That what he was afraid of, his *Aunt Sally*, was the cramped intimacy of family. The intimacy of love. He had fallen in love—or seemed to have, at least—with Clara, slightly younger though better educated than he. She was the perfect helpmate for him—frugal, where he was extravagant; level-headed, where he was too quick to pursue his fantasies—but as soon as their first child was born, Edward had lit out. He was gone two or three days every week; then a whole week at a time; then for a month. Soon he was out in the territory, among the tribes, for six or seven months.

I had always thought that what he was running *from* was the imprisonment of domestic life; from Clara, from their children. Then I took that trip to Pine Ridge and ended up spending the night in Wall, South Dakota, an outpost of ANGLO cowboyism outside the rez where tourists to the Dakota Badlands and Pine Ridge stop to spend the night, eat beef, booze up and buy the fake Sioux tat that passes as real Indian SOUVENIRS. Curtis is an *industry* in a place like Wall—I had known that postcards of his photographs were big out West but it hadn't sunk in until I saw a six-foot rotating display in Wall Drug of his reproductions made small. It was the same day I'd had my little *crise* with the land and the sky and the agoraphobia so I was still feeling the effects of *panorama*. *Panorama* was all I could think about: the immensity out there: the uncompromising BIGNESS. And then I came face to face with a display of Edward S. Curtis postcards and all I could think was *Oswald, Oswald, Oswald, Oswald*—one after another—*Oswald, Oswald*, the disgusting Lee Harvey slang attribution for a HEADSHOT.

All the Curtis postcards were HEADSHOTS.

A whole rack of them.

And I realized: *you don't go into the West to make* HEADSHOTS.

You go into the West the way Ansel Adams did—the way Timothy O'Sullivan and William Henry Jackson and Carlton Watkins did: for The Big Picture.

For the Views.

The *pan-o-rama*.

But there they were, lined up on a metal rack in Wall, South Dakota: face after face after face of *intimacy*—and oh, my Aunt Sally: *who are we kidding when we think we can run?*

You can flip through the entire Curtis *oeuvre*—all his photographs from Arizona, the Dakotas, Montana, Nevada, Idaho, New Mexico, Wyoming, Utah, Colorado, Washington, Oregon and my beloved California—more than 50,000 photographs in all, and you'll find that less than half of them were photographed *outside*.

We reveal ourselves in everything we do. We reveal ourselves even when we think we're hiding, even when we think we've got the wagon streamlined, when we think we've left the stuff we need to get away from far behind us.

It's a tricky business, this invention of identity.

So I make the call:

"Hello, good evening, it's Marianne Wiggins calling again."

"—oh, hello, Miss Wiggins, what can we do for you?"

"I just wanted to let you know I decided to make the trip, maybe I can help you figure out who this guy is, posing as my father. But it looks like I won't get to Vegas 'til the middle of the night."

"Go to Emergency. I'm on 'til six. Have them call me and I'll come and get you."

And then, even though I know the man cannot be my father I ask, *"How's he doing?"*

"Still unconscious. They don't think he'll linger long. You know, *his age.* The Indian's still with him."

" . . . the—??"

"—man who called the ambulance. Looks to be some kind of Indian. Truth is, *we can't get him to leave . . .*"

Out in the dark, sheep gather like reflecting pools of moonlight. I realize I'm wearing sandals in snake country and climb up on my car roof. I lie down and gaze up at the stars. I *know* this man is not my father. Just like I know HAN JIN containers come all the way from China even though my sensory logic tells me *the world is only what I see.* Maybe that is ultimately the reason anyone lights out. To learn how big the big world is.

To find *stories.*

What can one 83-year-old stranger posing as my father tell me? He's *unconscious,* silent as these stars. Silent as a photograph. You think you know someone by looking at his face but what can one face say about the thousand thoughts behind those eyes. Edward Curtis claimed he lit out for the territory to document a race of people he believed were vanishing before the nation's eyes—*The Vanishing Race* was what he called the first photograph in Volume I.

He believed that the indigenous peoples of the United States were laid out on their deathbed, in their final throes, that he better light out for the territory to verify identities.

And maybe I am lighting out for Vegas just like Curtis did—for some *final oath*. We love the best we can and light out for the territory all our life, hoping for the button that says PRESS TO LEARN, fooling, maybe, no one on the way about who we are and where we're going and the things we think we've left behind as we drive onward into silence past one great roadside attraction after another, never even knowing 'til we get there that we've carted our Aunt Sally with us, sound asleep, dormant, snoring, right behind us.

the mad greek

Try leaving all those family ghosts behind you when you're on The Mother Road.

That's what Steinbeck called Route 66 in *The Grapes of Wrath*— the Joad Road. Is there a Father Road?

Or is every road, every ribbon toward mirage, presumed to be the road to masculinity, the road each one of our American fathers had to take at some time in his life?

Thunder Road.

Highway 61.

Highway out of boyhood. Springsteen and Dylan hammering the licks, their testosterone passed off as social contract, their pretense of melancholy a pretense of some greater ethos called "freedom."

When it was drawn, graded and paved Route 66 clove to the old railroad routes like young Plato to ol' Socrates. Wherever there were train routes in this country, automotive roads would follow. "No nails, no Christ," the poet Donald Hall has written. No Socrates, no Plato. No railroad, no interstate highway system. Before 1956, when the Interstate Highway Act was written, there were already "national" roads—the Dixie Highway, north to south, from Michigan to Florida; the Lincoln Highway, east to west, from New York to

San Francisco—but there existed nothing on the scale of what President Eisenhower envisioned, 4- or 6- or 8-lane superhighways built not necessarily as connective tissue between two primary destinations, but for the mandated task of hauling freight across long distances as fast as possible with no unnecessary stops.

To eat, for instance.

Or take in a museum.

Sleep in comfort.

See a show.

Haul ass was the mantra of the new inter-state of being, so we got these monster roads where no roads had gone before, which forced us to face the fact that we could cross the country now in record time without ever seeing, stopping in or pausing at a real place or a real town.

And you may ask yourself, David Byrne reminds us, *"Where does that highway go to?"*

This one goes to Vegas and beyond, following as Route 66 sometimes did, the Union Pacific and Amtrak route into the Mojave through Barstow and Baker toward Nevada.

But Amtrak doesn't serve Las Vegas anymore, not by train, anyway, only by bus (then why call it "Amtrak"?), so the trains one sees running beside Interstate 15 are blue-collar rigs, trafficking in bare necessities, not leisure.

Beyond Victorville I lose The Mother Road as I-15 heads toward Barstow. 66, also called "The Main Street of America," used to wend from here toward the settled towns north of Victorville, but the Interstates were plotted to cut to the chase and cut out the Main Streets. At Barstow 66 will cross my path again, intersecting I-15 to turn toward Daggett, now a ghost town, Ludlow, Needles and on to

Arizona. So much of Route 66's lore is now about its role as a "historic" road, a *ghost* road, decommissioned from its active status as an official U.S. "Route" in 1985. Yet it never trespassed on Nevada, a state renowned for ghost towns. Bypassed, converted or overpaved by newer roads along its 2,600-mile stretch between Santa Monica and Chicago, 66 is now, in parts, CA2, CA110, I-210, I-10, I-15, I-40, I-44, I-55. *"Please help us save this invaluable piece of Americana before it is only a memory,"* reads a brochure from the National Historic Route 66 Federation that I pick up at a gas station on the Interstate in Barstow. It makes me think of Curtis, driving out through the unpaved desert to "help us save" the Indians before they were "only a memory." Well, hell. What's the whole of our experience if not "only a memory"? My father and mother are "only a memory" to me right now, but so is my daughter's childhood, and my own, and she and I are both alive— what's so regrettable about something being "only a memory"?

Unless of course we're talking about a race of people.

Or the soul of a marriage.

Or love.

But *a road?* Can we justify nostalgia for *a road?* Far younger than the Silk Road or the Via Appia, Route 66 was a road whose working existence spanned less than fifty years, roughly twice the average life span of celebrity. What was celebrated about Route 66 was, first of all, its place in the memories of those who came to California from Oklahoma and the Panhandle during the Dust Bowl years, like Steinbeck's Joads; and then, for later generations, what was celebrated about Route 66 was not only that there was a song about it but that there was a TV show about it, too. The song (. . . *get your kicks on Route 66 . . .*) was written by Bobby Troupe who was from my hometown and whose father owned the best music store there. Bobby and his chanteuse wife Julie London always made the front page of the *Lancaster Intelligencer Journal* when they came to town in the 60's, Julie's dramatic bosom generously displayed in whatever outfit she was wearing. I can't remember whether Bobby's Route 66 song was the theme song for the Route 66 TV program, but I do remember the Corvette and all the driving around through western scenery and that it costarred George Maharis, who, like my mother Mary, was a first-generation Greek American. His family came from Corfu and owned a restaurant and Mary watched the show each week because she had a crush on him. Neither of my parents ever traveled farther West than Chicago so their image of Route 66 derived from what they saw on television. In black and white, like a Curtis photograph.

Instant *vintage.*

What my parents knew about the real Route 66 approximates what I can know about Theodore Roosevelt by looking at Curtis's photograph of him. Did he have yellow teeth? Russet highlights in his hair? Indigo coronas around the pupils of his eyes? Except for paintings of him, every image that I've seen of Teddy has been in black and white, just like the images of the West on television back when all the broadcast world was shades of gray. When I was still in high school, no fewer than sixteen shows a week were Westerns. *Hopalong Cassidy* and *Gene Autry* in the 40's, *Roy Rogers* in the 50's, and then in the 60's there were dozens of them—*The Rifleman, Have Gun Will Travel, Wagon Train, Gunsmoke, Palladin, Tales of Wells Fargo, Death Valley Days, Big Valley, Bonanza, The Virginian, Broken Arrow, Cheyenne, Cimmaron City, Rawhide, The Lawman, High Chaparral, Laramie, Colt 45, Maverick, Bat Masterson, Wanted: Dead or Alive.*

Cowboy shows.

Cowboys *and* Indians.

My first concept of a walking, talking Indian was Tonto on *The Lone Ranger*—ever wise, ever loyal, deferential to his *kimo sabe,* never one to waste a word, never one to smile. And you might ask yourself, *Who was that masked man?* but did you ever ask why, at the height of post-war consumerism and suburban expansion with look-alike streets and look-alike houses, why the legend of the cowboy was so popular?

Think of the TV shows that have taken over the ratings since the terrorist attacks of September 11, 2001—shows that put the pieces of the puzzle back together, shows that solve the crime through diligent and thorough science, shows that find the missing, shows that revolve around an active, wise and super-vigilant government agent, shows that feature ghosts and the crime-solvers who co-operate with them to make the world a safer place. Sometimes we get the heroes we deserve but we *always* get the television shows our fears dictate.

The current top-ranked series for the past several years speaks to our need, as a traumatized nation, to believe that logic and order reign in the world, that crimes leave discernible fingerprints and that nothing—no thing—arises from unpredictable sources. The series takes place in Las Vegas, which is no random choice, because there is something in our national psyche right now that needs Vegas, needs the idea of it, rather than its base reality. Which may be why each segment of the series opens with an aerial view, different each week, glitzy, shimmering, of Sin City and its environs. Thirty seconds, tops, a bird's-eye view of neon Vegas, Vegas as mirage—then the show leaves all trace of the town behind for the cool and blue interiors of the crime lab. We know that no municipality on these beloved shores could afford a state-of-the-art glass and gizmo graced lab as the set of *CSI* pretends, but we believe it, anyway, the same way we believed in Lorne Green's accent in *Bonanza* and Miss Kitty's anachronistic foundation garments in *Gunsmoke*. Because PRINT THE LEGEND is one of the great lines from one of the great Westerns, and because when the daily reality presents itself as uncomprehendable, we fashion our own myths and then hold those phony truths to be inalienable.

The concept of cowboys *and* Indians, for instance.

The West had both of them, but those iconic scenes of Injuns chasing John Wayne in his Stetson could hardly be more mythic than an extraterrestrial on a flying bicycle silhouetted on a rising moon.

Indians fought Army men, not cowboys.

Cavalry.

Yellow hairs in navy blue wool uniforms.

G.I. Joes on Union wages.

But I didn't grow up watching boys play *Custers* and Indians. I grew up thinking Indians were on the side of *bad*. That the cavalry was *good*.

The power of the entertainment industry to skew our moral compass is older than the industry itself, it's as old as the first myths. Revelatory and marvelous, these myths sustain us, even when they are promoting points of view that were never true—and all I have to do is look up through my open sunroof at the desert sky to find supporting evidence in all the Greeks up there, storying the constellations.

Cassiopeia and her daughter Andromeda.

Perseus.

Pegasus.

Orion.

Hercules.

Neptune.

The Pleiades, all seven of them.

It seems the first great Greek diaspora was upward—a Greek APOLLO program to people space waaay before the added boost of jet propulsion. It's a big wide plasma screen of Greeks up there—as many reruns of Greek myths above me as TV Westerns in the 1960s. And once upon a time people *believed* in them, believed Orion was exiled for eternity into the sky just as people, not so long ago, believed cowboys went with Indians the way pepper pairs with salt. *No cowboys, no Indians.* But myths are passionate belief systems that have ended up in someone's attic, mothballed to the sky. They were irrefutable, once. Once, they were sustainable, and the fervor with which they were maintained illuminated the dark reaches of our ancestors' fears.

Ask yourself what you believe in, and you'll find out who you are.

Know thyself—the ol' Socratic oath. (Do normal people start channeling the mad Greek on their way to Vegas?) It's always HERE, on this leg between Barstow and Baker, that things begin to fray, and by THINGS I mean radio reception, cold reality, and stamina. Even in the dark I know there's nothing out here but grit, salt pans, deadbrush and mineral deposits on either side of the road—one-horse desert outposts named in honor of the ground. BORON. I stopped there, once, in daylight, shadowing Curtis's route through the Mojave. There's a cemetery there, dedicated to men who died laying the railroad through this desert. Their names are bleached away, but the small quadrant of sacred ground near the Union Pacific tracks evokes the labor of their lives with crosses made of railroad ties. Once you leave Barstow, let me tell you, you are out in no-man's-land—no stops—no recreation—just a long long stretch of straight straight road under godforsaken heat until your first sighting of a billboard promising your first sign of civilization fifty miles ahead.

Souvlaki, friends.

Homemade *baklava*.

The Mad Greek. A Greek restaurant. In Baker. In the middle of the desert.

Greeks! you gotta love 'em! and I'm not saying this just because I'm half Hellenic (well, yes, I *am* saying this because of that), but because Baker is a place that is basically a crossroad to Death Valley, a service road beside a railroad lined with gas stations, Bun Boy and the Bun Boy Motel and a couple of Mexican joints, one of the last places you would expect to find a Greek restaurant serving reasonably authentic Greek food, bursting with *rembetika*, open all night long.

Just when you need it.

Just when, out along the road, in the desert, you were starting to believe that you are seeing *eyes* . . . The promise of feta and olives arises.

The place is all lit up and the Amtrak bus is pulled up in the packed back parking lot, and as soon as I open the door and step inside I may as well be in any taverna in the Plaka or Piraeus.

The walls are white, trimmed in St. George blue, the blue of the Greek flag—the booths are the same unadulterated blue, the whole place *floats* with light, like an oasis. Plastic grapes and rayon bougainvillea grace the windowsills, and frescos of Mykonos and Santorini fill the two front walls along with a movie poster of *Zorba the Greek*, a translation of the Greek alphabet and the English lyrics to the Greek national anthem.

> ("*From the graves of our slain shall our valour prevail,*
> *As we greet thee again, Hail, Liberty, Hail*"!)

Tourists on their way to Death Valley congregate here, though not at this time of night, so I reckon most of my fellow diners will be of two varieties—those on their way *to* Vegas, those on their way *from*—and you can spot the differences between these two by where their body language registers on the *adrenal*-ometer.

If you ever wonder about the health effects of a stay in Vegas you should run a random survey among departing gamblers, wannabes and tourists at the rest stops between Primm and Baker.

The ones standing very very still in line have most definitely just departed. Ditto, ones with the dead eyes. The ones in ruined clothes.

Talky ones in freshly pressed polo shirts with toothy wives are on their way in their vintage Continentals, most likely for slots, the house buffet, Wayne Newton.

I take my place at the end of the line in front of the counter and survey the menu suspended from the ceiling.

TIROPITA. SPANAKOPITA. CHICK PEA DIP. GYROS. THE ORIGINAL ZUCCHINI STICK.

A foursome of moody stoners in varying degrees of undress wait petulantly in front of me. Brentwood brats, I reckon: Crossroads grads. A wall-sized plaque of FAMOUS GREEKS and HONORARY GREEKS is next to us and one of the laconic ones stares at it and then, almost by mistake, starts to read aloud: "'FAMOUS GREEKS,'" she monotones. "'Telly Savalas.'" She flatlines on his name. "'The Trojan Horse.' Yah, I think I saw that. 'HONORARY GREEKS,'" she reads without expression. "'George Hamilton. Lord Byron. Jacqueline Bouvier Kennedy Onassis.' Like we're supposed to know these people."

"She was 'Jackie O,'" another of her group registers real slow. "John-John's mother."

"'John-John'?"

"John Kennedy."

"Which one was he?"

"He's dead."

"I thought they all were dead."

"'Anthony Quinn. James Joyce. St. Paul. All Macka- Macka—'"

"*Macedonians*," I offer.

"They need to get that Nia person up there. That Nia person. Last name starts with 'V' or something. Made 'My Big Bad Thing.' You know."

"—big *Fat*."

"'My Big Greasy Wedding.' Couple years ago. *You* saw it—"

"Like I'd go to *that*. I'm not Greek. Who *is*?"

"Jennifer Aniston is Greek. I'm pretty sure."

"Well there you go."

"—half Greek."

"Chennifer—not even Grik name. I *speet* on her."

This from a rasping voice behind me.

I turn in time to see her dry-spit into her open palms. A fierce tiny woman in a black dress, in her 70's, I'd say, with dangerous eyes, no makeup and what I've come to recognize as female Balkan facial hair.

"Only thing Bra-*Peet* is ask is bebi. *Adonis*. I would sell my eyes to have his bebi. So I speet on this Chennifer." (She dry spits, again.) "She ees eembarrassmant to all Grik wimmin."

You don't want to be alone in a dark alley with a woman like this and it both frightens and enlightens me to think I may have one of her vintage enlivening my lineage but what captures my imagination most about her and her type of village crone is their ownership, their absolute and resolute assurance that they own the only info, that they're in the know not only about which village neighbors have been feuding for a hundred years or how to extract oil from olives but also about what Brad Pitt was thinking when he left his wife. The scary thing about this woman and others who talk about celebrities as if they know them personally is that the exercise squanders civic involvement. Unlike voting in a real election, voting in a *People* poll accomplishes absolutely *nothing*, but we're still encouraged to believe in celebrities as modern mythic gods. Modern-day heroic fallacies. Zeus screwing around behind Hera's back. Icarus getting high on too much ego. Innocent Ledas losing their cherries on the casting couch.

I place my order, pay and am given a white plastic *tipi*-shaped marker with a number on it. I take it to a booth in the front room in the corner under the poster of Anthony Quinn as Zorba. Behind me the Brentwood kids are still debating the relative merits of Angelina Jolie versus *Chennifer*, and to hear them talk, you'd think they are revealing secrets about members of their coterie and I start to wonder how this appropriation propagates itself. They sound as if they believe they *know* these distant entities, these stars, these misnamed goddesses. As if they and the celebrity luminaries were *down*. Me an' Angelina. Brad an' me an' me an' Brad, and to that extent, celebrity is a form of identity appropriation, identity theft, not unlike the man in the hospital in Las Vegas who's appropriated the identity of my dead father.

But, no: a celebrity relinquishes exclusive ownship of his or her own life.

A celebrity doesn't *steal* a life, she or he gives her or his life away.

To us average schmoes.

To the great unknowables, the undercelebrated me's and you's of the undercelebrated ordinary world.

And that's one thing for which I applaud my Mr. Curtis—for raising uncelebrated Indian faces to an iconic status.

We may never know these Indians' names nor how they lived nor whom they loved, but we will know their faces.

Curtis knew his craft, he knew how to commemorate a face, how to make it memorable with shadow, light and shallow focus, because by the time he started driving to the reservations he was a celebrated studio photographer in Seattle who had captured national attention when Theodore Roosevelt asked him to photograph his daughter Alice's wedding at the White House.

It was the party of the year, that wedding, and Alice Roosevelt was as appropriated and *oohed* and *aahed* over as any 21st-century media celebrity. Songs were written about her, a color was named for her and magazines sold out overnight every time Alice graced the cover. The public clamor for details of the wedding—details of the dress, the cake, the guest list—was so distracting from the business of running the country that Roosevelt's personal secretary issued a formal statement stating that the press was not welcome on the wedding day and that the only wedding photographs that would be made available to the nation's newspapers and magazines would be those taken by the official wedding photographer who had been chosen expressly by the President, himself.

EDWARD S. CURTIS.

In with The Man.

And one of the things that fascinates me about the life stories of so-called self-made people is how they get from *there* to *there*, how one gets born into obscurity and day-to-day economic strain and ends up telling Mr. President *smile. Say cheese.*

If you look carefully at the portrait that was the official White House release of that happy day, it's really not a great portrait at all, as a window into the souls of the bride, her shell-shocked-looking groom and her famously boisterous father. Congressman Nicholas Longworth, the groom, poor man, seems to be artificially propped up, barely touching his bride, clutching his gloves in one hand, his glassy expression frozen by the apparent thought, *Here I am with this stranger, her acre of dress and The President.*

Roosevelt, on the opposite side of the bride, is visibly leaning away.

In the center, Alice plays a subordinate role to the deluge of fabric that swamps more than half of the frame, and the reason I'm so fond of this picture by Curtis is that this is, first and foremost, a picture of something I love, a picture of A TRAIN, Alice's wedding gown train mounded like an elaborate meringue, its mass diminishing, like real railroad tracks, from the foreground into a distant focal point.

All three of the wedding group look pissy, as if Curtis had been holding them since dawn against their wills while all the champagne in Washington was flowing freely in an adjacent room.

And where's the LOVE?

Is there any visible LOVE among them?

Granted, it was 1906 and not the convention of the day to wear one's heart in public on one's sleeve, but as far as wedding pictures go, this one is a straightforward piece of stylized propaganda, not the least romantic (unless your passion is for French organza). It's not mythmaking in the way that other Curtis pictures are. It does not address our need to *believe* in any of these people, believe in their involvement with each other, their LOVE for one another, nor for their future as a loving couple and a loving family.

Perhaps LOVE doesn't photograph, but I believe it does, I believe something damn near approximating it does, a human-ness that isn't on display for us in this wedding picture. You can almost hear Curtis saying, *Lean a little to the left, Mr. President,* and although T.R. readily complies in a compositional gesture meant to offset the bridal couple, leaning away from his oldest child was a stance to which T.R. was well accustomed. He had been leaning away from Alice since her mother died when she was two days old. Alice Lee, Roosevelt's first wife, died in the same room where she had given birth to their infant daughter on the third floor of the Roosevelt house at 6 West 57th Street in New York City, and eight hours later, Teddy's mother died of typhoid in a bedroom on the floor above. After their funerals, Teddy left the infant Alice in the care of a fond aunt and traveled to what he called the OLD WEST to ride rough, eschew the company of women and shoot animals.

It has been said that his experience out West changed Roosevelt forever, and if it's true that the OLD WEST changed T.R., then it's also true that T.R. returned the favor in his subsequent commitment to the preservation of its beauty. The energy some men squander chasing women, T.R. expended romancing the West and all its myths. And although he remarried when Alice was three and rapidly had five more children, he was never his most natural self in the feminized domestic world "He wants to be the bride at every wedding, the corpse at every funeral and the baby at every christening," Alice told the press about her famous father.

In other words, he wanted to be the center of attention.

And perhaps he is leaning away in the wedding photograph not on Curtis's instruction, but on his own Presidential instinct, not to draw attention *to* the bride, but *from* her. And maybe the future of the wedding couple *can* be seen in the image Curtis made—Nicky Longworth would have affairs and Alice would have affairs and they would eventually divorce—and maybe that destiny was manifest, even on their wedding day, and all Curtis had to do was hold the shutter open and let that light record itself.

Curtis was thirty-eight years old the February morning that he made this wedding picture, and it was soon after this that T.R. wrote his letter to J.P. Morgan commending Curtis as an outstanding photographer of that soon-to-be-depleted asset of the OLD WEST, the great American NATIVE.

Meeting Morgan would change Curtis's life, but meeting Morgan had depended on meeting Teddy first—*no Roosevelt, no Morgan*—and Curtis had impressed him in ways that were bound up in a distinctive brand of mythic masculinity that the two men shared.

Both Teddy and Curtis cut a kind of cowboy figure, with or without a horse. Both enjoyed the rakish slant of cowboy hats, the feel of boots and the psychic boost of self-promotion.

Both preferred the company of men to women.

Both were men who disappeared into their pursuits and left their families in the exclusive care of wives and nannies for long periods of time.

If I were to make odds on which of the two was the more attentive father—more demonstrative, more forgiving—I'd have to go with Teddy.

We can imagine hugging Teddy.

We can imagine Teddy hugging back, even if his bear hug nearly killed us.

I can even imagine Teddy as the character of Zorba, like Anthony

Quinn in this poster on the wall, a mad Greek, dancing solo on an Aegean shore beneath the stars.

I can imagine Teddy heartbroken, mad with grief at the death of his young wife, blustering his way out of that despair and into new-found LOVE.

I have a harder time imagining that impulse-toward-happiness in Curtis, not because I haven't tried, heaven knows I've tried, but because the evidence that he was ever *comfortable* or *happy* is too thin.

I could find only one photograph of him in which he's smiling, and it's when he's reunited with his children who were then middle-aged adults, very late in Curtis's life, three decades after he and Clara were divorced, two decades after she had died. In this photograph Curtis is standing awkwardly—*posing*, as he always did—his hand on his hip, eyes averted from his children, who are laughing: but he's *smiling*. As if to say: *happy* is the way I want you to remember us.

This is us when we were happy is not the message the photograph of Alice Roosevelt's wedding delivers, and isn't *this is us when we are happy* the whole point of these commemorative portraits?

Whether they're stylized and formal or rapid from-the-hip snapshots, aren't these pictures supposed to deliver a true feeling for the moment, a re-creation of it, a re-run, not only visually, but viscerally?

And you would think in the archives of a renowned photographer there would be a treasure trove of just such captured moments, little golden artifacts like the ones furnishing a pharoah's tomb. If I was going to write about Curtis in a way that was meaningful to me then I had to search for his Kodak moments, search for any evidence that I could find of Curtis letting loose his inner Zorba. On that February morning in 1906 when he brought Alice and her fresh groom into focus, he, himself, had been married fourteen years. His oldest child, Harold, was thirteen; and he had two daughters, Beth and Florence, ten and eight. All three lived back West, in Seattle, with their mother Clara. All three called their father CHIEF, the appellation he preferred since he'd started traveling extensively among the native tribes. Even Teddy, one imagines, didn't ask his kids to call him CHIEF when he was home. Of Edward's and Clara's wedding ceremony, I could find no photographic record. Nor a single portrait he had ever made of his beloved. I found a lovely Curtis Studio portrait of her—her eyes are kind, if not suggestively wary—but it had been made by Edward's photographic assistant, Adolph Muhr, not by CHIEF, himself. By 1906, Clara and Muhr were managing the Seattle studio themselves, barely staying ahead of Edward's rising costs as he spent more and more time and more and more money photographing Western tribes.

He was rarely, if ever, home.

And unlike Alice Roosevelt, who continued to be an unrepentant thorn in her father's side, even after Teddy's death, all the Curtis children never stopped believing CHIEF could do no wrong, never stopped believing CHIEF was the perfect father, even after absences of many years, never stopped seeking CHIEF's approval.

He became, by disappearing from their daily lives, not a father, but the MYTH of one, a myth they needed to believe in to survive. And despite his actions, despite all contrary evidence, they needed to sustain that system of belief, even if it meant altering their memory, creating a false memory, a false identity, of who their father really was.

If Edward, the disappearing father, was to be the GOOD GUY in their system of belief, then someone—anyone—had to play the villain, because, surely, there was real unhappiness in their home, in everything around them, and someone, never Dad, no, never him, someone *else* had to take the blame.

The person who was doing all the yelling when the bills came in.

The person who was too tired to cook dinner after working all day long. That other unromantic parent asleep at the stove in her flannel slippers. Stressed out and exhausted.

Mom.

And if the bullet traces of the disappearing fathers are scattershot all across the fabric of our nation's family stories, who's to blame for all the exit wounds?

Who's to blame if men keep taking off, lighting out for unknown territories?

Must be the woman's fault.

Must be something that the woman did or did not do.

Even I, like the Curtis children, harbored a suspicion it was my mother's fault when my father disappeared. And when he was found dead, I secretly blamed her. Too much the good daughter, I never formed a verbal accusation but I allowed my secret blame to color our relationship for years. And then at some point I lost the energy to blame and decided to believe that in the beginning of their lives together, in their young marriage, their young love, they had found a kind of joy with each other.

I decided to believe something about them, even if it wasn't true.

I decided to create my own self-sustaining MYTH.

Besides, it *might* be true.

In fact, I have every reason to believe it was. I have the photographic evidence.

Because my parents eloped, they never had a formal wedding portrait taken, but I unearthed a picture they had kept of the two of them soon after they were married, when John was still a captain in the Army, stationed at Ft. Lee, outside Petersburg, Virginia, where they'd met. I think the picture might have been taken in 1945, soon after the war had ended, because clearly there's a party going on, everyone looks happy and relaxed and there are couples dancing in the background, you can see the Army guys' arms around the women's waists, holding them real close. John and Mary are seated at a table, their dinner plates still half full in front of them, across from another Army couple who are leaning forward, smiling for the unknown photographer. Whenever I asked my parents who the other couple were, they'd say, Those are THE HOUPASES and *the Houpases* became one of those commonly accepted but patently eccentric names that families toss around to indicate the couple in the house next door, the family on the corner or the mom an' pop who run the grocery store. We all have them, every family does—THE BREGUNDERS. THE BINSWANGERS. THE OTTS. THE HOUPASES. Mr. Houpas appears to outrank my father, if I'm reading the stars and bars on his uniform correctly, and I think they must have taken their discharges around the same time after the war and returned to civilian life, because some time before I was born John and Mary took a road trip to visit THE HOUPASES in, I think, Keene, New Hampshire. But in the picture, Mary's hair is artfully arranged in a style popular among the starlets of the day. She's wearing a single strand of pearls set against a tricolor paneled jersey dress, neither particularly eye-catching nor chic, but her fingernails are freshly painted and she presents herself as someone who's made an effort to look better groomed than she can afford to. John is leaning back a little in his chair so the photographer can get a good view of his new bride, and both of them look slightly posed, but still I like the way they look and it's my favorite picture of them. I have it in a frame in the room I write in and I'm sure I look at it a couple hundred times a year. I like to look at the people dancing in the background. But more and more, especially when I was writing about Edward and Clara, I started looking at THE HOUPASES and wondering about them, these two people whom I never knew nor will ever know, inextricably bound to John and Mary in this picture in my writing room. I Googled HOUPAS a while back just for the hell of it but all the search delivered was a Greek composer from Crete and a misguided florist in Ohio offering "authentic Jewish wedding *houpas.*" If they're even still alive, the couple in the picture would be in their eighties or nineties. And yet here they are, with me, every day, leaning forward on their elbows, smiling. People perpetually unknown to me, yet whose faces are imprinted on my memory. People whose evident love story I can only fabricate in my imagination, like lovers in a myth. Where are they now? Did they divorce like Edward and Clara? Did they fall to bickering each night? Or am I allowed to believe, because I want to, that they got up from the table later in the night and joined the others dancing? Drank too much retsina and joined Zorba, dancing on the beach? *Everything worth knowing is a secret*—maybe that's just the Greek half of me talking, in a Greek restaurant, under the influence of Greek music and Greek food. I look at John's face, sometimes, in this photograph and wonder if he ever had a clue about what he was in for among the brothers and the cousins and the related *dramatis personae* in my mother's mad Greek chorus. I doubt he had ever thought about a

Greek outside the Gospels and the Scriptures before he joined the Army. But there he sits with his Greek wife and his Greek Army buddy. And for a couple moments every day it doesn't matter to me how their stories ended. Because *This is who we are*, their faces say.

And we are happy.

vegas, baby

I should have known that at a distance, after midnight, it would appear, first, in the sky.

The *vega*—in Spanish, a fertile plain, a meadow, a tobacco plantation. And that's what its heat and radiation, its vibrant reflection on the underside of clouds look like from twenty miles away—a copper-colored meadow in the sky: *las vegas* : too gassy and nebulous to be a constellation, more like (another Greek word:) a galaxy.

I've driven this eighty-mile stretch between the Mad Greek Restaurant in Baker and Las Vegas half a dozen times; never, before, at night, and I have to say the night drive is the easier of the two, less tedious, more reflective. You've got the sixteen-wheelers riding up your back but you've got them in the daytime, too, although in the day they're less jacked up on caffeine or amphetamines or their own personal nighttime desert demon.

Vegas. Upward of thirty million tourists leave their money with casinos, on the tables, in hotel rooms, at the restaurants every year— to the tune of thirty billion dollars. Gaming is the city's leading earner, followed very closely by tourism, construction and the military. It's no coincidence that in Nevada ADAPT OR DIE, the desert's scorching motto, is also capitalism's slogan, and it's easy to forget as you drive into the state how much land has been co-opted by the federal government as a good place to detonate a bomb and shoot at targets with nothing between you and the bull's eye for miles and miles around whether you're standing with a rocket launcher on your shoulder or gunning the horizon from your F-16. Nevada is the state that owns the trademark *Ground Zero*, for good reason. Between 1962 and 1992 eight hundred nuclear devices were detonated here, in the atmo, before they started "testing" underground. To the north, northeast and the northwest of the city, tracts of land larger than Rhode Island and Delaware are owned and operated by the Feds. Nellis Air Force Base, the National Atomic Test Site, Area 51—our federal government owns more land in Nevada than in any other state—nearly eighty percent of it. So as Las Vegas tourism expands, so does the need to house its service community—the croupiers and waitresses, the spa receptionists, the nurses, palm readers, the cosmeticians—and you can see the spill of endless stucco homes and red-roofed planned communities flooding across the valley, threatening the boundaries and the no-go zones of the bomb and gunnery ranges.

Like Los Angeles, Las Vegas is a horizontal construct, but Clark County (named for William Clark, another railroad mogul) has knocked against Uncle Sam's wall on all four sides and has nowhere to go in this new century but *up*. Adapt or die. The existence of the military in Nevada proscribes how the state can manage its expansion and construction which in turn is in demand because of tourism. Which has its roots in the dirt of gaming. No wonder people come—it's all so freaking improbable. Triple-digit temperatures are not uncommon five months of the year and yet this is the city that fills sixteen of the twenty largest hotels in the world each season. The city where New York and Napa Valley celebrity chefs come to clone their branded *brandades* and *boudins*. Come to test their *bombes*. Growth fuels growth, that's what this city tells you from afar, If *I* can do it, against these dry as bonefuck desert odds, then imagine what *you* can do inside my magic circle.

Thirty million tourists is a lot of people every year and even from out here on I-15, with the megawatt attractor beam signaling space from the top of the thirteen-acres-of-glass pyramid of the Luxor in the distance, I can understand this city's calculated spike to our adrenaline. Even endangered bats with complicated sonar reflexes cannot resist the Luxor's artificial highway to heaven, so how are we supposed to feel about it? The beam is *huge* and now NASA is telling us it wasn't true about the Great Wall of China being seen from the moon but—hold your helmets—this light beam from the Luxor Hotel and Casino in Las Vegas *is*. Who wouldn't want to come here just to witness *that*? To say nothing of the fact that if you can't afford a trip to Venice, guess what. You can ride a gondola without ever passing Customs. You can eat a Nathan's hot dog on a fake New York City street. Enjoy *moules frites* under the Eiffel Tower. So I get it, I really do. *Ersatz* experience, but, still: experience. Not for me, but, still: I understand the appeal of this *Strip*-ped down impersonation. I understand why thirty million people come here every year.

What I can't imagine is my father ever coming here.

As I knew him, I would have to say. As I knew him for the last, and lasting, time.

Which was more than thirty years ago.

Whoever this John Wiggins is in cardiac intensive care at Sunrise Hospital, he can't be *my* John Wiggins. He must be an artificial version like this city, a *Mirage*, as the hotel is named, an imitation, like the frescoes and faux marble at Caesar's Palace, a master illusionist like the headline acts of David Copperfield and Siegfried & Roy, a fake like the Eiffel Tower at the Paris, a con, like Bugsy Siegel, an impersonator like the Elvis, Sammy, Dean and Frank acts working Fremont Street, a *fatwa morgana* on reality. Because unless he'd lost his mind or undergone some radical surgery on his personality, I can't imagine John in this milieu—Vegas, old or new, in the 50's or in the year 2000, would never be my father's kinda town. I can imagine him doing many things—leaving his rural Pennsylvania farm for the Army, falling goofily in love with my mother's exoticism and good looks—but I can't imagine him in Vegas, especially at eighty.

Nevertheless here I am, one hour after midnight, paralleling the Strip, as Mandalay Bay, the Four Seasons, the Luxor, Excalibur, New York-New York and the Monte Carlo sail by on a filmy sheen of megawatt-enhanced reality and the intoxicating shuck of all this human folly filters through my open sunroof in the moonlight.

I exit at Flamingo.

Not the shortest route to the hospital, but Flamingo is a street I know, having driven it in daylight on previous visits and the truth is even though I like to think I talk the talk of a road warrior, I'm really a pansy and driving alone in the West on an unknown road after midnight isn't a trip that I seek out on purpose. To my way of thinking right now Flamingo feels safer than the Desert Inn exit because Desert Inn winds past the Wynn golf course and the Las Vegas Country Club, both of which might be deserted and spooky at this time of night but who am I kidding. I'm acting like this is Los Angeles, weighing which exit I should *take* when in fact this is a town where the concept of "night" has no impact on traffic.

But Flamingo is jammed.

There are people, in shorts, mobbing both sides of the Strip like it's lunchtime on a crowded beach and the air, still hot, smells of automotive exhaust, popcorn, baked cement and beer. You could read, if you needed to, in the ambient light. You could perform vascular surgery.

It takes twenty minutes to thread through the Strip intersection, past Bally's to Koval, and then the light dims and the flat grid with strip malls and one- and two-story buildings takes over and the Strip's specificity trails behind me leaving me with the sense that this scene could be Anywhere—Phoenix or Tucson or Bakersfield—any place where the shadows of mountains can't reach, flat and hot.

I pass the Atomic Testing Museum, spectrally dark, on the right, then the UNLV campus. At Maryland Parkway I make a left and the Stratosphere, tallest structure west of the Mississippi, looms like a giddy launching gantry. All nite *carnitas*, all nite tattoos, all nite check cashing, all nite drugs—you would think that this part of the city doesn't exist at all in daytime. All nite pawn and all nite easy credit—*Casa de empeños, facilidades de pago*. Traffic is light, but the buses are full, transporting kitchen staffs and hotel crews back home to the rundown adobes and cheap seats north of Bonanza in West Las Vegas. I pass the sprawling Boulevard Mall— Dillard's, Sears, Macy's—shuttered for the night, the cleanup crews waiting by the bus shelters under the feline green and purple Citizen Area Transit (CAT) logos for their numbered buses to arrive—109, 112, 203, 213—poor man's roulette. Then, crossing

Desert Inn, I see it, high-rise buildings on both sides of Maryland Parkway, Sunrise Hospital, largest public health facility in Nevada. Largest parking lot, too, and for a couple of confused moments I circle, looking for the right entrance until a wailing ambulance turns in from Maryland and highlights the route. I find a space under an orange-burning sulphur lamp and get out and stretch. At the back of the lot, under another lamp, two late-model station wagons are parked back to back, tailgates open. Hospital workers, some smoking, all in pastel scrubs, lounge in lawn chairs. Two of them are camped out in sleeping bags in the back of the station wagons—the scene looks like a pastel-themed NASCAR tailgate party, and I take note that if I need to catch some shuteye in my car tonight, this could be the place.

Emergency Receiving is surprisingly small, and therefore fully populated. There are whole families here and I'm reminded how much misery can come down in any given household after supper. Mothers, brothers, sisters, uncles—everybody has that *oh, shit* look, except the kids, and there are plenty of them, playing Game Boys on the floor. There's an ATM against the wall next to a flower-arrangement machine with sprays of pink and white carnations on rotating shelves, a machine dispensing Get Well cards, a Coke machine and posters warning about sexually transmitted diseases. And there's the smell. That HOSPITAL SMELL—three parts disinfectant, two parts fear. Five parts institution food. Chemically enhanced "beef"-flavored gravy.

There's a single woman on duty behind a sliding glass partition and I tell her why I'm here and she tells me, "No visitors until nine tomorrow morning." I repeat that I'm here at the hospital's request and that I've driven all the way from California and that if she could only call the cardiac nurse on duty in the cardiac department we could get to closure here and make this work between us.

She makes the call and after asking me my name again tells me someone's sending someone down to come and get me. "You can wait in there," she says, indicating the open door across the hall from us marked CHAPEL.

Just what I need right now: a moment alone with MY THOUGHTS with visual prompts from OUR LORD. But the Chapel is that rare attempt at interdenominationalism that succeeds, in a quiet but weird way. Two pews deep, it's a pentagon-shaped blue-tinted refuge featuring an altar, of sorts, which is more of a lectern on which there are some candles, some pre-printed card-sized excerpts from the Gospels. *Please God,* one line in the ledger reads, I give up drinking and I give up women then you help my little girl. *Milagros,* pinned to the altar cloth with safety pins, rattle when I brush against them. Pictures of children, those photo-booth standards of our public schools, are stuck in the frame of a portrait of the *Virgen,* while on the less Catholic side of the shrine a pebble sits on a starched linen doily next to a glass *Shabat* light. *You for the cardiac?* a voice sounds behind me.

I turn and nod at the security guard, armed and not dressed in pastel.

Let's go, then, she tells me and leads the way down the hall to the steel doors of an elevator which she opens with a key on a chain on her belt.

I step inside.

She inserts her key in the touchpad and hits the 5 button, steps back and tells me, "You have a good night," and the doors close.

When they open again, they open on quiet.

Most of these hospital floors, wherever you are, are the same: nursing desk faces the traffic. Nursing desk faces the elevator.

I approach and state my name.

The place is so very quiet I can't help being aware that this is the floor where the heart patients sleep or lie awake listening for things like their pulses. *Sign in, please, Miss Wiggins,* I'm told and I sign a sheet on a clipboard and note the time: one fifty-two. *He's in five-oh-nine down the hall,* I'm instructed. "The door's open, it's a semi-, but he's all alone."

I turn and face the dim hallway.

One of THOSE MOMENTS when walking seems surreal, when the force propelling me forward seems to exist somewhere outside my body, when what I am doing seems to be at the behest of some other me, a me who is watching all this and cursing her shoes for the sounds that they make, the only sounds I can hear that might be described as sounds that are human, the only sounds audible over the beeps that percuss through the doors like the pings of lovelorn dolphins' code. And the rhythm, the steady rhythm of my steady steps keeps me from stopping outside his door, keeps me going for fear of breaking the spell and then I'm there in the room, in the weak light, facing him. His eyes are closed and there's no comfort in watching an unconscious human attached to his guardian monitors, no sense at all of who he might be on his own, *inside,* behind the closed eyes and the lax-jaw expression. His arms are placed on top of the sheet and I lean down to look at the name on the blue plastic strip on his wrist and notice he's wearing a thin yellow-gold wedding band.

I pick up my pace heading back to the nurse and I'm sure now my footsteps sound louder. She's waiting for me but she doesn't stand up.

"You know," I remind her, "I've just driven all night to come here all the way from L.A."

She has steady eyes, which I reckon might come with the job.

"Don't you think you might have mentioned to me when you called that your John Wiggins is a *black* man?"

Those steady eyes do not flicker.

"And I know this is the twenty-first century and we don't make these racial assumptions anymore about parents and children," I say, "but that is a *very old* black man in there and when he was born and when *I* was born it was the previous century and people in hospitals were not as cool as we are today about mixed race families so I just think somebody might have *asked* me oh by the way aside from being *dead* was your father by any chance African American?"

"So what you're saying is—?"

"The guy's not my father."

"But he has your father's name. And your father's date of birth and Social with you listed as his closest relative."

As she speaks she takes a transparent plastic bag from the lower shelf of a rolling cart behind her and withdraws a brown leather billfold from it and lays it on the desktop between the two of us. On one side is a Nevada state driver's license with a picture of the slightly younger-looking man down the hall identified as John F. Wiggins and on the other side is an organ donor card with the word *Daughter* and my name written in the space following Nearest Living Relative. From within the billfold itself she withdraws a yellowed newspaper clipping.

"—*you*, no?—once upon a time? I can still see the likeness . . ."

"—jesus," I can't help muttering.

The clipping is from a 1965 *Lancaster New Era* article announcing a production of the play *Our Town* at Manheim Township High School and there are two thumbnail pictures of the play's leads, me (EMILY WEBB) and Dennis Landis (STAGE MANAGER), a kid I went to high school with.

"—how *the hell?*"

I make a point of memorizing the street address on the license before she snaps the billfold closed and seals it back up in the plastic bag.

"I'm really sorry," I tell her. "I don't know what to tell you. I don't know how this man came to have that picture of me in his wallet."

"Well maybe Mr. Shadow can help shed some light on this."

I blink.

"—Mr. Shadow."

Maybe she's been talking to the dying for too long.

"He's down the hall."

"—Mr. Shadow is?"

"Yes."

"—is that your way of saying *Death?*"

"My way of saying 'death' is d-e-a-t-h but if you want to find out more about our Mr. Wiggins you should go and talk to Mr. Shadow down there on that bench at the end of the corridor. The Indian. He was with our Mr. Wiggins when he had his cardiac event."

I stare down the hall and notice for the first time a single figure sitting upright on a bench against the wall, presumably asleep.

"Hasn't budged for hours," she whispers. "Won't leave. Some sort of *tribal* thing . . ."

At my approach the man doesn't move and I'm convinced that he's asleep so I kneel down to where our faces are parallel and touch him lightly on his sleeve. "—Mr. Shadow?"

Immediately his eyelids open and I'm instantly his focus. "Lester," he tells me. I introduce myself and we shake hands, his more callused palm engulfing my smaller, softer one.

"Are you the daughter?"

"—no, but he seems to be using my father's old identity."

Lester frowns as if the concept makes him sad.

I sit beside him.

"I understand you came in with him," I say.

"The medics wouldn't let me in the ambulance. I followed in my truck."

"What can you tell me about him?"

He looks at me and says, "He's going to die."

I hold his gaze for a long moment and there is nothing uncomfortable about it, merely two unrelated strangers recognizing an apparent binding truth.

"How long have you known him?"

I can see him count: "Sixteen hours."

"I presumed you were—"

"He came into my daughter's store just after ten o'clock yesterday morning—the first customer. My daughter and her husband run a native craft cooperative in a building on Sahara that used to be a pawn shop. People come in with their pawn because they think my daughter's place is still a trading post." He grins. "I came across from Tuba City to mind the store while my daughter and her husband are in Teotihuacán, Mexico. She's working on her Ph.D. in indigenous societies."

"You're Navajo," I venture.

"What gave it away—?"

He flashes another grin and pulls his single silver plait forward from his neck so that it falls across the placket of his denim shirt. Then he lets his hand drop to an object wrapped in jeweler's felt beside him on the bench which he moves onto his lap and carefully unwraps. "He came in and I could tell he was there to try to pawn or sell me something and the first thing he puts in front of me is this. Museum quality," he says and with both hands holds up a headdress made of beads and quills and silver coins.

"I've seen one of these before," I say and he, again, focuses his dark eyes on me. "In a photograph. By Edward Curtis."

He starts *playing Indian*, looking ancient and severe which kind of creeps me out but then he lowers the headdress onto the square of felt again and touches it. "No one in my family will ever trade in tribal pawn, we will not touch it, most of all the pieces that you see in jewelry stores in Santa Fe and Phoenix have been stolen one way or another, sometimes from burial sites. They tell you in those stores that native people have brought the pieces in for cash to purchase liquor or to make the next support payment but that's not the truth. A piece like this—how much do you think the Heald Museum would offer? I'd have to ask my daughter but I think this is Plains Indian, perhaps Chinook or Nez-Percé, from the 19th century. But—touch it—it feels as if it's just been made. Someone's taken expert care of it. When I looked at it I had to ask myself what is this elder Negro gentleman doing with this artifact? He saw me hesitate and I think he thought I had no interest in it so he quickly showed me *this*." He unwraps a second item from the felt, a bracelet. It's made of very high standard molded silver but the square stone in the center, two inches on each side, is unlike any that I've ever seen.

"—bone?" I wonder.

"Snow turquoise."

"—snow?"

"*White*. White turquoise. Very, very rare. But look at it more closely."

He passes it to me and I turn it toward the light. A copper vein runs through the center of it, almost in a perfect oval and within the oval shape other copper-colored lines delineate some features while two distinct round shapes of *blue* turquoise stare out, like eyes.

"It's a face," I marvel.

"My father called this piece The Shadow Catcher. And he's the one who made it."

He turns the bracelet around and shows me the silversmith's stamp on the back in the shape of a standing bear. "That's my father's mark. 'Owns His Shadow.' That was my father's name. Bear Clan."

"So of all the pawn shops in all the cities in the West—"

"Native craft cooperative."

"—so of all the native craft cooperatives in all the cities in the West this guy with my father's papers and your father's bracelet walks into—"

"This is not my father's bracelet. *This* one is."

He slides up his sleeve and shows me a similar one, not a duplicate, exactly, made of the same stone but with only a trace of the other's distinct facial image.

"He made two bracelets from the same piece of snow turquoise. One he kept for himself. That's the one that I wear. The other, with the face in it, he gave to his friend because the face inside the stone looked so much like him."

I stare at the image in the piece of turquoise—copper-colored hair and beard, two piercing blue eyes . . .

"Who was his friend?"

"Edward Curtis. The photographer you mentioned."

"Are you messing with me, Lester?"

I have to ask but I can tell he isn't.

"When the man showed me this bracelet I must have looked as if I'd seen a ghost. I couldn't help it. I looked at him and said, 'Who *are* you?' And his eyes grew round and he parted his lips as if to speak and clutched his chest and then fell down. I went around the counter and I held his head and he looked at me, desperate. I had to leave him on the floor to go call 911 and when I came back I could see he'd had a stroke, one eye was closed but that other eye—" He stops, then tells me—"*pleading*. I think he knew that he was going to die. He was trying to tell me something. So I had to follow him to here. With these"—he indicates the jewelry—"and these." He shows me a set of keys and I notice what appears to be a house key among them.

"He's wearing a wedding band, so he must belong to *someone*."

"He left his car in my daughter's parking lot. I was thinking I could search it for his address. Then they told me they had found his closest living relative, and that you were on your way."

We stare toward the open door of the room where Mr. Wiggins lies unconscious.

"I saw his driver's license," I mention. "I know where he lives."

We exchange another look, and Lester weighs the old man's house keys in his hand. "Middle of the night," he mentions. "Can you stay 'til daylight?"

"Sure."

"I don't want to leave, in case he wakes up."

"I can understand that"

"I have a duty to him."

"Yep."

"Even if he has a wife, she would be very old, like him. We don't want to wake her up and scare her. Another heart attack."

"—still. I think she'd like to know. Given his condition."

"Better that we wait 'til morning."

"—okay. You've got a point. I know what those unexpected calls are like. The news that you don't want to hear."

He studies me. "—your father?"

"—for starters."

"How did he die?"

"Suicide. —yours?"

"—in his sleep. We didn't know his age but figured ninety-seven."

"And he really knew Edward Curtis?"

"Owns His Shadow scouted sites and translated for Mr. Curtis in ought-eight, ought-nine. Owns His Shadow spoke the English Mr. Curtis liked. He had been transported from the reservation to the Carlisle School in Pennsylvania when he was still a boy, so he had learned the white man's ways before he broke with all of that and made his brave escape back to the Navajo. I have a picture of them. Owns His Shadow and Mr. Curtis."

"I would like to see it."

"Well it's home in Tuba."

"I haven't been to Tuba City for a while."

Again, that focused look. "What were you doing in my nation?"

"Research."

"—on the rez?"

I pick up The Shadow Catcher and hold it so the spectral image in the stone faces both of us. Invisible at first, the image forms before my eyes the longer that I look at it, as if it were exposed but still invisible light held captive on a page of photographic paper floating in the shallow pool of a transparent chemical bath. After several seconds a familiar likeness gathers in the fine lines of the stone. "*This* man, actually. Curtis." I turn the bracelet in my hands, appreciating every subtlety. "This is really beautiful," I say.

"Father said that Curtis thought so, too. I'd like to know how he let it go from his possession."

"Well he's been dead for fifty years. And in his last thirty years or so he was always scrambling just to make ends meet. Lost everything. Gave away the copyrights to all his American Indian work to J.P. Morgan's heirs to cancel out his debts to them. In the end he went a little crazy and spent a couple decades right here in Nevada just prospecting for gold."

"Father lost all touch with him."

"I'm not surprised. Aside from that one picture that you have of them, did he photograph your father?"

"*Owns His Shadow?*" Lester grins. "Father would not let another steal his image."

"But you said there *is* a picture—"

"In it, father looks away. And points. Like this." He swivels on the bench and points away from us, toward a sign at the opposite end of the hall that reads EMERGENCY EXIT.

"But your interest is with Curtis, not my father," he intuits.

"Used to be. I wrote a book about him."

"And it's finished?"

"Yes."

"And you talked to those who sat for him and had their shadows stolen?"

"No."

He makes a little bubbling sound deep in his throat and whispers, *oh.* He looks toward the open door into the dying old man's room again. "You should have waited."

"For what?"

He inhales deeply and resumes the posture I had found him in, but with his eyes wide open now, not closed, his eyes locked on the open door.

"Until the silent ones have spoken," Lester murmurs.

clara and edward

The great Seattle fire started on the lowest floor of a wooden building owned by Mrs. M. J. Pontius on the northwest corner of Front and Madison Streets in the city's harbor district.

Jimmy McGough, a paint store operator, leased the lower floors from Mrs. Pontius and the first fiery accusations pointed to an untended glue pot in his back room, but the spark that set the conflagration roaring actually leapt to life from the hands of John E. Back, a careless cabinetmaker, working with a combustible shellac one floor below.

The paint store only added volatility to what would have been a bonfire, anyway, with nothing but rows of timber buildings standing between the initial tongue of flame and the quenching water of the harbor. Twenty-nine blocks, in total, burned, destroying the entire business center, the railroad terminals and all but four of the port city's many wharves. Seattle's population on the morning of the fire was estimated between twenty and thirty thousand and it had only recently instituted regulated ferry service on the Puget Sound as well as a civic agenda to replace hollowed-out logs with lead pipes in the sewer system. There was an electrified trolley in both the lower and upper streets, but indoor plumbing was a rarity and a recurrent tidal ebb of sewage perfumed the smudgy mudflats by the shore. There were two newspapers in English, another in Norwegian, and an occasional lynching of an Indian, a Chinaman or a Negro. After the fire came the first of many population booms, the city's numbers rising to 42,837 in 1890 owing to the open importation of cheap labor to rebuild the city. The governing white class welcomed even more Chinese and Indians into the population as exploitable non-union crews and within a decade the Klondike gold rush doubled the city's numbers again. By 1910, twenty years after the fire, the city's population was a quarter of a million. Meat packing, fur, export-import, timber, shipbuilding, breweries and the U.S. Gold Assay Office gave Seattle an annual income of more than $174 million before the century was done, but it was the summer fire of 1889 that lighted the Sons of Profit's firecracker fuse. The fire, it turned out, was *good*: it killed the rats. And, like other city fires—the Fire of London, the Chicago fire—the Seattle fire made the city reinvent itself, for the better. No more timber roofs, plank sidings, cedar shakes and clapboard shanties—having had its heart destroyed, the city turned to stone, refashioned its foundations with rock-solid cornerstones, replaced its former wooden public face with brick and slate and granite.

As Clara did, after Edward left her.

She strengthened her resolve and steeled her heart with harder stuff—burned once, she would not allow herself to be the victim of that firestorm again.

But here he stood, his hands around the halter of the buckboard's lead, his eyes intent on the woman in the driver's seat above him. He had been twelve days on the road, on foot, living in the rough and still, she couldn't help but note, his fingernails were shaped and clean, his beard was trimmed and he had nothing of that ruddy unkempt look that displaced travelers carry on them.

"Where are you going?" he asked her, while his eyes begged a different, deeper question.

"Where did *you* go?" she countered.

And then, seeing his perplexity: "—*without a word?*"

"What would you have had me say?"

"—'good-bye.' '*Thank you.*' "

His confusion spread.

"Why state what's obvious?" he said. "Come down from there, Scout. I have things to tell you."

Clara gripped the reins and glanced from him to Asahel, standing only twenty feet away beside the road, his face revealing his astonishment and pain at witnessing what would have appeared to any passing stranger, not only to him, a lovers' quarrel.

"Come down," Edward repeated. "I've thought of nothing else. I've worked it out. I can make a go of it, I know it, Scout. With your help."

"Please do not address me as 'Scout,' Edward. My name's not 'Scout.' "

Again that look of pained perplexity: "—but it's my name for you."

"I'm not yours to name. Like a slave or like a piece of . . . like your chattel."

"—but it's who you are to me."

He gripped the harness and pulled the pack mule to him with his other hand, tying the mule's lead onto the buckboard's tackle.

"—don't do that, Edward. Let go. I'm going to Seattle."

"Plenty of time for that."

He raised himself onto the boards and sat beside her. Without knowing how she had relinquished them, she saw he'd taken up the reins.

"Will you want to come to Seattle with us, Asahel?" Edward called and waved his hat. "We'll be going there to make our fortune—!"

Asahel raised a tentative acknowledgment and started to walk toward them. In the brief time it took for him to join them on the buckboard Edward turned to Clara and stated his proposal. It was five words long. *We shall have to marry.*

She stared at him.

"We shall have to marry," he repeated, "if we're to live the way I want us to."

She would remember flies were buzzing on the mule and mares, she would recall that flies were on their ears and asses and that the air around her smelled of mammals and that the man in whose presence she always found herself to be most helpless was paying the leathers through his fingers, his gaze focused not on her but on the road ahead when the proposition that would change her life had been put forward as if it were a point of trade at a livestock auction.

"—live the way you want us to?"

Still, he didn't look at her.

"What way is that, Edward?"

He turned and met her gaze.

"You know . . ." He was having trouble speaking. "*That* way."

She felt her color rise.

"—as man and wife," he finally said.

What did he know of men and wives, she couldn't help but

speculate, this man who'd lived outside the company of women for most his life, who'd never lived within the compass of a loving household or a loving couple, whose own parents had been apart for more than half their married lives. He was not like her, whose expectations for the marriage compact had been born of firsthand observation, whose parents had flirted and cavorted openly before their children and had lavished kisses on them and on each other.

"Do you even . . . have you any feelings toward me, Edward?"

"—of course."

"I mean . . . have you love for me?"

She was aware that Asahel had clambered up behind them and was now within earshot of all they said.

"I have *need*," Edward whispered to her.

He took her hand and then moved to hide the gesture in the folds of her skirt. But Asahel had seen it. So he was not surprised when, early that same evening, at the family compound, Edward made an uncharacteristic appearance at the supper table and announced to everyone, "I will be taking Clara for my wife."

"I knew it!" Hercules exclaimed and ran around the table to embrace his sister. "*I asked mother and father to get you a quick husband*," he whispered in her ear. "I prayed to them. So you wouldn't have to leave me." He scurried, not to Edward, but to Asahel and embraced him, too. "Does this make us brothers?" he asked hopefully.

"I already have a brother," Asahel remarked, his eyes riveting first Edward, and then Clara.

I don't understand, Ellen generally lamented. "—Amelia? What about . . . that man you're already married to?"

"*When?*" Eva icily inquired.

Clara was surprised by her displeasure.

"We're going to Seattle in the morning to secure arrangements," Edward announced.

We *are?* Clara thought

"Who'd have thought you'd find a husband before I did?" Eva mused, not charitably. Only Asahel, among the Curtises, was kind enough to raise a toast. To Clara and Edward, he announced: *God help you.*

Edward left the kitchen as abruptly as he had appeared and Clara followed him across the porch into the yard as he continued walking, unaware that she was shadowing him. She called his name and he stopped and turned and she came up very close to him.

"Edward, what is this about—?"

He looked at her intently and for one careless instant she believed he was about to kiss her but instead he touched a stray lock of her hair and smoothed it back along her head. He kept his hand beside her face and traced the delicate bone of her ear. "You must let me call you what I want to call you," he said, and she nodded, once, as if entranced, and, once again, he almost smiled.

"Read this," he said and handed her a folded piece of newsprint from his shirt pocket. It was a small notice, torn from a page of a Seattle newspaper, seeking capital investment in a local business.

"A photographic studio," he pointed out. "A going concern. Already established. I wrote to him. The owner, Mr. Rothi. I told him not to take a partner on until I came to see him."

"How much does he want?"

"—what does it matter? If he's got a full setup I can start to print my photographs. We can make a business of it—you and me . . ."

He looked so hopeful she leaned to kiss him as an affirmation but he turned his head aside, so her lips touched his bearded cheek and when she threw her arms around his shoulders she could sense that something wasn't natural in the way he stood, in his resistance, a specter of reluctance in his flesh.

He didn't come to her that night, although she only half expected that he would, now that his mother and his sister were returned. Edward was not a man to compromise her virtue in their eyes, she knew—but she also knew that he was not a man to let anything come between himself and what he wanted, once he wanted it. She hoped, against her rational judgment, that he would wait until the household was asleep and come to her again to lie beside her. She thought she had been cured of this longing that arose unbidden every time she thought of him, but his reappearance, the physical effect he had on her, had proved her wrong. She placed her palm flat on the pillow where he had slept and tried to ease her disappointment in the present with thoughts of their future life together, not a single night but a succession of nights and days, with Edward. *Happiness* should have been her natural state—she knew she should be happy—but some occluding doubt, or lack of faith, diffused that vision. They were to be married. If there was some less-than-gratifying aspect of their present contract, she believed, they would find the means to make it better in their future years together, as a couple. She loved him and he needed her. And that was all that mattered.

They left as dawn broke the next morning, Clara wearing for the second day in a row the only traveling clothes she owned and Edward dressed in a worsted three-piece suit she'd never seen, cut high beneath the arms as had been the fashion several years before. His shirt was starched but on close inspection she could see the collar had been turned. He wore a silk cravat tied at a rakish angle and carried a moroccan leather portfolio of deep burnished cordovan stamped in gold, in an exquisite flourish underneath the handle, with the letters *E.S.C.* They took the buckboard and the two dray mares Hercules had at the ready for them and reached the boat landing in less than half an hour. In another hour they were on the water, plowing through the coastal fog as if sleepwalking in a dream, the points of reference otherworldly, passing them as phantoms. Clara stood with Edward by the rail, their faces and their clothing growing damp with moisture from the air that formed a blanket visibility, a *surround*, a seeing-but-not-seeing, which intensified the mystery of things one heard. A loon. Two loons. A distant bell. *Sound*, she thought—no wonder this body of water was called Puget *Sound*—sound defined the world out here, not vision. It reminded her of snow, of the way snow falling in the evening in St. Paul had baffled sound around their house, of the way her mother had led them out onto the porch to listen to sound's heightened intensity under the influence of falling snow. Her mother would have loved the echo chamber that this fog created, Clara thought—it was like a tunnel, snug—and as she bent across the rail she had the feeling that if she leaned out far enough it could nullify her being and subsume her, render her invisible and swallow her as snow had devoured both her parents—

Edward! she breathed, reaching for him as a safety. She had never told him how her parents died, only how she and Hercules had been forced to carry on without them. She had never told him of her mother's sensitivity for sound, only of her father's artfulness, and now she felt she had to tell him all about Amelia, how the music lived inside her, how she played, how she transformed into another being, an instrument of sound, when she sat down and started touching the piano.

"—Edward, I so want to tell you how my mother . . ."

"—yes, I know you're fairly bursting with excitement, aren't you, Scout? You are *so good for me!* You've changed my life! Those books— you must go on giving me more books to read! You must teach me everything you know—!"

He kissed her fingers through her glove.

"I've brought along this gold nugget," he said, showing it to her. She had seen it—or one like it—on his writing desk, when she had visited his spartan room: it was small and brown, the shape and color of a relic tooth.

"For our wedding bands," he said.

From the size of it she could see how thin the bands would have to be, but she was touched.

"A fellow gave it to my father, for saving his wife's life through prayer. The woman had a fever and my father sat with her three nights and prayed. While we waited, this fellow told me how he'd gone out west to California when the gold was struck, one of the first, in '49. He told me how he'd found a strike and mined it— not a panning site, a placer find. From that moment I was gold struck—so many things to do in one life, Scout! That fellow ran out of strength before the gold ran out and he showed me on a map where it was and he asked me if I would go with him. Would I! I'd have gone in a heartbeat but for father weighing in against it."

He rolled the nugget in his hand.

"This nugget was all that he had left and when his wife was cured he pressed it into Father's hand and said, 'She's worth it.'

Father didn't know what it was worth. If I hadn't taken it from him he would have squandered it."

"—you took it?"

"I *conserved* it."

His look declared his self-acquittal. Some people, it seemed to say, cannot be trusted to appreciate the value of the things they own, cannot be trusted to safeguard their heritage. It was not so different, she supposed, than her own conservation of her father's paintings from the debt collectors. And she was even further moved to understand that Edward was now willing to convert this talisman to rings to pledge their troth.

It had already slipped her mind that she had started to tell him something dear to her, about herself. When he had interrupted.

They had not known each other long enough for her to see a pattern, yet—everything they did together was still new, a singular event, so when they docked, and disembarked, into the bruit and push of the rough and tumble ferry slip and Edward strode ahead of her, leaving her to struggle through the crowd alone to catch him, she thought the pace he set was from their shared excitement, not his single-mindedness.

The docks, striving for a state of operability after the destruction of the fire, were a labyrinth of stacked raw timber and improvised sawmills, coils of rope as thick as trees and stoves of steaming tar. Mud was everywhere underfoot—mud mixed with ash and charcoal soot—the broad planks serving as pedestrian walkways slick with muck the color and consistency of wet tobacco. Her dress boots, soles worn thin from years of walking St. Paul's cobbled streets, offered no protection from the viscous slime and she could feel damp starting in her heels and rising to her ankles. She slipped and fell against a barrel-chested man with an iron cudgel hammering an anchor chain, whose breath, when he turned to catch her, reeked of ale and onions. The air, less dense with fog than on the water, filtered light as if through muslin and was thick with unfamiliar smells, acrid, metal and marine, laced with the pungent spice of charring fagots that the Chinamen were burning to fry meat and nests of noodles in hammered bowl-shaped pans the size of carriage wheels.

This was not the city she expected.

Everything about it was rough and *go*, not civilized so much as *being* civilized and as she pushed through the clotted knot of people to catch up with Edward she felt comforted that he was there with her and wondered how she ever could have dreamed of managing this frontier alone.

As the city rose—and it rose in steppes, hill after hill—it became more tamed.

She followed him onto an esplanade, then up a paved incline into a street that began to prompt her memory of what a proper city had to offer. There were trolley tracks and sidewalks—a bakery, a tea shop, a stationer. The late summer sky was still a dismal gray but the rawness of the dockside blocks gave way to the patina of a better neighborhood as Edward finally came to a full stop and peered around a corner. This is it, he said.

"—it's an *alley*," Clara couldn't help but noting.

"It's that building, there," he said and pointed to a shop at the head of the dim cul-de-sac with a sign that read, PHOTOGRAPHIC PORTRAITS.

The alley, though short, was wide enough for two carriages and must have originally been built as a mews to stable carts and horses, because midway down the short block there were distinctive stable doors and the remnants of tackle designed for lifting bales of hay. The little street was paved with cobblestones and was not the bleak dead-end that she first thought—on one corner there was a ladies' milliner next to a gentleman's cane-and-umbrella shop. On the other corner, a goldsmith and jeweler.

Carriage trade, she rightly assessed. "On second thought," she said to Edward, "this could be a good location."

They proceeded to the entrance, Clara conscious of the rising mudline on her skirt, as if it were a shore, and were surprised to find a neatly printed notice—CLOSED—hanging on the inside of the door. Edward rang the bell and a faint instruction inside informed them that the door was open, and they entered. "Is that you, Mr. Curtis?" the faint voice inquired.

A man emerged toward them—thin as a rail, lost in a brown suit of clothes several sizes too large, his head balancing on his emaciated neck, glowing yellow like a golden orb inside a gaslight globe.

"I am Rasmus Rothi," he announced and extended a frail jaundiced hand but Clara took an immediate step backward, pressing Edward back as well, while covering her mouth and nose with her linen handkerchief.

"Do not worry, I am not contagious," the jaundiced man informed them. "It's my liver, as you see, but it's specific to my person. And the reason I can no longer entertain the public trade myself."

Edward took the gentleman's hand and introduced himself, while Clara still held back.

"Would you like to see my photographs, Mr. Rothi?" Edward asked, proffering his monogrammed portfolio.

"I would rather see your money," Mr. Rothi said.

"In that case I will have to see the darkroom."

"In the back. Studio is up these stairs," he pointed, "where there's light. Skylight on the upper floor," he started to explain but Edward had already disappeared behind the counter through a door toward where the photographs were printed.

"I'm sorry you are ill, Mr. Rothi," Clara said, still keeping her distance, but before she had even breathed another breath Edward had returned, racing up the stairs. She could hear his footsteps on the floor above and then, within an instant, he was back. *How much?* he asked.

Clara took a small step toward him.

"—perhaps Mr. Rothi would like to show you his accounting, Edward," she said, but he waved her off.

"One hundred and fifty," Rothi said. "For half share of the business."

"I'll give you a hundred."

"And I'll give you the door."

Clara watched the two men stand off with each other.

She wondered how Edward had acquired so much money, or if he even had it, but noted that nothing in his posturing before the older man suggested otherwise.

"I'll work the difference off—work without a share in profits until the balance's paid," Edward offered.

"One hundred and fifty. Cash in hand. That's my final," Rothi told him.

Edward tendered their farewell and turned and left and Clara followed and once outside he grasped her wrists and said, "This is what I *want*—I could learn *so much* from him! What a tough old character, a man like him could teach me all I'd need to know about how to operate a business—"

"Edward," Clara had to ask: "Do you have a hundred dollars?"

"—why, of course. Salary from all those years, odd jobs, and from the sawmill. I can raise the extra fifty, I suppose—I could sell the homestead, Father paid three dollars an acre for it—fifteen acres—plus, now, there's the house and barn . . ."

"—but, Edward, if you do that . . . where would your mother and sister live?"

"—here. Seattle. They could live *with us.*"

Clara held her breath.

"—but, *dear,*" she argued: "Where would *that* be?"

"—we'll find the rooms to rent . . ."

"—rooms for *six*? The city's overrun with boarders from the fire. How would they pay? Where would the rent come from?"

"Asahel has work. Asahel has money saved. I could borrow—"

"Do you really *want* this, Edward?"

"So much, Scout. So very, very much . . ."

"—then *here.*" She reached into her bodice for the money she had left from Lodz.

Edward looked at the money then took it without speaking, nursing it from her fingers without touching her, though his eyes spoke an emotion she interpreted as ratified devotion.

She waited outside the building, watching the sun slide above the rooflines, pushing the shadows to one side of the street, while Edward went inside to deal with Mr. Rothi. She could hear a church bell clanging on the hill above her and detect a buttery aroma from the bakery nearby and she began to reinhabit the delights of city living, that sense of feeling others close at hand who share one's cultural language and experience. She watched a carriage arrest at the corner where a well-turned-out gentleman descended, top hat and cane, and helped a lady in a fashionable dress dismount onto the pavement, as he took her arm and nuzzled his head close to hers before they saun-tered, slowly, out of sight. *I will have this life again*, Clara thought. She felt her heart quicken—with a surge of pride she thought, *I have* paid *to have this life again*. She smiled, and told herself: with *Edward*.

He emerged from Rothi's shop, his face more radiant than she had ever seen, and announced, "It's done." He took her arm and backed her up into the middle of the mews facing the building and swept his hand across its bland façade. "'Rothi and *Curtis*,'" he pro-nounced. "'Photographers.' *Thank you*, Scout."

She felt that she might cry from joy.

"Now let's go see about these wedding rings," he said and started toward the jeweler on the corner at the trot she was learning was his natural speed.

"Where did you get this, sir?" the jeweler, assaying the gold nugget, asked from behind his loupe.

"Why do you want to know?"

"I *already* know," the jeweler said. He assessed Edward and Clara more carefully. "I want to know if *you* know."

Edward held his gaze without answering.

It had been forty years since gold was found at Sutter's Mill but superstitions and suspicions still swirled around the protocols of discovery, as if the gold, itself, were the product of alchemy, not na-ture, and it was *un*natural to give away details of its provenance be-cause of the vestigial fear of being claim-jumped.

"I would wager California on the Nevada line," the jeweler said. "There are traces of BORON in the fasciae."

Edward didn't blink. "Are you saying that the nugget isn't pure?"

"It is *very* pure. Outstanding carat. And for that very reason I am loath to melt it down. But I will tell you what I think it's worth and you can use the trade to purchase rings from my selection of hand-crafted wedding bands."

Clara watched him write a figure on a piece of paper and pass it to Edward—she saw Edward's color rise—then the jeweler passed a wooden tray to them, lined in purple velvet and gold wedding bands.

"What will you do with the nugget?" Edward asked.

"I will preserve it. Make a tie pin of it. Very elegant."

Sir, Edward said and reached to stay the jeweler's hand.

Edward explained who he was and that he had just entered into an agreement with Mr. Rothi, the jeweler's neighbor, and that he and the jeweler were going to be commercial residents on the same street and that if the jeweler would consider holding the nugget as surety against the cost of the two wedding bands Edward would like to reserve the right to come back in three months' time and pay him for the two rings as well as paying for the jeweler's craftsmanship to convert the nugget to a tie pin.

Clara watched without a word—watched Edward wield persuasion as an enticing snare of conversation, charming the jeweler with that same unyielding focus that could sometimes distance but that never failed to win her over.

They chose two beveled bands, identical except for size, Clara feeling, again, that she would weep, when she tried hers on.

"And what sentiment would you like engraved inside?" the jeweler asked.

Edward shook his head, explaining, "None . . . we need to take them with us, right away."

"I can do it while you wait," the jeweler offered, and Edward's face went blank.

"I would like," Clara piped up: "I would like, inside of mine, the single word—*Edward*."

"—and you?" the jeweler asked, turning to Edward.

Edward held the ring and stared at it then looked at Clara, seeking her permission.

"*Scout*," she told the jeweler: "Etch in the word 'Scout.'"

They waited while the jeweler took the rings to his engraving desk beneath a window, Clara passing the time by looking at the jewelry in the cases—filigreed necklaces and ladies' watch fobs, earrings strung with freshwater pearls, pink and green with iridescence.

"—let me know if something takes your fancy," the jeweler told her and she blushed, feeling she should turn away for lack of justification, from such opulence.

Meanwhile Edward surveyed the shop, judging the way it was assembled, how the inventory was presented to the public. He particularly took notice of the nearly empty walls—the lithographs hung as meager decoration to make the customer feel at ease among the products.

"I see you are a '*connoisseur*' of Mt. Rainier," he told the jeweler, pointing to the framed art.

Clara kept her head down to suppress a smile. *Connoisseur*. She had taught him the word. His pronunciation was a perfect duplicate of hers.

"It is my own 'mountain of mountains,'" he added conversationally. "Perhaps I can interest you in purchasing my photographs of it to enliven your emporium."

Clara smiled again at Edward's language.

"Are you a mountaineer, Mr. Curtis?" the jeweler asked.

"I have ascended to Pinnacle Peak. *Twice*," he answered. "Carrying my dry-plate camera. Fourteen thousand feet."

The jeweler stopped and looked at him.

"You have *photographs* taken from the peak?"

Edward nodded.

"Then perhaps I can interest *you* in showing them to our Mazamas Club. Have you heard of us?"

Edward shook his head.

"We are the premier mountaineering group of the Pacific Northwest. Do you mountaineer, as well?" he asked of Clara.

"No, I'm sorry. My pursuits are more interior . . ."

The jeweler turned his attention back to Edward: "I'll put you in touch with the Club leader, we make several expeditions a year into the Cascades and Olympics . . ."

As the men talked Clara began to see into a world of symbiotically connected links, a society like the one she had known her parents to have had in the art world when she was growing up in St. Paul, formed of men and women whose interests overlapped. But then the jeweler said, "It will help your business," and Clara realized there was another aspect to the world of *mutual pursuit* that she had yet to learn.

The bell on the door chimed and what appeared to Clara to be a beggar woman entered with a damp smell accompanying her, rising from the crude reed basket that she carried covered with a cloth. She was all of four feet tall, almost equally as wide around her hips, with a faded blue bandanna tied around her weathered face from which tiny crescent eyes peered at Clara without expression over thin down-turning lips.

"Good morning, Princess," the jeweler greeted her with what

Clara thought sounded like mockery. "What have you got for me today?"

The woman opened her fist, palm up, in front of Clara in a gesture Clara assumed was meant to ask for money until she noticed tiny ivory pearls the size of apple seeds scattered on the incised map across her palm.

"Pearls," the woman said.

"Let's have a look," the jeweler told her.

She crossed to him and showed him what she had while Edward watched her closely. The jeweler counted out the tiny pearls across the counter, then handed her some coins.

"Clams?" she asked, exposing the fresh shellfish in her basket. "Mussels?"

"Not today, Princess," the jeweler said.

She looked at Edward, and Clara could see that he was studying her every feature.

Then, without a word, she left.

"That was Princess Angeline," the jeweler told them. "Quite the fixture around here."

"That's somewhat cruel, don't you think?" Clara braved. "To call someone like her a 'princess'?"

"—but she *is* a princess. The daughter of Chief Sealth. The Suquamish head man from whom *Seattle* takes its name. She and her ilk dig clams and mussels on the reed flats down by Eliot Bay . . ."

He showed the finished rings to them for their approval and asked, "Anything else I can help you with this morning?"

"Yes," Edward said. "Tell us where we need to go to find a judge so we can marry."

It was the courthouse and within two hours, and without ceremony, they were man and wife. They had stood next to each other
without touching but when the moment came they had turned to
face each other, and had smiled.

When it was over Edward led Clara to a nearby restaurant and
held her hand across the table as the waiter brought them glasses of
ice water in leaded tumblers with real ice. It was thrilling, Clara
thought.

"To 'Rothi and Curtis,'" Edward toasted.

"Yes," Clara concurred. She raised her glass. "And to *us*."

She looked around the room and began to anticipate the excitement of their life together in this invigorating place. She squeezed
his hand. "I have a single favor I must beg."

He waited.

"Hercules," Clara said. "I trust you will allow—"

"—of course," Edward affirmed. "I already think of him as my
own brother." He pressed her fingers. "—even as my son."

Thank you, she breathed.

She could not imagine greater happiness. At a nearby table a
woman laughed and Clara turned in time to see the woman's escort
bring her fingers to his lips and kiss them and then press her hand
against his heart. She felt Edward lift his hand from hers and by the
time she turned back to him he had tucked a napkin in his collar
and was lost behind the menu.

Through the meal he sought her advice on designing stationery
and his business card and asked her help composing the notice he
would place about his partnership with Rothi in the newspapers.
He had determined he would stay on a few days and begin to work,
begin to look for rooms for them to rent and when they reached the

top of the entrance to the dock he asked if she needed him to walk her all the way down to the ferry.

"I can make it on my own," she said.

"That's my *Scout*."

He took her by the shoulders then and kissed her on the check and when she turned to wave to him after several steps he was already gone.

The sun had still to set on her wedding day when she brought the mares to a halt before the house and Hercules came running from the barn.

"I shod my first horse—!" he cried. "All by myself! The farrier let me shoe her!"

Clara waved her finger with the wedding band in front of him. "I guess we both got shod today," she joked.

He embraced her and she walked beside him as he led the horses.

"Edward bought a business."

"—what kinda business?"

"Pictures."

"—oh that's nice. Like father's?"

"Photographs."

"—oh I've seen him do that in the barn."

"Yes but now he's going to do it in Seattle."

Hercules stood still.

"No," he said.

"Hercules, it's a wonderful city—like St. Paul. You'll meet lots of boys your age—"

"You were supposed to marry him so we could *stay*," he said. "—so *you* would stay."

"I'm not saying we will be apart . . ."

"*I am.*"

She blinked.

"I'm not going to Seattle," Hercules said with grave finality. "You can't make me."

"Why are you behaving like this, Hercules?"

"I'm *happy* here—"

"—we will still be happy in . . ."

"I'm happy here where I can be with horses."

"There are horses in Seattle," she began to argue.

"—*these* horses."

Clara took a moment to assess her brother's mood.

"I *talk* to them," he said.

She watched him smooth the fine soft hairs along the gray mare's cheek.

"We can always visit—"

"—no I talk to *them*," he told her.

She stared at him.

"—inside the horses," he tried to explain to her.

"You talk to . . . ?"

"—mother and father."

"—*inside* the horses," she finally repeated.

"—don't ask me to explain it. I didn't want you to find out."

He began to cry.

"—no, no . . ." she comforted him. "It's a good thing that you've told me, Hercules."

"I can feel them. In the ponies. When I pet them. And I know they can feel me . . ."

She watched him lean his head against the horse's flank and

close his eyes and she laid her hand against his back and patted him.

"Tell me something," she said after a while. "Which horse is it?"

"All of them."

"—every horse?"

"Every one I've ever met," he said. "They just know me. We just fall in love. There has to be a reason *why* . . ."

"—you're a very special boy, is why. And we'll have to find a way to make sure that doesn't change."

"—even if it means we have to be apart?"

That was a condition Clara did not want to have to think about—because unlike Hercules, she had not found an entity, other than herself, to act as a repository for her sorrow or in which to store the memories of what their parents were in life, the space that they had filled, the way they'd sounded. It had not yet been a year since their deaths and yet she found she had to struggle to recall the fleeting things about them—the shape of her father's hand, the timbre of her mother's laughter—and she needed Hercules at hand to validate the little she remembered and the sum of what they'd lost. If Hercules should be parted from her, if he should ever go from her daily life—as almost certainly, some day, he would—her diminishment would double.

But she was also on the brink of an enriched life, a potentially *growing* family, rather than a decreasing one, and she could not allow a yearning for the past to sabotage the happiness that was her future. Besides, she was not convinced that Seattle was the less enlightened choice than this backward rural one for Hercules's education and well-being—until Mr. Silva, the farrier, paid her a visit two days later, bringing with him a tall stranger.

The Curtis women had, oddly, treated her marriage with gloomy passivity, Eva showing signs of nervous curiosity only when Clara told her of Edward's partnership with Rothi. She gave scant notice to Clara's wedding band and seemed interested only in knowing if this Mr. Rothi was a single gentleman. Asahel had made himself invisible ever since her return so she was alone, without counsel, when Mr. Silva stepped up on the porch and rapped on the screen door, his hat in hand, and introduced the stranger.

"This is Mr. Touhy, miss, he's from Tacoma."

Clara held her left hand up for the gentlemen to see and said, "It's *missus*, Mr. Silva. Mr. Curtis and I were married just two days ago."

"Which one, ma'am?"

"—*Edward.*"

"—oh well congratulations, I didn't know. Mr. Edward, he's a fine gent. Mr. Touhy, here, breeds fancy horses."

"You're a long way from Tacoma, Mr. Touhy. What brings you to the island?"

"Actually miss—*missus*—he's come to take a look at Hercules."

Clara asked the gentlemen to sit, which they did, not comfortably.

"I don't know if Hercules has told you, but I've been coming by most every week to give him skills."

"He *has* told me, Mr. Silva, and I'm grateful to you."

Nevertheless, she kept her eyes on Mr. Touhy.

"Hercules is very fond of horses," she explained.

"Well that's an understatement," Silva grinned. "I'd say, frankly, Hercules is one in a million."

" . . . and what would you say, Mr. Touhy?"

Touhy ran his hat brim through his fingers and told her, "I would say the boy has got the touch."

"He talks to horses," Mr. Silva chimed in.

"—yes, I know," Clara told them.

"Well do ya know *nobody* does that?"

"What do you *want*, Mr. Touhy—?"

He wanted to apprentice Hercules to his breeding ranch. Clara's instinct was to forestall making a decision until Edward had returned so he could advise—she knew nothing of the kind of life they were describing and Edward, after all, had been apprenticed to his father from the age of six and seemed to have come out the better for it in terms of working for a living and being trained in many skills. But when she called Hercules from the barn to join them it was clear the boy knew what he wanted. Asahel could not be found and rather than allow Hercules to leave with Mr. Touhy, as the gentlemen suggested, Clara agreed that either her husband or her brother-in-law would deliver the boy, pending an inspection and approval of the site, itself.

That night Clara sat up waiting in the kitchen in the dark for Asahel to finally come to get his supper. She struck a match and startled him and said, "You've been avoiding me."

"Call it what you will."

She lighted the lantern and told him, "A man named Touhy came to visit me today."

" . . . the horse breeder."

"—you know him?"

"He has a reputation. —a *good* one."

"He wants Hercules."

Asahel sat down across the table from her with a plate of cold ham and cold potatoes, and began to eat.

"I'll miss him."

His manner, his dispassion, seemed as cold to her as his plate of food but she chose to let it ride and said, instead, "I need your help," then tempered the request by adding, "Hercules and I do. I trust you. You know I do. Will you take him out to Tacoma and tell me what you think?"

"Why not ask your husband?"

"Because I'm asking you."

"—or because you know Edward wouldn't do it?"

"Edward's busy—"

"—when is Edward *not*?"

"Are you *angry* with me, Asahel?"

"Let's just say I know my brother. Better than you do. He takes what he wants, when he wants it, as if it is his due. As if all the years at Father's beck and call earned him the right, now that he's free, to finally be the selfish cur he was cut out to be—"

"—he puts food on this table, Asahel, and a roof over your mother's and your sister's—"

"—and you think I *don't*? —is that what he's told you?"

"He hasn't 'told' me anything about you, your sister or—"

Asahel threw his fork down, pushed his chair back and stood up.

"That's because he's a kingdom of one, Clara."

He picked up his plate, left it in the basin and started for the door, not meeting her eyes.

"—and I'll do anything for you and Hercules. Anything you ask."

He turned and finally looked at her.

"—forget what I've said. I haven't slept for two days. I'm working double shifts at the sawmill . . . mine and Edward's."

Still, she sat in judgment of him, and he felt it, so he told her, "Maybe you will change him—maybe *love* will change him," then he left.

Love, she couldn't tell him, the word *love*, had never been spoken as an avowal between herself and Edward—nor did it need to be, she reasoned. They had an understanding, a workable arrangement, shared interests, a sympathy and need for each other, an enjoyment in the other's company: but, foremost, they had Edward's *work*. And Edward's work was all-consuming. Once they were situated in their first residence in Seattle—four rented rooms in a brick Georgian house on 2nd Avenue—Clara rarely saw him. He never ate at home. He hardly slept. If she woke when he came into bed in the middle of the night then she struggled to wake again to see him off before the dawn. She had read of ancient Spartans' regimens of work but she had never known a single man to set himself the task assignments of a regiment: he was teaching himself to become a master printer, and at the same time he was teaching himself to become a master engraver, setting for himself levels of perfection that he, alone, could judge. He was joining Clubs, appearing in public to lecture with his signature gold nugget tie pin: he was lobbying for influence. He was leading the Mazamas Club, after only one meeting with them, up Mt. Rainier, following in John Muir's renowned footsteps but also making innovative forays of his own. Within the year he had outgrown his use for Rothi, sold off his share at profit and entered into a second partnership with an established photoengraver by the name of Thomas Guptill, becoming the most sought after engraver north of San Francisco. He persuaded Asahel to leave the sawmill to come and learn darkroom techniques and by the spring of '93, when Clara first suspected she was pregnant, Edward had sold the homestead on the island and all the Curtises—Edward, Clara, Asahel, Ellen and Eva—were reunited under one roof once again, this time in Seattle. Hercules had long since gone to Touhy's ranch in Tacoma and although she saw him several times a year, especially at Christmas, Clara thought a great deal more about him once her own son was born, that November. They named him Harold, after Clara's father. Edward lavished his attention on him and Clara believed the child's birth might be a turning point in Edward's emotional devotion, that following on the birth of their son, he would forswear some of his projects to stay at home more often. But his reputation as Seattle's first-rank society photographer was just coming into bloom, even as his scenic landscapes of Puget Sound and the Cascades were gaining notice in national publications. He won a competition with his studio portrait of Princess Angeline in her faded bandanna, and his moody studies of the Suquamish clam diggers were the favored wall art in Seattle banks and law offices. For her part, Clara had learned early in her history with Edward that if she was going to capture his attention she had to do it on his terms, putting herself somewhere he would be reminded of her, somewhere he could see her and that meant putting hours in at his place of business, catering to clientele, overseeing the employees, holding up her end of the social ladder he was so determined to climb. She was active in the Arts Club, active in arranging *musicales*, even active, for a while, in his mountaineering outings until successive pregnancies and the effort of the frosty climbs with ice picks in those mandatory *skirts* exhausted her.

Their first daughter Beth was born, followed by Florence, named for Clara's father's favorite city. Edward split from Guptill, moving to a new studio of his own the same year he bought their first house and even though they were more comfortable than they had ever been and his career was flourishing he could not have foreseen the skyrocketing success of Seattle in 1897 when gold was discovered in the Klondike in Alaska. When the first ship from there docked below 1st Avenue in Seattle it was said five hundred millionaires got off. Edward dispatched Asahel by boat to send back dry plates for engraving to distribute to the nation's papers and he, himself, journeyed up along the Alaska coast by a second route. If the city had seemed a boom town in the two decades before, it now felt like the mecca that invented *manna*. But with it, mining mania brought concern from the nation's new breed of conservationists, on alert for gross misappropriation of water, land and mineral rights in the wake of scandalous governmental bequests to the railroads.

Which is how, one unseasonably warm March weekend in 1898, unbeknownst to Clara, the elements that had been ready to impact on Edward's life and change its course away from her, irrevocably, finally converged.

And they were, to put it simply: three lost men. On a mountaintop.

Dr. C. Hart Merriam, Chief of the United States Biological Survey; Dr. George Bird Grinnell, Editor of *Field & Stream*; and Gifford Pinchot, Chief of the United States Division of Forestry, had lost their bearings in a sudden vicissitude of weather halfway up the face of Mt. Rainier and had become dangerously disoriented in an isolated col, separated from their camp and without supplies when their cries were answered by a dashing young adventurer in rakish hat and bold cravat who happened to be summiting that afternoon with his Premo dry plate camera.

Edward led them down to safety and, from that chance encounter, back in Seattle, found himself on the receiving end of profound and lavish gratitude from three of the most influential men he had ever met. Individually dedicated to the cause of preserving the nation's scenic and God-given resources, the three men opened their circle of robust camaraderie to embrace Edward into their fold—especially after he had brought them all into his studio to show them his portfolio of Pacific Northwest landscapes and portraits of Puget Sound tribal people.

The three took Edward to dinner two nights in a row at the Cosmos Club, where they were lodging, and upon departing by train on the third day pledged they would maintain their bond through letters until such a time as a reunion could be planned.

Each one left with a gift of a signed Curtis print of Mt. Rainier—and in the process Edward had sold them a total of eleven other photographs, at discount, of course, but still for seven dollars each.

The evening of the day of their departure he came home unexpectedly while Clara was still sitting with the children at their supper. "What should I write to them?" he fretted. "I want to write to them before they write to me—especially that Bird Grinnell—I took to him enormously. Or do you think I ought to wait until they write to me—? What should I do? What do you think?"

"I think I've never seen you in this state," she marveled. "Who thinks Father's got a bee in Father's bonnet?" she joked with the children. "Let's all make a buzzing sound and show him how we're little bees—"

"*Clara*," he said suddenly: "This is a serious matter."

It was only on rare occasions, anymore, that he chose to call her "Scout."

And those were only when he was moved to thank her for compliancy. In bed, or out.

"Edward, you do not need my advice on social discourse with *men*. Men are charmed by you, as are women—you're a charming person."

"But I write stiffly, so you told me."

"Then write to them as if in conversation. In your imagination put Bird Grinnell in front of you and simply *talk*."

"Good *Scout*," he said and kissed her lightly on her head—then kissed Harold, Beth and Florence exactly the same way.

The letters paid off.

Grinnell was a friend of Edward Harriman's, the railroad tycoon, who had just bested J.P. Morgan for control of the West Coast Union Pacific line and was under doctor's orders to take time off from acquisitions to ease his choler and his heart. Harriman, never one to relax, consequently put together a scientific expedition to Alaska with a view to collecting samples of the fauna and documenting natural wonders. He chartered a boat, hired hunters and taxidermists and paid for twenty-three biologists, zoologists, geologists and naturalists to join him on a two-month catered jaunt into the Yukon—among them John Muir, Merriam, Pinchot, Bird Grinnell and—at Grinnell's urging—Edward, as the official expeditionary photographer.

In preparation, Edward depleted his bank account on new cameras and equipment and a new wardrobe and borrowed several hundred dollars more to have custom leather trunks and luggage made to transport his portable laboratory.

"I will make more than a hundred times this money back," he told Clara to counter her concerns. "*Official* photographer! Everyone involved will want to buy my photographs of this experience—Harriman's a millionaire!—and if we have to miss a payment to the bank and keep the children's piano teacher waiting for her money, then so be it."

"I will never keep *a piano teacher* waiting for her money," Clara pledged.

And she didn't—she found ways to economize—but still: Edward's expectations of an economic windfall from the journey proved to be unfounded.

And a harbinger of how his expectations, his tendency toward grandiosity, would fail to deliver the anticipated "gold" at the end of those rainbows again and again. Mt. Rainier had led to Grinnell who had led to Harriman who would lead to Teddy Roosevelt—a chain of surrogate, older brothers—who would lead Edward to J.P. Morgan who would advance him seventy-five thousand dollars—a future sum the future Edward enthusiastically expected Morgan to earn back from the future sale of all those future photographs. He would squander Morgan's money, in part, on custom clothes and custom camping gear, on Italian printing papers more exquisite and valuable than any that Da Vinci had, and he would end up signing over all his copyrights to Morgan as a consequence.

He did not foresee, in 1899, that a group of men of the caliber that Harriman had summoned would bring cameras of their own, that they would show up with what he termed "push-button apparatuses," easily portable Kodak box cameras supplied with easy rolls of negative film, and enjoy the experience of taking spontaneous pictures, themselves, *snap* shots, from their own points of view.

Although Harriman had ordered a private folio edition of seven hundred printings from Edward at the completion of the expedition, he never reimbursed the cost, and Edward was left scrambling to recover from the debt but also drowning in expensive prints of Inuit villages and rugged ice that no one seemed to want.

Clara tried to be supportive, but Edward couldn't understand why anyone would prefer to have a Kodak quick-and-easy photographic record over what amounted to a lasting work of handmade art. His portraits and landscapes were "painterly," he knew that— that was his purposeful effect, an effect he tried for over the crisper images of, say, Asahel, whose photographs were often sharp enough to slice through steak. The question of where photography was *going*, what it *was*, was the leading subject of the journals he subscribed to—the *avant-garde* coming from New York City and the Photo Secessionists led by a Mr. Alfred Stieglitz who propounded the theory that a photograph should *be*. That it should be a *thing-in-and-of-itself*, like a sonata or a poem, not something that appeared, self-consciously, to have been produced through the mechanics of an apparatus. The East Coast journal, overseen by Stieglitz, was called Camera *Notes* while the West Coast journal, to which Edward frequently contributed, was called Camera *Craft*—a distinction between *theory* on the one coast, and *craft* on the other, which more or less summarized the East Coast elitist view that photographers out West were not only provincial, but uninteresting to boot.

Edward thought the Stieglitz point of view was junk, though Clara championed it.

"I'm not convinced," was his final verdict whenever they discussed it. "A photograph shouldn't *be*, it should tell you what some thing *is*."

He worried, in light of the Harriman expedition debt, that his photographs weren't *interesting*. He worried that his focus, that the subjects that he chose, were falling short of capturing the public's interest. So he was wary when Bird Grinnell wrote to ask if Edward would accompany him on a journey to Montana that next summer to be among the few white men invited to attend the Plains Indian Sun Dance.

"I am loath to bring my camera," Edward wrote back, in acceptance.

"But you *must*," Grinnell responded.

In purely economic terms Clara could not see how the business could sustain another out-of-pocket cost. Their bread-and-butter, Edward's society portraits of debutantes and heirs, was already showing symptoms of decline owing to his absences. "Mr. Curtis oversees each print himself," was her front office line when clients voiced their disappointment that Edward, personally, was not behind the camera, but, "Mr. Curtis oversees each print himself," could hardly float when the Seattle papers advertised that Edward was in Alaska for two months. Or going to Montana. She had cut costs everywhere she could—she had no domestic help, herself, in a household of eight people, except for a laundress and a daily char. She employed a part-time woman, when she could, to help her cook and although she resented Eva's passive presence in the household she was reluctant to ask either her or Edward's mother to take on the duties of a servant. She encouraged Eva to develop interest in the business, in the darkroom processes, but Asahel, alone among the Curtises, was the only one on whom either she or Edward could depend for active help, and his absence in Alaska had been sorely felt. Still, she knew, the person on whom all of them depended most was Edward—and if he was determined to make the journey to Montana she would help him any way she could.

Little did either know that *love* was waiting.

As it always does: in ambush.

On the evening of his departure Clara heard Edward come home as she was putting the children in their beds upstairs. She heard the front door close and heard his footsteps toward the study. Minutes later she heard the front door open and close again and then the sound of other footsteps toward the study and within moments after that she heard the sound of two male voices raised in heated argument, below. She put the children down and closed their doors and went to listen on the stairs.

Edward had never raised his voice in all the time she'd known him.

But he was shouting now—and the voice that countered his and overpowered it, was one she recognized:

Asahel, returned.

She crept forward 'til she reached the bottom tread.

As best as she could fathom, through the door, Asahel was shouting about *shadow*, about being overshadowed all his life by his older brother, every act of his own "*stolen for the greater good of Edward! And now my photographs—*"

"—it is common practice for a studio to sign its name . . ."

"—'*its*' name! But the name you printed on my photographs says '*Edward Curtis*'—"

"—that's the name of—"

"—not the '*studio* of Edward Curtis.' *Ed . . . ward . . . Curt . . . is!*"

"—*yes!* The man who *paid* for you to make those pictures—"

"—the man who *paid?* —so that gives you the right to *own* them—?"

"—absolutely."

I swear I hope this comes to bite you on your backside one day, brother."

"Get out of my house—!"

Despite herself Clara had edged into the entrance hall to hear them and the sudden violent exit of Asahel caught her stranded, off her guard, as he slammed the study door behind him and swept past her in impassioned heat. Several feet away from her he stopped and turned and swung around to her, forcing her against the banisters, feeding her his mouth until she couldn't breathe. She raised her hand to strike him but he caught it in mid-air, and then released it.

"Now you *know,*" he said: "You married the wrong brother."

Then he was gone.

Clara took several minutes to compose herself, then rapped on Edward's door.

No! came the answer.

He would never speak to Asahel again, so long as they both lived.

If he saw him on the street, in Seattle, he would cross to the other side and not acknowledge him.

Such were the things playing on Edward's mind when he left Seattle for Montana—and whether it was his doubts about his own career, in the public's seeming lack of interest in the photography he cared about, or whether it was his doubts about his words and actions toward his brother—or neither of these things—when Edward reached his destination on horseback he was in a frame of mind that was, uncharacteristically, open to emotion.

And what he saw was like nothing he had seen before.

He had traveled out by train to Butte where he and Bird Grinnell had hired horses and they'd camped a night and then pressed on to where the several tribes of Sioux—Lakota, Apsaroke, Piegan— were gathering as one great nation.

Their approach was from higher ground and as they neared, Edward saw the Sioux had chosen a broad geological depression in which to congregate their tipis, all white and of the same design but different sizes, hundreds of them, thousands, arrayed across the valley floor like totems from another world and as he gazed down at them he had the sense that he was flying, flying out of present time into a visible history, and later he would write that in that moment he experienced the most profound feeling of emotion in his entire life.

Love.

He would never call it that, but Clara knew it in a heartbeat, as soon as he began to try to tell her why he had to go, go back to the place where he had felt it first, keep going back, to try to reinstate that moment of original devotion.

In 1900 he was gone five months.

The next year, seven.

Following Clara's good advice he wrote the children letters from the field as if, in his imagination, they were right in front of him— and they thrived on eighty words, perhaps a hundred, for as long as he was gone.

He took Harold with him, every summer, and Harold, following camp protocol, was the first among the children to begin to call him "Chief." Home for a rare visit when Harold was thirteen, Edward informed Clara that he had arranged for Harold to be educated by some friends of Mr. Roosevelt's "back East."

"What do you mean? —*what* 'friends of Mr. Roosevelt's'?"

"A banker and his wife living on Long Island. Childless. Harold will live with them and they will pay his schooling."

"Harold has an education *here*."

"He's going to New York." Then: "Don't look at me that way, Clara. You let your brother go, and he was younger."

"They gave you money, didn't they?"

He waved her off.

"*You sold your son.*"

"It will be good for him."

"—it will be good for *you*."

"He will thank me later."

"—and who in God's name will *you* ever thank?"

After Asahel had left, the Curtis women had moved in with him—and with Harold gone, and Edward gone most months, Clara was alone with Beth and Florence in a house that suddenly seemed too big, with too many rooms. She looked into the possibility of selling it but discovered there were several liens against it and when she advertised for female boarders she was surprised to find that not a single applicant was willing to pay rent in a household that included children. Her children were, after all, her single greatest joy, their laughter echoing in the empty entrance hall, proof that happiness existed, even in a vacuum, and that her life had had a purpose and a meaning. Beth and Florence, in their banter and their games, mirrored what was best about the life that she had made with Edward, and she kept his accomplishments and his adventures in the forefront of their conversations so they would remember him, so he would remain a presence in their daily lives. But the truth was, without Harold to remind them of the energy of boyhood—and with an absent father—the household became, inevitably, centered around girlish things, reading stories, playing make-believe in dress-up clothes and linen sheets discovered at the bottom of their mother's painted trunk. The games they played, the stories she encouraged them to tell to each other, established heroes in their minds— princes on white horses slaying dragons, impoverished boys who learn one day that they are kings. The men they saw each day, however, were the milkman and the greengrocer down the street, the trolley driver and the man who swept the gutters.

It was no small surprise, then, when, late one afternoon, a cowboy in a broad-brimmed hat and riding boots appeared.

Hercules.

"—you should have told me you were coming!" Clara greeted him, not meaning to admonish, but embarrassed by her lack of preparation, self-conscious of the way she looked.

"—I've aged," she fussed, seeing how he looked at her.

"Are you a *real* cowboy?" Florence asked.

"He's your real *uncle*," Clara told her.

"Father is an Indian *Chief*," Beth announced. "That's what you're supposed to call him."

Hercules had grown into a man and Clara couldn't keep from smiling at the rugged, easy figure that he cut—too large, it seemed, for anywhere but the outdoors. In the last ten years he had gone from boyhood into acquired wisdom of a sage, from Tacoma to Wyoming on to Colorado where he had his own small ranch. He had brought a show horse to a client in Portland and had decided on impulse to board the train to come and see his sister.

And he could see at once that something weighed on her, despite her grace.

Her eyes were not the eyes that he remembered. Her confidence, so strong when they were in their youth, had left her.

"Let's have some tea, and you will tell us all your news," she said and led him to the kitchen where, he noticed, she suddenly seemed flustered. He watched her open one cabinet, and then another, seeming to hunt for things that were not there.

"Do you like fried bread?" Florence asked him. "We have fried bread for our supper."

"Every day," Beth added. "Except when we have soup."

Clara prised the lid from a canister she'd found, peered inside and murmured, "Oh. It would appear we're out of tea . . ."

He took the two girls with him to the grocer's, returning with some chops, some eggs, a cake and tea, and after they'd had supper and the girls had gone upstairs, he sat with Clara at the table in the kitchen and said, "Truth time."

He took her hand so she would talk but still she kept her silence.

"Whatever it is, Clara, we have been through worse. Together. And back then it was *you* getting *me* to do the talking."

His hand was so rough—she turned it over, ran her fingers on his callused palm, as if, like the magic lamp, rubbing it would release the genie she once had inside.

"Edward is never home," she finally said.

"But that is Edward."

"Yes, but . . . He has changed."

"How?"

"He has a . . . mission."

"—he's found *religion?*"

"No . . . Well, in a way."

She looked into her brother's eyes, surprised that she could see there both the boy and this new man.

"I think he's fallen out of love with me."

"Oh, Clara . . ."

"I think I don't exist for him. I think he doesn't *see* me . . ."

"Has he . . . —is there another woman?"

"—oh *lord* no."

"I will go and talk to him."

She squeezed his hand.

"You can't."

"—why not?"

"No one knows where Edward is."

"Who's running the business?"

"I am. With the people we employ."

"And where is Asahel?"

"He and Edward . . . They're not speaking."

"—*why?*"

"Something . . . They had a falling out."

"Clara . . ." He stared at her. "—what did you *do?*"

"—oh please. You think that all of this . . ." She waved her hand around the room: "—is *my* fault?"

"Of course not, but—"

"—when a man leaves his wife, when a marriage fails, it must be something that the *woman's* done . . ."

"*Has* your marriage failed?"

She waved her hand around the room again: "I would not exactly call this a success."

"Then you need a lawyer."

"—oh Hercules: it hasn't come to *that*."

"That's what Lodz would tell you."

"—that's because Lodz *was* one."

"—and we needed him."

"—we sure as shooting *did.*"

They almost smile.

"—surely Edward's making money?"

"Edward's *spending* money."

"—and the business?"

"—bleeding money to keep Edward and his mission alive."

"But I thought Mr. Morgan—"

"—all that money's gone."

"—on *what?*"

"Look around you. I am living in a house with seven bedrooms. Everything that Edward does is *grand.* —*grand scale.*"

"You can come to live with me in Colorado."

She hadn't smiled as much in months, even with her daughters.

"I am going to make a 'mission' of my marriage," she announced. "But it's good to know that I have somewhere else to go . . ."

He saw a glimpse of her old self in her, and smiled.

"How are the horses?" she inquired: "—still talking?"

"I'm surprised that you don't hear them, Clara."

"Perhaps some day I *will* . . ."

When she thought about it, in her final hour, that last afternoon with Hercules might have been the last time she felt young again. It would take years—another decade—for her to finally gain the courage to admit defeat, to finally realize she was beaten, that she finally had to follow the advice of Lodz and Hercules and hire an attorney, because another's life depended on her stamina to stay alive and well, just as, those many years ago, her brother had once needed her.

As a result of an abrupt and unexpected, brutal and ungentle final coupling nineteen years after their first union, Clara found that she was pregnant, yet again, at a time when her other children were old enough to be leaving home, themselves.

Edward was not present for the birth but came to visit Katherine once, when she was still an infant: and then did not see her again for eighteen years.

Once the divorce proceedings were initiated, all three of her older children turned their backs on her.

It was as if someone had taken the portrait of the three of them hanging in the chamber in her mind and turned the picture to a wall.

Their outrage toward her, for her legal action against Edward, was such that when she was awarded the Edward Curtis Studio in full, Beth contrived to steal her father's glass plate negatives and break them so their mother couldn't profit from their father's work.

When Edward was cited for contempt of court for failing to pay child support for Katherine for nine years, Clara had him arrested in the Seattle train station while he was passing through, on his way to California from Alaska.

From that day her older children, in the Curtis fashion, never spoke to her again. Stopped speaking to her, fully.

Turned their backs on her.

Still she held a distant hope that someday she might go to Colorado.

It was a fantasy, she knew—what would she do in Colorado? — she, whose passions had always been the bookish kind, who was far more at home inside the reverie attendant to a sonnet than to the outside where the panorama made her feel diminished and afraid.

So when the first police reports were sent to Beth and Florence, both of them—with Harold—concurred there must be some mistake.

Clara . . . in *a boat* . . . alone? On Puget Sound—?

This must be another case of mistaken identity.

Their mother had never rowed a boat in her life, as far as they all knew. Their *father*, on the other hand, was a renowned adventurer.

But she was not the type.

They refused to believe that she had perished in a boating accident.

Her body had not been found.

But the police described the clothes that had been bundled in a linen pillowcase and tied to the oarlock: the pillowcase had Clara's maiden name initials embroidered on its edge, and both Florence and Beth remembered dressing up in clothes from Clara's painted chest identical to those that had been found.

Still, they did not believe it. Their mother had apparently been missing for some time before the rowboat was discovered on the shore of Puget Sound seven miles from Seattle and how were they to know the letter from Denver had arrived, from Hercules's lawyer, explaining he had died, trying to save a horse from drowning in a rapids. How were they to know the comfort that their mother found in the muted sound out on the water when the mist was thick and still.

How it made the world into a concert hall where every drop of water could be heard.

How the mist reminded her of snow, and of her parents.

How the way she thought about the passage of her life had been reduced to those few moments she could count as purely joyous.

When she had realized that she loved him.

When she had filled a copper tub—that little boat—and taken off her clothes.

When Edward had appeared.

When the thought had run through her like Revelation: *stand.* Stand *up.* Stand up so he will *see* you.

She had tied the clothes that she was wearing in a bundle.

And through the mist the man she loved had called to her.

That name he had for her.

So long ago.

And once again—so proud, so free, so joyous—revelation shot through her.

And she stood up.

an american place

I wake up in my car in Vegas, in the parking lot of Sunrise Hospital, to realize I've been dreaming of the dead.

My unzipped sleeping bag is rutched around my knees, my neck is stiff and it takes a couple moments for me to realize the persistent beeping in my ear is the alarm clock that I set at three o'clock this morning to go off so I wouldn't miss my rendezvous with Lester Owns His Shadow at seven. I adopt what the yoga people ominously call the "corpse" pose and close my eyes to focus where I am and I realize I've been dreaming about people who are dead—except by dreaming them, I'd made them come alive.

Which is normal for a novelist because we dream non-living characters and animate them with our words but I'd never dreamed Red Cloud before which is probably my mind's way of processing yesterday's encounter with an Indian.

In the dream Red Cloud and I were standing at a precipice that sometimes looked like the North Rim of the Grand Canyon and other times looked like the edge of Acoma Mesa facing out across the plain. I knew who Red Cloud was in the dream because he looked exactly like the famous Curtis photograph of him, which means his head was down and his eyes were closed when he addressed me and I remember saying that he looked a lot like Dante in that pose, the way Signorelli painted him, which happens to be the portrait on the cover of the Penguin Classics version of *The Portable Dante* I found in the back of my car when I was making up this so-called bed at three a.m., left there after a Great Books discussion at a professor friend's house a couple weeks ago in Santa Monica.

How the average person dreams is pretty much how the average novelist puts a page together. Random bits of seen material float in, dismembered parts of memories, skeins of information knit and shred in contrast to their logic.

In our dreams, as in our tales, we use the dead to tell us things we'd otherwise have to admit that we are saying to ourselves.

We dream the dead in ways that serve our needs, exploiting them for our unrecognized agendas, for our investment in the continuum of history, searching for a thread by which the meaning of our lives might hang. We dream the dead to stop the hollow longing in ourselves, and there were never two more potent dreamers of the dead than Dante in his hell and Red Cloud in his Ghost Dance on the Trail of Tears. So stick that in your subconscious high hat, Zigmund, that explains it: I'm an average dreamer. I meet an Indian, I end up dreaming one the first shut-eye I get. I see a book at bedtime and hey, presto. But that hardly explains the many times I've dreamed my mother and my father, the conversations that I've held with them in dreams for decades since their deaths. *In dreams begin responsibilities.* I remember standing in the Colorado Historical Museum in Denver a couple years ago, staring at a painted hide that once had been the sacred document of a Plains tribe's winter count. The "winter count" was a tribal history, a sort of census taking, but rather than tally the living and their demographics, as our current census does, the winter count tallied how many in the tribe had died during the year and what had caused their deaths. The dead were painted as small hollow figures, their outlines waiting to be filled with detail and with tint. The empty ones had died of natural causes, but the ones filled in with red and yellow dots had died of smallpox and year after year there were more and more of them until the hide looked like a field of ocelots, overpopulated with bizarre and freckled corpses. Those were the dead that Red Cloud told his people could dance to life again through active dreaming—dance until their minds achieved a spirit level of entrancement, a wormhole through consciousness into the other world, like Dante's *purgatorio*, where the dead remained, suspended in a state awaiting their rebirth. Red Cloud promised his people that the Ghost Dance would bring back the dead—not as ghosts or zombies but *alive*, their former selves intact, the way they had been before contact with the white man. *Reunion* was the subtext of his promise—and isn't that what dreaming is, the union of our conscious with our sub-? Once or twice a year for several years after my father died I dreamed he'd visit me, knock on my door one sunny morning and tell me he'd been living in another city all these years under an assumed name and that he'd found new meaning in his life and that he was doing swell and fine and he was happy. These dreams left me feeling a burden had been lifted from my conscience—for however briefly these dreams lasted I had a sense of great relief that I didn't have to try to figure out how to keep him active in my mind, how to place him in a setting excised from reality: he was in a *city*, he was fine and swell and I'm guessing I can't be alone in dreaming death as some nearby Philadelphia, some Tampa or utopia where the departed go to take on new, improved or different lives. The necessity for Heaven—as a *place*—must be essential to our chemistry and, like water, maybe we can go without it for a while but ultimately every one of us succumbs to thirst. Every one of us must find a place to put our dead. The idea of miraculous return is an ancient one and I'm certain Uncle Freud would choke on his cigar if he found out how quick I was to pack the sleeping bag and jump into my car to find out if that "city" I had dreamed my father into, after death, was Vegas. *We are lost*, Red Cloud was saying to me when I dreamed him last night, *lost in a pathless wood. Exiled from ourselves.* This, of course, is Dante's theme in his first Canto—that he's lost in a strange place. Homesick. Exiled from his city, Florence, forcibly removed, as Red Cloud's people had been from the land they loved. Both men summoned the dead to ease the pain of their homesickness—Dante built his fictive hell in circles that resemble Florence and Red Cloud told his people to transport themselves from hell on earth through dance into a psychic, fictive history. Homesickness, in other words, is the distance that we put between who we are and who we used to be, between our present and our past. And we are lost only when we have lost our dead, when we exile them from our lives, because the city where they live is us. *I am my father's Philadelphia.* The place he went to start his second life. But somewhere there may be someone still searching for the old man upstairs, plugged into a machine to keep his real—and false—identity alive. And maybe that's the shape of the despair that Lester saw in this man's eyes—his final homesickness, as a man who's stolen someone else's shadow and has no one in whom to live when he is gone.

I get out of the car, take a deep breath and stretch my muscles, grab my ditty bag and head through Receiving to the public bathroom. Receiving has become more crowded since the middle of the night, there are more families with more kids, most of them still in their pyjamas, and when I push through the door into the Ladies there's a woman in there with a toddler outside a stall. *I'll be right here, Tiff,* she's telling the child. I lock myself inside the next stall and sit down on the toilet when Tiff says, *Mommy, close the door,* and I hear the woman pull the stall door shut. Then I think I hear Tiff ask her mother where flat daddy is and the next thing that I know a life-size cardboard head and shoulders of a grinning man in an Army uniform looms up above my stall and looks at me then bounces over like a friendly puppet to Tiff's side. This is going to make for *interesting* dream time tonight, I tell myself, and flush. If not for me, at least for Tiff.

"Sorry, did we scare you?" the mother asks as I walk by her to the sink.

"Not in the way you think." I had heard about these cut-out family members on the radio, cut-outs of service men and women missing-in-family-action, that the Army and the Guard offer to their loved ones at home, but I'd never seen an actual flat daddy doing duty. The Army's version is a full-body photograph mounted on piece of foamboard cut out along the real dimensions of the real soldier in question. But this type of artificial dad is hard to keep upright, he blows over in the wind and can't go mobile, can't travel in a car to soccer practice or McDonald's and seems ominous, standing there in uniform, at bathtime and at breakfast. The Army wants us all to call these one dimensionals FLAT SOLDIERS, but FLAT DADDIES has the cultural cachet that flat soldiers can never have. "Can I see him?" I ask and the woman holds the cardboard up so it's facing me but Tiff immediately screams, "*Gimme back flat daddy!*" Theirs is the National Guard version, a HALF FLAT, a daddy from the head down to the chest, a portable flat daddy who can be propped up in a chair at dinner and travel in the backseat of the family car when duty calls.

"Where's the real one?" I ask this woman and she mouths *Iraq*. She leans toward me and whispers, "*But we tell Tiff he's somewhere else.*"

"*Philadelphia,*" I conspire, and she looks at me real funny.

"*Reno, actually.*"

Your dad's in Reno, Dad's in Philadelphia, Dad's at work, your dad's with Teddy Roosevelt, he'll be back someday but this week he's with Red Cloud, he's learning the Ghost Dance, he's on the space shuttle and orbiting the moon. He's taken someone else's name and gone to Vegas.

Outside, I see Lester waiting for me on the lawn beside the parking lot—doing something with some sprigs of vegetation. As I watch him I call my sister from the car—*Hey, bird,* I say when she picks up.

"Where are you?"

"Vegas. I got in last night. Listen—this guy. He's not daddy."

"Well I coulda toldya. Next time you want to take a trip to Vegas, Cis, just go. Without the drama."

Lester lights the sprigs of vegetation with a lighter and waves them in the air until they start to smoke a thin blue smoke.

"Who is he, then?"

"Some poor old guy who had a heart attack. No one thinks he's going to make it, which is sad to watch. Still, he's using daddy's I.D. so I'm gonna stick around a while and try to find out how he got it."

"—and check out all the restaurants on the strip in your spare time. Check into the Bellagio."

"No, that's your *other* sister. I spent last night in my car . . . Look, I'm sorry but I gotta go. The Indian I'm with is about to tangle with Security."

"—*another* Indian? —*again* with the security?"

An obscure reference on my sister's part to my previous relationships with men.

"—ha ha," I say. "I'll callya later."

"—always an adventure," she acknowledges.

I intercept the security guard before he gets to Lester. "He's harmless, sir. I can vouch for him." I realize I look like I slept in my clothes, I don't have a spot of polish on and I'm definitely a ringer for that lady who comes to Vegas, craps out at the tables and camps out in her vehicle before going crazy. Lester, on the other hand, looks like the guy doing that weird Kevin Costner *pas seul* thing in *Dances with Wolves*.

"What's he doin'—?"

"I think it would be safe to say that he's invoking spirits, sir."

"—oh that's not good. —with *smoke?*—in front of a *hospital?*"

Lester raises both arms and starts to hum. Then he stands on one foot; holds the pose. Takes a big step forward, lifts the other foot. Repeats. And hums.

"—now what's he doin'?"

"I think it would be safe to say that what he's doin' is a little dance, sir."

"—with the *smoke. Again.*"

The smoke, and not the insurrectionary nature of the ritual, seems to be the safety issue here and the security officer isn't happy until the burning vegetation suddenly goes out. He leaves and I sit down on the ground to wait 'til Lester finishes.

"Was that a prayer?"

"Navajos don't pray."

"It looked like a prayer to me."

"People who need prayers see them."

Who does he remind me of when he talks in only aphorisms? Tonto. Maybe even Zorba.

"How's our guy?"

He shakes his head.

"Did he wake up?"

"No."

"Is he *alive*?"

He nods.

"Shall we go and look at where he lives?"

"I'll drive," he says and guides me toward his truck.

"You reminded me of Zorba back there, with the dancing. You know, Zorba the Greek—that scene in the movie when he dances by the fire on the beach. You don't have a clue what I'm talking about, do you."

"I know there is a nation called 'Greece.' Get in."

The pickup has some age and a couple areas of body work on it, and I'm reminded of Sherman Alexie's joke about how you can tell a ride that's from the rez: the only gear it works in is REVERSE. The leather seat is polished to a soft patina, a single raven feather dances from the rearview, and in the ashtray there's a half-burned cone of piñon incense, like a miniature volcano.

"Do we know how to get there?" he asks.

I take my notebook from my shoulder bag. "I Mapquested the place before I went to sleep last night. Take Maryland and then stay straight across Flamingo. It's a little street behind the University."

"Far?"

"Not far."

"I only have a quarter of a tank. Gas is so expensive off the rez! How do you people manage?"

"That's what I like about the tribal nations. No state and federal tax."

"And all the bars are right across the border."

"And the Navajo have universal health care."

"Part of our last treaty. Our own hospitals. Yes." He nods solemnly at something I can only guess at. After a brief silence I ask, "Is there a Mrs. Lester, Lester?"

"Rose. Dead seven years next Sunday. Cancer took her."

"—oh I'm sorry."

"—thank you."

I roll the window down.

"You're not married," he observes.

"No, sir."

"I don't think our mystery man is, either. I don't think we'll find a wife where we are going."

"Well I hope we find someone. Someone to remember him."

"We'll remember him."

"—not the same. Without his history he's another unknown person."

"—not true. I looked into his eyes. And saw his face." He shrugs, as if it will make the memory fit better. "Faces, eyes—take for example your Mr. Curtis and his photographs. When we look at them, we know those people. They are not forgotten."

"—not the same," I say again and I can hear the sadness in my voice. "Those photographs. Maybe without them there would be no record of those people's lives. Or there would be a different record, a more private and, therefore, diminished one. They're beautiful, his photographs. But to me they're still flat daddies."

On Lester's look I tell him to take Harmon then make another right and soon we're in a warren of untraveled narrow streets named after shore birds—Blue Heron, Egret, Swan—where the houses are called "courts" and are situated in circular formations perpendicular to the sidewalk as if they were built to accommodate guests in the style of motor courts along old Route 66. There are neighborhoods in Hollywood that look like this, blocks of row residences built by the studios to house their contract workers around a central court or meeting space like little Melrose Places. But who built these mini-houses on these mini-streets in Vegas—or why— escapes me. All the houses look alike, despite their individual decorations—a set of shutters here, a little weather vane atop an artificial vestibule.

Tipis, Lester registers as we get out.

"It should be that one over there," I say, pointing to the small house at eleven o'clock on the circle. The house beside it is the dominant house on the court, larger than the others, and as we approach we can see a ramp built to its door and connecting, by a separate boardwalk, to the door of the house we're heading for.

"Is our guy—?" I start to ask.

"—seemed fine to me, when he walked in. Before he fell. Walked fine."

I look back at the connecting house. Like all the other houses on the court its blinds are closed, no sign of life inside discernible. The place in its abandonment feels like an empty backlot movie set. Lester rings the doorbell and we hear it chime. He rings again, then opens the screen door and knocks. We wait, and nothing stirs. He tries a key from the old man's set of keys—the tumbler turns, the handle turns, and we walk in.

It's dark—not dark, but dim, the blinds are closed, and Lester

leaves the door ajar for light and we each, tentatively, call out *Hello*—?
The house is the size of a log cabin—square, divided down the middle by a central partition walling off the kitchen and the eating area to the right, from the "living" and "sleeping" ones on the left. I go toward the little dining room while Lester walks without a sound through the living room into the bedroom at the back and returns to say, "There's no one here. The bed is made."

We start to case the place, Lester shadowing me through the dining room where there's a table and four chairs and a glass-fronted hutch. Much as I claim you can't know a person's history from a photograph, I still believe the photographs a person chooses to display speak volumes, and the old man who's stolen my father's name has a gallery of Polaroids taped onto the glass panes of the hutch and onto the surrounding walls—all of them of him in a spiffy hat, white gloves and a well-pressed uniform, smiling for the camera with his arm around another person.

"He was a *doorman*," I realize. "Look at all these people—"

"—who *are* they?" Lester asks.

"—Dean Martin. Ann-Margret. Phyllis Diller. You don't recognize them—? Shecky Greene. Robert Goulet. Phyllis McGuire . . ."

I realize there's no reason why Lester should recognize these come-and-gone headliners from a culture not his own. Even I have started to forget them: "—Phyllis McGuire . . . of the McGuire Sisters? She was an It girl around Vegas years ago—Sam Giancana's mistress. Wayne Newton, you don't recognize him? Buddy Hackett. —Liza Minnelli . . . ?"

There's a goldfish bowl full gambling chips that Lester lifts to look at.

"—*tips*," I tell him. People in this town tip the hotel staff with gambling chips, and if he was working as a doorman—" I study the building in the background of a Polaroid. "I wonder what hotel he worked at?"

There are leather books stacked on the hutch, the top one reading AUTOGRAPHS. I flip it open:

Johnny—
When Opportunity Knocks
Make Sure You're the Doorman
Howard Hughes
1970

There are other autographs—Paul Anka, Barry Manilow, Liberace's signature candelabrum—four volumes' worth of brief encounters, the earliest dating from 1970, the latest, 1991.

"There's nothing here to explain how he got the headdress and the bracelet," Lester says. "Nothing at all." He drifts back into the living room, I follow. On a table next to the sofa there are boxed games—Scrabble, Monopoly—and decks of cards beside a neat row of score pads. "He must know *someone*," I comment, "you can't play Monopoly alone, that's an oxymoron . . . *Greek* word," I add for Lester's benefit, even though he's turned his back to me to investigate the shelves of paperbacks arrayed on a low bookshelf under the window. I wander to the bedroom. The bed, a standard double, is neatly made and covered with the common cotton bedspread anyone can buy at any box store. There are two standard bed tables with drawers, crowned by two bedside lamps—no pictures, nor any ornamentation, on the walls. I slide open the drawer of the nearest bedside table and discover aspirin, a tube of Rolaids and a ubiquitous

amber canister with a white plastic cap signifying a prescription. LIP-
ITOR. A STATIN, for high cholesterol, prescribed by a local doctor,
filled by a local pharmacy, for JOHN F. WIGGINS. *He even took my
father's middle initial,* I note. I close the drawer and walk around the
bed, hesitate before I open the closet but then tell myself *oh what the
hell* and do it. Two doorman long coats, one burgundy, one sky blue,
both with more brass buttons than a circus ring leader's, hang, like
curated opera costumes, in plastic bags. I lift the bag of the sky blue
one and read the words emblazoned on the buttons: THE SANDS. I
search the top shelf of the closet for some hidden clue, search the
floor behind the shoes but everything I see and touch tells me this
mystery man, although he had his secrets, kept them to himself,
dressed in regular clothes, lived in a regular house and lived an ordinary outward life.

Nothing here can tell me where he came from or who he was
before 1970. The year my father died.

Not expecting to find anything revealing, I open the one remaining drawer of the bedside table on the far side of the bed and
probably because the set-up is the same in countless hotel rooms I've
stayed in across the country I'm not surprised to see the Bible there
and almost close the drawer again until I notice that this Bible
doesn't look like the standard hardbacked version placed beside Best
Western beds by the Gideons, this Bible is worn, its leather cover
soft and pliable and in the lower right-hand corner, stamped in gold,
a name: CURTIS EDWARDS.

I take the Book and hold it in my hands. Inside the cover, fixed
to the left flyleaf with a piece of tape, dry and brittle as a shed snake-
skin, is a Teamster's Union membership card dated 1946, with a
black and white photo of a young black man, a younger version, I

recognize, of the old man in Sunrise Hospital, his face slicked with optimism under a hat barely containing his oiled wave of black hair. The card identifies the man as CURTIS EDWARDS, his employer as the PENNSYLVANIA RAILROAD, and his occupation, PORTER.

Another piece of history slips out from beneath this one—a wallet-size photograph in color, one of those ubiquitous elementary school sittings that rose to popularity in the 1950s. This one's of a boy, probably eight or ten, all grin, his adult-size teeth too big for his still child-size face, his dress shirt buttoned up to just below his adam's apple, punctuated by a black bow tie. Across the bottom of the frame, as if to prove its mug shot origins, a black banner with white letters announces, ELKTON ELEM SCHOOL—ELKTON, VIRGINIA.

Next to these two pieces of real evidence, lodged into the gutter of the Book, is a newspaper clipping, the color of toast, folded down the middle, and as I peel it open, carefully, the headline hits me,

BODY OF PENNSYLVANIA MAN
FOUND IN NATIONAL PARK.

Don't read this, races through my mind, *Stop reading this,* but my eyes, trained to a page for hours every day, speed over the words that say the body of a Pennsylvania man was discovered in the early morning hours of April 28 in Shenandoah National Park.

The cause of death was apparent suicide.

The body of the man, whose identity has not been revealed, pending notification of the surviving family, was discovered just after dawn yesterday by Mr. Curtis Edwards, a resident of Elkton.

Mr. Edwards, an employee of Pennsylvania Railroad, discovered the body on National Park lands, near the road.

Mr. Edwards, a porter on the transcontinental Pennsylvania Railroad train service, was driving home to surprise his son on his 10th birthday.

"After I called the police, I went back and waited with the body 'til they came," Mr. Edwards told this paper.

"It seemed like the right thing to do."

Mr. Edwards and his family live in Elkton.

I guess I've sat down on the bed because the next thing I realize Lester is crouching down in front of me asking, "Daughter—? Are you all right?"

I hand him the news clipping and he reads, aloud, all over again, "Body of Pennsylvania man found in national park. The body of a Pennsylvania man was discovered in the early morning hours of April 28 in Shenandoah National Park. The cause of death was apparent suicide." He seems to read the rest in silence, to himself, before he looks at me. "The 'Pennsylvania man,'" he says. "—*your father?*"

I nod, realizing, late, that he's laid a healing hand on me.

"Our guy stole my father's wallet," I say, my voice sounding, even to me, like a shadow of itself. "—why would he do that? —why would anybody do a thing like that?"

Lester's face lets me know that given who he is and where he comes from he doesn't understand why people do the things they do, but that they *do* them, *have* done them and will *continue* to act beyond the range of decent social action and that their choices are a brutal fact of life in these united states and I must learn to live with them.

There will be times—and places—for my outrage, but this isn't one of them.

"He had a son," I say and pass the picture of the boy to him. "—*has* a son," I correct myself, hoping to suggest that it's my duty, now, to try to find him.

Lester pats my knee and is about to say something when we hear the screen door slam, accompanied by a blast of angry language—is it *Spanish?* —from the living room.

Lester's on his feet, heading for the source. I hear a rapid, overlapping dialogue in two competing foreignnesses, one voice shouting at Lester in what I now recognize as Mexican Spanish and Lester speaking back in what I can only guess is Navajo.

When I appear before the two of them, still clutching the Bible, the noise arrests. Then, in English, "—*who are jou? —what are jou doin' in thees house? —where's Johnny?*"

A tiny woman weighing maybe ninety pounds, dressed in a cotton nightgown and a flannel robe, her hair still bedhead, sits in a motorized wheelchair, shoeless, one foot lividly discolored and the other one replaced by a pink prosthesis.

With one hand she operates the joystick on her wheelchair, caroming back and forth in short, small spurts, threatening Lester with a cane that she wields with her other hand, jabbing at him, repeatedly, in the chest, as he backs up, hands above his head.

"Who are *you?*" I ask.

"—*jo* Mendoza. —*jo* landlady. —how did *jou* get in here? —*where is Johnny?*"

"Miss Mendoza," I explain, "My name is Marianne. My companion's name is Lester . . ." Lester grabs the butt end of the threatening cane and just *stops* it. " . . . and yesterday Johnny . . ." (I have trouble speaking the false name): " . . . Johnny entered Lester's place of business and had a heart attack."

Miss Mendoza bites her fist.

"We let ourselves in—Lester, show her the keys—" He does. "—because we . . ."

"—hees die?"

"No."

"—hees hokay?"

"He's in Sunrise Hospital."

"—I tol' heem: 'Johnny, jou nee' home-cook. Jou nee' stop eatin' these fry stuff. Hees, how jou call, high *cholo*-steeral . . ."

"Would you like to see him?" Lester interrupts.

Miss Mendoza nods.

"We'll take you," Lester tells her.

She looks at me clutching the Bible and asks, "Are jou from church?"

Before I have a chance to answer she wheels around and heads out the door, saying, "I put dress on. Follow me."

Lester follows her, but I hold back, taking time to reexamine the display of Polaroids.

Ever since my father's death I've rehearsed a single version of how his body was discovered, how he was found, and now I try to re-create how and when that version entered my unchallenged memory.

I think my mother must have told me.

I think Mary must have told the version she remembered from the State Police. A milkman, she had said. A milkman had discovered him on his morning route through Shenandoah National Park, and for years I thought about that milkman in his milk truck on his milk route through the milky morning in the Park and how he must have felt coming on a body of a man hanging from a tree, the horror and the shock of it, and what he did that instant, if he got out of his truck right away or if he prayed and what he told his wife when he got home that night and if he had trouble falling asleep and if the image of my father gave him nightmares.

I had always felt that different waves had radiated outward from my father's death, one of them capsizing my mother, another over-whelming my sister and myself, still others touching on the lives of those who stood beneath him on that day and had to bring him down.

I think of this each time there is a circumstance that calls for the retrieval of the dead, when crews go through the parishes in the af-termath of Hurricane Katrina, when crews tunnel through remains, encrypted under the twin towers. Once the dead have entered on the world that we inhabit, once they're *here*, in front of us, how can we pretend that life and death do not exist in one continuum?

Sometimes I wonder if the milkman quit his job that morning or took a long vacation, moved to another state or went back to work next day as if nothing extra-ordinary had happened.

The degrees of separation between the milkman and myself were too few, and too intense, for me to ever exile him completely from my mind, but now, in light of what the story really was that April morn-ing the milkman version seems a fairy tale and I'm surprised I never asked myself, Who the hell *is* there to get a milk delivery in a Na-tional Park, anyway? *You*, I almost say out loud, touching my finger to an image of Mr. Edwards in his doorman uniform, *you're* the man that I've been looking for. And maybe if we're lucky, you'll recover from this incident, regain consciousness so we can talk.

Because life just throws those miracles our way, doesn't it?

I take two Polaroids—the ones with Ann-Margret and Dean

Martin—and slip them inside the Bible just as Lester presses his head against the screen outside and says, "You need to see this. Right away."

I follow him along the ramp to Miss Mendoza's door, at which he steps aside to let me enter, and my initial response is, "What *is* this place?"

A *museum*, it appears.

The layout is the same as in the former house, but larger, the walls have been pushed back but the relative dimensions are identical. In the living room, to the left, low bookshelves skirt the perimeter, every inch of shelf space filled with artifacts—Kachina dolls, reed baskets, clay pipes, beaded bags, black and red clay pottery, drums, carved fetishes. They radiate an inner life, each one of them, and the temptation is to take each treasure in hand—to touch—which may explain why the only times I've seen such items on display there's a protective pane of glass between me and their powerful attraction.

On the floor and draped over the sofa are hand-woven rugs emblazoned in the geometric patterns of the Plains tribes, and in the center of the longest wall two beaded buckskin dresses hang from a carved pole festooned with leather fringe and feathers.

But what captures my gaze is the array, on every wall, living room and dining room, of framed black-and-white and gold-toned photographs.

These are *Curtises*, I breathe.

Not gravures, which are as common as salt and cheap to manufacture, over-produced by galleries for the gullible at a couple hundred dollars a pop. No, these are *originals*, hand tinted prints from Curtis's glass plates, worth—I'm guessing—tens of thousands of dollars each.

Miss Mendoza zooms around the dining table, a coffee pot in hand, and tells us, "I don' change a thin' in here from time that I inherit"

"—you *inherited* all this?"

"This house, the one next door."

Lester draws the bracelet and the headdress from his shoulder bag and sets them on the table. "I believe these must belong to you."

She nods.

"Every now an' then I sen' Johnny out to sell some thin's. When I need money."

"My father made this bracelet," Lester tells her. He shows her the jeweler's mark that matches the twin one on his forearm.

"Then jou mus' keep it."

"Please, Miss Mendoza—"

"—Clarita."

"Clarita. I don't think you understand what this is worth."

"—plenty more where it comes from."

"But Miss Mendoza—" I begin.

"—Clarita."

"Clarita. I'm no expert, but—"

"—you're sitting on a fortune," Lester volunteers.

"How did you—where did all this come from?" I ask her.

"—was Tio Rico's. With *el jefe*. They live here."

"—*el jefe?*"

"Tio 'Uardo. They were, jou know, how jou say—?"

She crosses two fingers of one hand in front of us.

"—*tight?*" I guess.

"—mens. *Two* mens. Tio Rico, hees my mother's brother, she live over there, in the house I rent to Johnny. Her house, with me, after I am born. She cook an' clean for thees house, an' for all other house." She draws a circle around the outside court with her outstretched hand. "She clean for all the boys."

"—the boys?"

"Jou know—nightclub boys. Dancers. Very nice."

I look out the window at the gingerbread fronts of the little houses on the courtyard and reason this was quite the community, in its *hey* day.

"But that doesn't explain where all this—"

"It was *jefe*'s. Tio 'Uardo's."

"*Ed*-uardo?"

"—*si.*"

"Do you have a picture of this *Eduardo*?"

She takes a scrapbook from the top drawer of the breakfront.

"Help *jourselve*. *Chicita* in the picture, she is me. Beautiful lady— Lupe, *madre mio*. Handsome man—Enrico, *tio*. Other man in how jou say *las gafas*—glasses?—that one ees Eduardo." She points the wheelchair toward the living room. "I go get dress."

She goes, and Lester and I page through the scrapbook. Someone kept it with a persnickety archival diligence and an unintentional comic flair for writing. "The Lovely Lupe in Her Floral Apron with Carne Asada" reads the caption under one snapshot of an attractive young woman posing with a platter of food decades ago in this very dining room. "Enrico, *El Toreador!*" reads the quip beneath another picture of a handsome young Mexican man, shirtless, with a pair of garden shears outside this very house. There are pictures of groups of men assembled at an outdoor party in the court—pictures of what appear to be camping expeditions in the desert—pictures of a tent beside a stream where some sort of gold-extraction apparatus had been set up—pictures taken in the bare Nevada mountains—and then a picture whose caption reads, "Our First Gold Nugget," where the handsome Mexican man holds a nugget of gold in his palm while he stares into the eyes of an older man in glasses, who stares back at him, adoringly. This is followed by a number of pictures taken through the years where the two men, never actually touching, pose in such a way, unguarded, that one, even after all these years, can hardly fail to sense their erotic charge nor fail to see that they're in love.

"—*Curtis?*" Lester asks.

I nod.

"'The Missing Years,'" I can't help saying, fondly.

"You aren't surprised?"

"I might have guessed. But I never saw the evidence. These pictures were taken in the 1930's, 40's. Something must have changed between Edward and Enrico."

"Maybe Enrico died . . ."

" . . . because in the late 40's he went back to California to be with his four kids."

"Maybe he missed them."

"He had never missed them before."

I recall the photograph of Edward I had found where he's posing with his children, the only one that I could find in which he's halfway smiling. Beth is in an eye-popping apron, Florence in an artless off-the-rack frock, and only Katherine and Harold look as if they dressed expecting there might be someone with a camera present. Edward, out of character, looks disheveled, down at heel, as if his diminishing eyesight is finally taking its toll on his ability to see a bright horizon. *This is us when we are happy* the photograph is meant to say. But when I think of Edward in that picture, I have to say I'm not convinced.

Clarita reappears—dressed, her hair combed—and tells us she is ready.

"Clarita," I ask. "Did Enrico die?"

"—sure, I already tol' jou he is die."

"No, I mean: why did Eduardo leave these things behind?"

" . . . worth a fortune," Lester adds.

"He leave them for Enrico."

"Enrico was still alive when Eduardo left?"

"*Si*—he go. Like that." She snaps her fingers. "—break Enrico, in hees heart."

"He left his wife in the same way." I snap my fingers.

"—he has wife?"

"—and four children."

"I don' understan'," she says.

I look at the pictures of Edward and Enrico again, *This* is us, they say, when we *are* happy.

But it was the 40s.

And he had once had the admiration and respect of Theodore Roosevelt and J.P. Morgan.

And he was working on his memoirs.

As ever, he was working on his MYTH.

When you've immortalized great chiefs of state, tribal chiefs and Presidents, when you've broken bread with Red Cloud, T.R. and Geronimo, what does your private life have to do with the way you want your name to be remembered?

In his own mind he was CURTIS, the signature—E.S.C., the monogram—and who on earth would care, in the gristmill of posterity, if the only thing it said on his gravestone were the two words, LOVING FATHER?

Lester tells Clarita there will be wheelchairs at the hospital and he offers to carry her to the truck but she insists on going in her *moto* because she doesn't like to "be push," and within minutes we're on the road, the two of them chatting up a storm in the front cab while I hold onto the wheelchair with both hands to keep it from rolling all around the flatbed of the truck, my hair flapping in my face as we speed along under the now predictably scorching Vegas sun.

I go inside with them so I can show the I.D. that we found to the nurse at the nurse's station on the cardiac floor and then while Clarita sits beside "Johnny's" bed I tell Lester I'm going to check into a hotel to work the phone and Internet to try to locate Curtis Edward's son before the weekend starts and places of information, like schools and businesses, shut down.

I give him my cell phone number and he agrees to call me later and in half an hour I'm standing in the middle of my own loft suite at the Alexis, an off-Strip hotel across the street from the Hard Rock but far enough away from the noise to guarantee some quiet. I draw a hot bath then get down to work checking the online White Pages for Elkton, Virginia, and then Mapquest to find out where the hell Elkton, Virginia, *is*. There are four Edwardses listed in Elkton and after I have my bath I call them all, asking in my best non-threatening I'm-a-nice-person voice if any of them are missing an old man named Curtis.

Not one.

If the son was ten years old in 1970, as the article says he was, he would have graduated high school in '76 or '77 so I dial Elkton

Regional High and ask to speak to someone who can help me trace a graduate, owing to a "family emergency." I get a really nice sounding lady who digs out yearbooks for those years and finds a Curtis Edwards, Jr., in the senior class of 1977.

"Would you happen to know if he went on to college after high school?"

She asks me to hang on a while and then she comes back and says they don't keep those kinds of records but that someone in the office remembers Curtis Edwards, Jr., and would I like to speak to her. I say I would and then a second nice sounding lady comes on the line and tells me she doesn't remember Curtis, Jr., himself, but she remembers he was well known in the town because he got written up in the local paper when he won a scholarship to the Air Force Academy "out there in Colorado."

I call Colorado Springs and ask to speak to the press office and tell the young man on the other end my tale ("family emergency") and after some time he's able to confirm that Curtis Edwards, Jr., graduated the Academy in June 1981.

"Is there any chance that you can tell me his address?"

"No, ma'am."

"The town he lives in?"

" 'Fraid not."

"Because of Homeland Security?"

"Because, I think, of the Constitution."

"Can you say if he's active or retired?"

"I can say that he's on active duty, ma'am."

"Can you tell me where?"

"No, ma'am."

"Can you tell me his rank?"

"Ma'am, why would you want to know *his rank?*"

I take a breath. Sir, I say: "I'm trying to find a man whose father has had a serious heart attack and may not make it through the weekend. This man's last name is Edwards. Aside from having an entire Air Force Base named Edwards, how many Edwardses do you think you might have on active duty? Ten, fifteen? Twenty? If I knew this gentleman's rank it would—"

"That would be a colonel, ma'am."

I Google Col. Curtis Edwards, Jr., and come up with nothing. I order lunch.

I think about how to find a colonel in a haystack, and then when my room service arrives it dawns on me to call Nellis Air Force Base right here in Vegas a couple miles away and ask to speak to a public relations liaison. Which I do, while sitting on the bed, picking at my thirty dollar salad. My call is passed from one department to another and while I wait I doodle the colonel's last name on the hotel notepad, followed by his first name. Then I draw two lines and stare:

EDWARD /S/, CURTIS

"How can I help you, ma'am?"

I explain the story (leaving out my personal involvement) to a man who says he's the public relations officer and then he asks if he can call me back after he relays my story to Personnel and I tell him no, I'd rather hold. After a while another person comes on the line and says, "I understand you'd like to speak to Colonel Curtis?"

"Yes, please. It's a family emergency."

"Please hold while I connect you—"

Are you kidding me? Is this a *trick*—?

"Colonel Curtis's office."

Um . . .

"—hello?"

Sounding like a prattling fool, even to myself, I give my name, my occupation, my nine-digit Social (am I *paranoid?*), my cell phone number and a brief description of the reason for my call ("I have information pertaining to the current whereabouts of his father") and am told with icy dispatch that my message will be passed on to the Colonel.

I put my cell phone down and stare at it because as everybody knows, that will make it ring.

Ten minutes go by, while I eat my salad. Fifteen.

Guy probably has a busy schedule.

Flying planes around.

Maybe, god forbid, he's in Iraq.

I pace, and think of other things I could be doing. I didn't handle this well. I should have left the number of the hospital. The important thing is not for *me* to talk to the Colonel but for the Colonel to talk to his father. But what if he doesn't want to? What if, after thirty years, he's made up a story in his mind about why his father disappeared, a tale that permits him to forgive or to accept the fact? Why would he want to hear a different tale—a counter-story—at this point in his life? We tell ourselves the things we *want* to hear, not necessarily the things that are the truth, and it's selfish of me to want to know what story the Colonel has manufactured for himself in the name of mental health.

Or what story Clara Curtis or any woman, for that matter, married to a man with more than one sexual identity manages to tell herself on those dark nights when the unspoken truth must be too obvious.

I don't love you.

Or perhaps I love you but I love someone else as well.

I love another way of being and this life is killing me by inches and I need to get away from here or die.

What did the Curtis children—Harold, Florence, Beth and Katherine—think about their father's disappearances? I know the stories that they told themselves had at their core a classic mythic entity—a larger-than-life Father, the Father as a Hero. I know they created for themselves the story of a spiritual antithesis, even if it wasn't true, of what a modern kid might do, of a false deity, a modern day Flat Daddy. For the Curtis children *el jefe*, the Chief, could do no wrong, even when *wrong* was all that he was doing. So I wonder how it was for this Air Force Colonel, and yes my self-investment drives my curiosity because I had to do a lot of magical explaining to myself in the years after my father's suicide and I'm frankly curious about how others—we, generic humans, as a *tribe*—create whatever stories that we need to just so we can *cope*.

At four o'clock my cell phone finally rings and it's Lester calling from the pay phone by the nurse's station to say that things aren't looking good.

"Heart function," he attempts to fathom as he speaks: "They're saying that he doesn't have enough."

"Where's Clarita?"

"She's here. I'm going to take her home. Then I'll come back and stay with him again tonight."

I tell him that I think I've found the son.

"That would be the miracle. To see the two united. I'll go tell the old one not to die just yet."

I call the general number for Nellis Air Force Base again and ask for Colonel Curtis Edwards. I get an answering machine with a female secretary's voice and this time the message I leave is a winner for its clarity and precision—I identify myself and say the Colonel's father is dying in cardiac intensive care at Sunrise Hospital in Las Vegas and leave that number.

Done.

Tomorrow I'll go home.

I walk up to the Strip and lose myself in the crowd, trek all the way to the Venetian for the kitsch pleasure of *prosecco* by the fake canal, then wander back down to the not-so-hip Mon Ami Gabi at the Paris for an early dinner of *moules frites* where I can sit street-side on the Strip and watch the crowd and catch the water show at the Bellagio across the street.

By ten o'clock I'm back in bed at the Alexis, sound asleep, too exhausted to even dream, because that's just the kind of Vegas party animal I am.

At six forty-five a.m. my cell phone rings. CALLER I.D. BLOCKED. A resonant male voice. *Am I speaking to Miss Wiggins?*

"You are."

"This is Colonel Edwards of the United States Air Force."

And I guess I *did* dream, I dreamed the speech that I would make to him if he called back because I find myself sitting up in bed and reciting a coherent argument for him to meet with me.

I tell him that two days ago I had received an unexpected call, myself, from Sunrise Hospital in Las Vegas claiming that my father had suffered a possibly fatal heart attack.

"My father died on April 28, 1970, in Shenandoah National Park, Virginia. A date and place you might remember," I say.

In the absence of a response I tell him the hospital representative had told me that the man in Sunrise Hospital had convincing documents to identify him as my father so I had driven from Los Angeles to Las Vegas to see him for myself.

"Events have proven that the man is, in fact, *your* father and that he adopted my father's name after finding his body in the Park that April morning." On his continued silence I ask, "Have you called the hospital yet, sir, as I previously suggested?"

I wait through another silence and then say, "I found your father's Bible at his residence, sir, with your boyhood picture and I'd like to hand these over to you if you—"

"Am I to understand from this that you're still in Las Vegas?"

"Yes, sir. If you'd like to meet I—"

"—in my office."

"I could be there in an hour."

"I'll instruct the Gate."

For a civilian, the combined terrain of Nellis Air Force Base and Range is as frightening a place as an orphaned foreign country under military occupation, or as segregated from the mainstream nation as the Sioux, Arapahoe or Apache were meant to be, on reservations. Maybe all our military bases are as tightly sealed as this one, but I doubt it, because with her multiple locations around Vegas, Nellie holds a record in land size as well as the questionable honor of having surrounded the nation's official Atomic Testing Site throughout the 50s and into the next decade, and if you approach the Bombing and Gunnery Range from Tonopah, from the north, on Nevada Route 95, you begin to see the twisted logic of our government's program of enlightened land use: there is just plain nothing else that could have been done with this godawful land so why not bomb the hell out of it and strafe it all to kingdom come.

When we were still marketing aboveground nuclear testing as NOT DANGEROUS TO YOUR HEALTH and a dandy source of pyrotechnic entertainment for your neighborhood, the flyboys out at Nellis used to post the bombing schedule in the local papers so Vegas denizens could power up the briquettes in their backyard barbecues and get out the lawn chairs for a little bit of awesome fireworks courtesy of uncle sam. The last time we blew something up at Nellie, albeit underground, was 1991 and I suppose there may be some conspiracy theorists out here who might notice that that was around the time the Vegas Strip started going pyro- and hydrotechnic in its own way with crowd-pleasing sidewalk shows.

The Gunnery Range is still a hotbed of half-life particles and conspiracy speculation but the Base, where Nellie's personnel are quartered, is tucked behind Sunrise Mountain, a twenty minute drive from the Strip, straight up Las Vegas Boulevard—and its entry regimen in these days of heightened Homeland Security is no laughing matter.

A smile will get you nowhere in this atmosphere.

Granted, I'm used to looser "secure" venues—even on the Sony lot or at Universal I have to show a photo I.D. to get through the gate and when I went for jury duty last month at the Van Nuys Court House in the San Fernando Valley I had to show *two* pieces of identification and have my bag X-rayed and walk through a microwave (just kidding). Rather than increasing my assurance in my safety these procedures make me feel the opposite of *safe*, they make me feel more vulnerable, less saved from *what*, exactly? From *what* exactly are these procedures designed to save me? *Pull over to the side and step out of your vehicle, ma'am, please,* I'm told at Nellie's super-fortified Gate. I *smile* and say I'm here to see the Colonel. A German shepherd on a tight rein has some olfactory fun around my Michelins and two guys in white helmets and combat gear go over every inch of my car's interior while another guy in a bulletproof vest investigates the undercarriage of my PT Cruiser with a tilted mirror on a stick. *That* makes me feel safe. A *mirror.* A device I use in my own bathroom. To tweeze my eyebrows.

A rectangular piece of plastic with the letter F is placed on my dashboard, the letter showing through the windshield, and I'm told to drive to the next checkpoint, several hundred feet away, and hand the piece of plastic to the MP there. He gives me another piece of plastic with the letter G on it and directs me to turn right, toward a parking lot about a quarter of a mile away down a well-patrolled thoroughfare, where I'm asked to show my photo I.D. again and then instructed where to park and where to enter the nondescript cement building straight ahead.

After a bag X-ray, a body screening followed by a full bag search in which every item in my bag is scrutinized, including the Bible, I'm directed toward a reception desk and then a woman in an Air Force blouse and skirt comes to get me and leads me down a gray-carpeted hallway to a closed door. She knocks, discreetly, twice, opens the door and I find myself in a large office, tastefully appointed in the Spartan manner, face to face with a tall fit man in his mid-forties who I can only conclude must be the Colonel.

My experience with military men above a certain rank is that they are very *clean,* almost impeccably clean in their comportment, as if training for the possibility that they might have to *kill* someone or at least order others to that duty, has had a compensatory effect of demanding of them unwarranted but perfect manners so before the Colonel can begin to charm me with his sugared brass I draw out the picture of him in elementary school and hand it to him with the Bible. *This is how I found you,* I explain. He takes these from me and points me toward a chair facing his desk. There's a sofa and two armchairs in the near corner of his office but he directs me, instead, to a place where his large desk will be between us. I slide the Polaroids of his father with Ann-Margret and Dean Martin across the surface and tell him, "There are more like these." I watch him read the newspaper clipping in the Bible and look at the photographs. I watch him as he starts to piece years and this new knowledge together and at a certain point, through his ensuing silence, I begin to feel that watching him invades the privacy he needs at such a moment so I look away. I let my gaze travel over the things he's chosen to display: *Maps.* There are maps on all four walls, framed topographical projections of the Earth, three dozen of them, with detailed isometrical pictographs and color washes defining rising elevations, mountains, ridges, canyons, flats in smooth concentric circles—maps drawn looking down on earth from somewhere high up in the air—and I'm reminded that this man across from me, by the very nature of his job, has seen the Earth in ways, at heights and speeds, that Da Vinci only dreamed of.

The Colonel breaks his revery by reaching behind him to a bookshelf and bringing forth a twelve-inch plastic model of a dark green painted helicopter transport with two rotors, the kind I recognize from the Wagnerian beach scene with Robert Duvall in *Apocalypse Now.*

"It was my birthday," the Colonel says. "I was ten years old." He spins one of the little model's rotors with a finger." . . . and I loved making model airplanes."

He looks at me.

"Pop had gone to F.A.O. Schwartz—that famous toy store in New York. To buy me this. And he'd been driving all night, straight back from New York City, to bring it home for me, in Virginia, as a surprise. It's an Apache," he explains.

"The rotors move."

He demonstrates.

A long silence passes between us. And then I have to ask, "—what *happened?*"

The Colonel, elegant, almost, in his controlled composure, shakes his head, as if to shake the question.

"He was in the house when I got home from school. What a great thing, for a boy. To have his father home, I have to tell you. Pop worked for the railroad on the coast-to-coast service, kept him away from home, on the job, sometimes, two, three, four weeks at a time. But those were great, great days, the ones when he was home. Nothing like it. He didn't have to do a thing—he could be sleeping in the hammock—the house was *lit* when he was there. Mother was all lighted up. But that day—something was wrong about it, not the same. He gave me my present and we ate my birthday cake but there was a thing unspoken, some thing I couldn't understand. I remember I stayed up late, working on this model. And I knew he was sitting in the kitchen, all alone. That night, and then the next. I could hear him. Two days later he was gone."

We stare at each other.

"I was a kid," he says, "I thought he had gone back to work. On the rails." He makes a pyramid with his hands and leans back in his chair. "When I figured out he wasn't coming back I gave my mother a hard time, went on for years. God bless her."

"I did the same. These dads who disappear get away with—"

"She died in 1982."

"I'm sorry."

"—saw me graduate. I brought her out to the Academy. That's when we finally had the *Talk*."

He looks at me again with something urgent in his eyes that makes me hold my breath.

"Do you know—can you *imagine*—what it must have been like for a black man of my father's generation to be driving home one morning on a lonely road down South and find somebody hanging from a tree?"

I feel the room grow small around me.

"That is a black man's nightmare. *Lynching*," he enunciates.

I hold his gaze.

"She told me Pop came home that day and told her what he'd seen. How he'd seen a car parked on the road and stopped to see if someone needed help. Got out of his car. And saw . . ."

Please don't say this, I am thinking.

" . . . a man. Hanging there. And . . ."

Shut up. Stop speaking now.

" . . . his legs were kicking."

I close my eyes.

" . . . his legs were kicking and my father told my mother that he only stood there. He couldn't move. He stood there. Couldn't save him . . . and he didn't know how he could live with that."

We sit together for a while in silence.

"Our fathers . . ." I begin to say, but stop. "He left you for thirty years."

"—and your father *didn't?*"

"How did you . . . what reason did you give for him?"

"What reason did *you* give?"

We wait the question out in silence.

"Didn't you ever ask yourself . . . *why?*" I finally ask. "I mean: he left. Your father *left*. You and your mother. Weren't you tempted to wonder if they were ever happy? —your parents?"

"—what does it matter?"

"I think it matters."

"I think if you think it matters: then, sure. What choice do you have, but to convince yourself that they were happy?"

"Your father still wears his wedding band."

The Colonel holds his eyes closed a few seconds, then he opens them.

"What was he *doing* there?"

"—my father?"

"—from Pennsylvania. What was he doing *there?* In Virginia. In the Park."

He liked to drive, I try to explain. It helped him think. "He went there once. With my mother. They went there on their honeymoon."

When they were happy, I almost add.

He stares at the model helicopter.

"Will you go to see him?"

"Pop—?"

Imperceptibly, he nods.

"I drew a map, in case."

I hand it to him.

"—you drew *me* a map."

"To the hospital. To show which entrance you should take."

"—but you drew *me* a map," he repeats and, for whatever reason, my drawing makes him smile, and that smile, I see, is dazzling.

I get there before him to find that Lester isn't waiting in the hall, so I slip inside the room where Curtis Edwards lies, not so much to see him or to commune with him in any way, but to see if Lester's with him.

But once inside the room I'm captured by the silent reverence, a sanctity around his body. How small he is. I hadn't noticed his frailty when I first looked at him a day ago—perhaps because I hadn't seen the pictures of his former self, robust and smiling for the camera, the shadow of his son's smile, I recollect. But now the man who made his son light up seems but a shadow, too, a frost of white beard, dusting of fresh snow, across his chin, his blood blue beneath his skin, his lips and fingers fringed in indigo. He is barely breathing and it takes a conscious effort on my part to convince myself that beneath his eyelids there is life. I stand and gaze at him awhile before I realize someone's watching me from across the room and turn to see Lester in a chair beside the windows on the far side of the second, vacant, bed, so still he's almost invisible. I go to stand beside him.

"Have you been here all night?"

He nods.

I touch his shoulder.

"You've done a good thing."

"So have you," he says and inclines his head to point in the direction of the door.

The Colonel has come in.

I had not intended to be present at the moment when the Colonel sees his father but now Lester and I are trapped by the choreography of circumstance and we both freeze, stop breathing, as the Colonel's gaze barely acknowledges us before focusing on the body of his father.

The Colonel has put on a jacket since our meeting in his office, he's in full dress uniform, and I can't help noticing his shoes, those military-issue shoes that always look too shiny for normal use. At over six feet tall he seems to take up all the space beside the bed and he stands at what I have to call ATTENTION for what seems like several minutes until, slowly, I see his edges blur, his sharpness soften like an image in a camera lens deliquescing out of focus.

"Pop—?" he carefully whispers.

Leaning in to look at him, he places both his hands on his father's legs beneath the blanket.

"Pop, what did you do?"

He waits, as if for an answer.

"What did you do with your life?"

He drops his head as if in search of something in himself and then he goes and gently takes his father's hand in his and I have to close my eyes. Because this is the moment, in the nation where I live, where we've become conditioned to expect the unrealistic ending, the Happy one, where, if this were a movie that my nation routinely makes, the father would return to life, respond, squeeze his son's hand in his, wake up and reconcile their shattered past, but when I open my eyes again the Colonel is still there, his hand around his father's unresponsive one, his act of touch a one-way communication, like a prayer, or like looking at a photograph, as empty or as full as visiting a grave. There is only ever one answer to the question *what did you do with your life,* and it's the same—fleeting and unknowable—for every one of us.

I lived.

the shadow catcher

B efore the Train, the grasslands teemed with herds of buffalo so thick and mythic in their numbers it was said that when they ran they ran as thunder raining on the earth. The men who hunted them could hear them coming miles away, could feel the ground around them shake and rumble with their roar as they barreled past, and maybe that's the sound I think I hear inside a train, the sound of animals, a sound the living earth once made, a plaint, the sound of history's demand to be remembered.

Or maybe I just love the sound the whistle makes, that twisted chord, rooted in C major or B minor but ranging, concordantly, some nights, to the uncharted note of the undiluted wanderlust that springs from sadness.

This is, singularly, a North American note, a U.S. of A. site-specific sound.

European trains sound like audible Twinkies, air-infused and artificial.

But an *American*, running like an unchained herd of half-a-ton horned animals across a plain, well, my friend, that's show biz, rock 'n' roll and jazz and ska and rap and Beat and MGM all tied into one:

The sound my nation makes.

And I can tell that Lester is trying to keep me from the road because he keeps bringing up new subjects for discussion.

"My daughter's coming home tomorrow."

"Lucky you," I say. "I'd like to meet her."

I'm already in the driver seat and he's standing by the passenger side, in the hospital parking lot. He hands me a business card from his daughter's craft cooperative through the open sunroof.

"I'll take her to Clarita's. Catalogue what's there. She can give Clarita good advice." He looks off to the horizon, then continues: "I was supposed to go out to the Paiute reservation this afternoon. See some craft people there. But I'll go see Clarita, too. She's upset there won't be any funeral."

"Colonel's decision, Lester."

"I know . . ."

He hands me another card on which he's written his mailing address and phone number.

"You should come and visit. Maybe in the spring. At shearing."

I blush because I realize I've never asked him what he does, how he makes a living, I had committed the classic Anglo thing, consigning Lester to the job of being Indian, as if his race were his profession.

"I farm sheep."

"—of *course* you do." What better *shepherd* do I know? "I'm great with sheep," I lie.

He sees right through me, I can tell, because next he says, "You'll have to change the book."

I'm not sure what he means until he adds, "The truth about your Mr. Curtis."

"*'Print the legend.'*" I recite.

"Truth is better."

"—*whose?*"

He nods in recognition and then tells me, "Some things are not open to interpretation."

"A person's life, Lester."

"What were these fellows looking for, do you think?"

By "fellows" I guess he means Curtis and Edwards.

But he may also mean my father.

"I don't know. Are you going to try to tell me they were searching for the Truth?"

He shakes his head.

"I think it's impossible to know another person's motives. Practically impossible to really know our own," I tell him.

"Maybe," he concedes. "When you come to my place I'll take you to see the Lands. And then you'll make a Vision Quest."

"That is something that I promise we will do," I pledge.

He sets a bundle wrapped in newsprint on the seat beside me.

"Medicine smoke. Branches from the land I live on. Find some place on your journey home and stop. And set these leaves on fire. Some place where you can be reminded of your friend. And of our friendship."

The packet has already perfumed my car with piñon, sage and mesquite, and as I head out for the road I'm enveloped in an incense that evokes a certain kind of West, high desert, the West made famous by the movies—Red Rock, Monument Valley—Navajo Land.

It's a land best wedded to the buffalo, not cattle, where sheep and goats can scratch a bare subsistence from the scrappy brush but where man's soul is better fed than his stomach. In parts, the wind can rip a person into shreds and finding shelter from one element can only leave you open to another—lightning, hail, snake, bear, sun, vulture, cougar. The Navajo named their clans for what could kill them.

And the only terrorists they knew wore hats, rode horses.

Safety was in numbers, the Navajo larger than the populations of the tribes around them, but safety came with ritual, as well, in knowing one was part of a cohering pattern, part of something greater than oneself. A renegade was truly that, a broken thread, an anomaly outside the unifying fabric. Each man would leave the tribe on his vision quest at the beginning of adulthood, only to return, again, as part of the tribe, once he had experienced the vision, specific to himself, of his spiritual identity. Armed with nothing but his wits and pride and a crude weapon, a boy began the journey that could last a week, a month or half a year. When he returned, he was a man. Or so Legend has it, because whether you were living before 1492 or after the atomic bomb, if you're going to understand your part in the fabric of Earth's life, then you have to take your quest for understanding to the source and live on earth as if your life depended on it—on its air, its water, its futurity.

CURTIS EDWARDS DIED THIS MORNING IN THE PRESENCE OF HIS SON.

That's why Lester gave these branches to me—to perform a ritual, the ritual of cleansing fire, the spirit medicine of smoke.

And there are plenty of places on this route out of Nevada— there's nothing here *but* place—where I could pull off down a dusty road to find a quiet spot, but as I head West for California on the highway running next to the Union Pacific tracks, it occurs to me that, for a good portion of his life, before that fateful morning in the Shenandoah National Park, Curtis Edwards was a porter, working for The Road, riding rails. He was a *train* man.

Head for *Barstow*, I tell myself.

If he had been working the transcontinental passenger line, chances are he would have passed through Barstow one way or another, it would have been a place he would have known.

I don't stop at Baker, don't stop at The Mad Greek, press on another hundred miles and exit I-15 at Route 66. The sun has just passed its apogee, tilting toward the West and there are hardly any shadows on the desolate Main Street to soften its appearance of stark and blasted bankruptcy.

A couple bars and resale stores are open but most buildings are vacant, either out of business or going and the feeling on this stretch of 66 down to the railroad yard is one of failure and foreclosure.

A trainyard without moving trains is certainly a sad and haunting place and I realize as I park the car that what thrills me about trains is not their size or their equipment but the fact that they are *moving*, that they embody a connection between unseen places. A train at rest is just another big machine but a train moving through a landscape is a process, and it carries with it all the mystery of journey, like a promise.

There are a couple stranded engines on the sidings, but instead of moving trains what the Barstow station has this afternoon are buses, two of them with Mojave Sun Country Tours written on their sides, disgorging tourists of the most obsessive kind, the ones who'll go to any length to photograph a Harvey House or a red caboose.

There are too many people here for me to carry out a ritual so I leave the packet on the seat and make my way around the tourists on the platform, down, onto the tracks.

When I'm out in the Dakotas or in places like Marathon, Texas, where the main streets of the towns have only one side and the train tracks run like a parallel street past the buildings, my favorite two games to play are Fry the Penny and Catch the Vanishing. I don't know whether it's the heat, the weight or the speed of the passing train that fries the penny I put down on the track but that damn coin comes out looking like it's been to hell and back. Catch the Vanishing is an exercise of hide and seek, and one I can do anywhere with a flat unbroken view of the horizon, but it's at its best on a train track because of the illusion that the vanishing point—toward which one can walk forever but never *catch*—is the point of union where two lines come together, join, as if the past might unite, somewhere, with the future. I look West down the long rail now to a point where it seems to disappear and think of Curtis Edwards, and of Edward Curtis, too. Edward Curtis thought the Indians were vanishing—he called them The Vanishing Race. He based most of his conclusions on that error of fact and photographed them with a false solemnity appropriate to his belief that they were expiring in front of him. That's part of why he made them look so beautiful—it was his funerary legacy to them. We think today that his accomplishment was to have captured all their faces in the midst of life, but, really, he believed that he was making images of people on the brink of their extinction, capturing them in death, at a moment when they were passing from one way of being to non-.

As the Colonel watched his father pass this morning.

For reasons that only a bureaucratic mind could understand, both he and I, as the deputed closest living relative on record, had to sign the hospital paperwork after Curtis Edwards died.

We waited in the corridor together.

"Can I ask you something—?" I began. "Do you ever dream you're flying?"

"—doesn't everybody?"

"—no, I mean: you really *fly*. So I wonder if your dreams are different from, say, someone else's. Your father, for instance. Do you think your father ever dreamed that he was flying?"

He stared at me.

"That's not what you want to know."

"—it *is*. Because sometimes I dream I'm flying in across the whole United States . . ."

"That's not what you want to *know*," he said again. "You don't want to know if *I* dream of flying."

"—no, I really do, I—"

"Your father hung himself. You want to know what *he* was dreaming, when he jumped."

When the papers came for us to sign I watched the Colonel tick the box for CREMATION on the form that designated where the hospital should send the body.

"I think that's best, under the circumstances, don't you?" he asked.

I couldn't answer.

"I don't see him lying in the ground beside my mother for eternity."

"What are you going to —What will you do with the ashes?"

"I figured I would take him *up*."

He pointed.

"—in a small plane. Or a chopper. Like the one he gave me."

"Where will you—?"

"I was thinking over railroad tracks. Or maybe over here, over Las Vegas. We lived here, fifteen years, within miles of each another, and never knew it. I guess I will decide when I get up there. Want to come?"

Maybe I should wait to enact the Indian ritual until I go back to Vegas when the Colonel and I release his father's ashes into the atmosphere but standing here in Barstow on the train tracks I have another idea about what to do with Lester's medicine smoke.

Forest Lawn.

They close the gates at sunset so I drive as if on a vision quest, stopping only once, for gas, and hit the Glendale exit while the sun is still high enough to burnish this California town with bold strokes of gold.

No one stops me to check my I.D. at the gate, no one asks to look inside my car, the security for visiting the dead is non-existent and I encounter no other cars as I wind my way, slowly, up the carefully landscaped road to where I know he is, by memory, surrounded by Harold, Florence, Beth and Katherine under a stately Norfolk pine.

I take Lester's packet and rummage for matches in the earthquake kit I keep in my car, then I go to sit beside his grave to start this ritual.

Pine needles and other debris have gathered on the nameplate set into the earth, littering his name LOVING FATHER, and as I clean the litter with my hands I speak to him, *You're going to like the smell of this, old man, you're going to be reminded of those places you lit out to.*

They want to make a movie about you—set you out there on a horse against the wild. I bet you'd like to shoot it, wouldn't you? All those beauty shots. And yet not once in your life did you ever photograph an Indian when he or she was laughing, eating, embracing, kissing—not once in your whole life did you ever photograph them all as if to say, *This is who we were, and we were happy.*

I peel back a bit of newspaper and take a few dry leaves and rub them in my hands, releasing the aroma of wet clay, baked earth, the green heart of fragrant growth buried in a desiccated stem.

I draw the sheet of newspaper from the bundle of bound leaves and then, around their stalks, I see the bracelet.

The *shadow catcher*.

"Oh, Lester," I say out loud.

I slip it from the stalks and place it on the grave marker and light the leaves and blow on them until a fragile thread of smoke twists upward toward the tree above.

I watch the smoke braid and rise into the tree, a shadow branching growth, a ghost, and I think about the ways that lives can intertwine, the way one life touches on another, our lives and all the lives of others a long continuous thread—a train—of independent yet contiguous actions.

I slide my hand inside the bracelet.

If this were Hollywood there would be a whistle rising in the distance now, moving slowly toward me, the inimitable sound of *train*, a sound my nation makes, but instead there is the stubborn uninterrupted susurration of lives stirring from their shadows toward sustaining light.

And I feel safe.

notes on the images

NAI: *The North American Indian,* published in 20 volumes between 1907 and 1930.

25   Found photograph. Collection of Lara Porzak.

28   *ESC: R.I.P.* Collection of the Author.   .

31   *Reds.* Collection of the Author.

42   Edward S. Curtis, *Waiting in the Forest—Cheyenne* (NAI, Vol. VI). Library of Congress.

51   Asahel Curtis, *Port of Seattle* (circa 1890s). Curtis & Miller/National Geographic Image Collection.

68   Pieter Brueghel the Elder, *Landscape with the Fall of Icarus* (1558). Scala/Art Resource, NY.

78   Edward S. Curtis, *Kachina Dolls* (NAI, Vol. XII). Courtesy Northwestern University Library.

80   Giotto, *Death and Ascension of St. Francis* (detail), Santa Croce, Florence. Bridgeman Art Library International.

119   Edward S. Curtis, *Watching the Dancers* (NAI, Vol. XII). Library of Congress.

120   Giotto, *Madonna*, Santa Maria Novella, Florence. Bridgeman Art Library International.

120   Edward S. Curtis, *A Favorite Cheyenne Costume* (NAI, Vol. XI). Courtesy Northwestern University Library.

120   Giotto, detail from *Meeting at the Golden Gate*, Arena Chapel, Padua. Bridgeman Art Library International.

153   Found photograph. Collection of the Author.

161   *John Wiggins's Civil War Discharge*/recto. Collection of the Author.

163   *John Wiggins & Mary Book.* Collection of the Author.

167   Edward S. Curtis, *Canon de Chelly—Navaho* (NAI, Vol. I). Library of Congress.

173   Found photograph. Collection of the Author.

acknowledgments

I am indebted to the novels of the late W.G. Sebald, whose interleafing of photographs with prose opened my eyes to the possibility of a new way of reading.

I thank the photographer Keith Carter and his light, Pat, for always wanting to know more about this lengthy work in progress.

To my sister, Johanne Wallace, more gratitude than can be spoken for the license to decorate our shared history.

I thank Denise Roy, Editor, for her grace and wit at all times.

I am grateful to these authors and these books for truth and inspiration:

Curtis, Edward S. *The Portable Curtis: Selected Writings of Edward S. Curtis*. Edited by Barry Gifford. Berkeley: Creative Arts Book Company, 1976.

Dyer, Geoff. *The Ongoing Moment*. New York: Pantheon Books, 2005.

Gidley, Mick. *Edward S. Curtis and the North American Indian, Incorporated*. Cambridge University Press, U.K., 1998.

Makepeace, Anne. *Edward S. Curtis: Coming to Light*. Washington, D.C.: National Geographic Society, 2001.

Marias, Javier. *Negra espalda del tiempo*. Barcelona: Ediciones Alfaguara, 1998.

ABOUT THE AUTHOR

Marianne Wiggins was born in Lancaster, Pennsylvania, and has lived in Brussels, Rome, Paris, and London. She is the author of ten books of fiction, including *John Dollar* and *Evidence of Things Unseen*—for which she was a National Book Award finalist in fiction, as well as a finalist for the Pulitzer Prize. She has won an NEA grant, the Whiting Writers' Award, and the Janet Heidinger Kafka Prize. She is Professor of English at the University of Southern California.

READING GROUP GUIDE

1. Marianne Wiggins's new novel, *The Shadow Catcher*, centers in part on the life of a real historical figure, Edward Sheriff Curtis. Discuss the unique process of weaving fact and fiction: What difficulties might it pose? What artistic freedoms might emerge?

2. The book features an unusual narrative technique, combining historical fiction with more documentary-style biography and history, as well as a personal narrative that reads like memoir. Why do you think the author chose to tell this story in this way?

3. The chapters in the novel about Edward and Clara are essentially told from Clara's point of view. Is this story ultimately more about Clara than Edward?

4. The intimate details of a personal relationship that unfolded in the past may not be documented in the way a public life might be. Is love a timeless emotion, or is the feeling influenced by the times in which it occurs?

5. The Edward Curtis presented here is a much more complicated man than the heroic figure that has come down to us through the legacy of his work. How do mythic elements of a human life arise over time?

6. Do you think Edward Curtis's story is a singularly American one?

7. There is a character named "Marianne Wiggins" in *The Shadow Catcher* who, on the surface, shares much of the history of the actual Marianne Wiggins. When you are reading a novel, does the feeling of making a personal connection with the author add to your experience?

8. In another unusual feature for a novel, *The Shadow Catcher* is peppered with images—not only some of Edward Curtis's photographs, but photographs from Marianne Wiggins's family and images of historical and personal documents as well. Why do you think the author included these?

9. This is not the first time a photographer has been a central character in one of Marianne Wiggins's novels. Discuss the art of photography as it might relate to fiction.

10. A watchword throughout this novel is "Print the Legend." Why do you think we sometimes cling to our cultural myths in the face of overriding evidence against their truth?

11. Late in the novel Wiggins writes, "How the average person dreams is pretty much how the average novelist puts a page together." Discuss the possible meanings of this statement.

12. Marianne Wiggins was born and raised in the East, lived in Europe for many years, and now lives in California. How might a person come to develop such an obvious passion for a region—in this case the Western landscape—not her original home?